PRAISE FOR SIX

★"Creative details . . . and an *X-Files*-worthy mystery keep the pages turning, but it is the supportive and loving Banks family that makes this story shine. . . . Inventive, entertaining, and thought-provoking."

—*Kirkus Reviews*, starred review

"A concept that is full of potential. . . . Particularly well done." —*Publishers Weekly*

"Readers will be drawn into the story with its swift, adventurous plot." —*Booklist*

"This action-packed science fiction novel is a page-turner. Vaughan has created characters that the reader will root for, especially with the strong bond that she has established between Parker and Emma. Her imaginative gadgets and devices will delight fans. Recommended."

—*School Library Connection*

SIX

M.M. VAUGHAN

MARGARET K. McELDERRY BOOKS

NEW YORK LONDON TORONTO SYDNEY NEW DELHI

ACKNOWLEDGMENTS

I am so fortunate to have had so many generous, brilliant people help, guide, and advise me while writing this book. Thank you Rūta Rimas, Tina Wexler, Stephanie Thwaites, Claire Nozieres, Emma Herdman, Joanna McCracken, Laura McCuaig, Becky Allin, Michela Ciardi, Alex O'Brien, Tony Keefer, Freya Latimer, Alice Mowbray, Kari Lia Sim, Candy Seagraves, Amanda Nixon, Jessie O'Regan, Mary Jane Vaughan, Peter O'Regan, Kathy & Federico Meira, and Mark Johnson.

And also a huge thank-you to the following for inspiring me more than they could ever know: Anya & Felix Donald, Oliver McMenamin, Annachiara & Federico Ciardi, Jacob & Emilia Sim, Spencer Roberts, Alejandro & Nicolas Reyes, Gracie & Elliot Meads, Toby Johnson, Lucia Meira, and, of course, Emilia Johnson—for the reward charts that kept me writing, and the invitations into an invisible world far more incredible than anything I could have ever dreamed up myself.

MARGARET K. McELDERRY BOOKS
An imprint of Simon & Schuster Children's Publishing Division
1230 Avenue of the Americas, New York, New York 10020
This book is a work of fiction. Any references to historical events, real people, or real places are used fictitiously. Other names, characters, places, and events are products of the author's imagination, and any resemblance to actual events or places or persons, living or dead, is entirely coincidental.
Text copyright © 2015 by Monica Meira
Cover art copyright © 2015 by Sam Kennedy
All rights reserved, including the right of reproduction in whole or in part in any form.
MARGARET K. McELDERRY BOOKS is a trademark of Simon & Schuster, Inc.
For information about special discounts for bulk purchases, please contact Simon & Schuster Special Sales at 1-866-506-1949 or business@simonandschuster.com.
The Simon & Schuster Speakers Bureau can bring authors to your live event. For more information or to book an event, contact the Simon & Schuster Speakers Bureau at 1-866-248-3049 or visit our website at www.simonspeakers.com.
Also available in a Margaret K. McElderry Books hardcover edition
The text for this book is set in Georgia.
Manufactured in the United States of America
0416 OFF
10 9 8 7 6 5 4 3 2 1
First Margaret K. McElderry Books paperback edition May 2016
The Library of Congress has cataloged the hardcover edition as follows:
Vaughan, M. M.
Six / M.M. Vaughan.—First edition.
p. cm.
Summary: When twelve-year-old Parker's father, on the cusp of a technological breakthrough, is kidnapped, Parker is determined to find him, but his search soon uncovers a sinister project that threatens far more than Parker's family.
ISBN 978-1-4814-2069-3 (hardcover)
ISBN 978-1-4814-2070-9 (pbk)
ISBN 978-1-4814-2071-6 (eBook)
[1. Science fiction. 2. Teleportation—Fiction. 3. Kidnapping—Fiction.] I. Title.
PZ7.V4518Si 2015
[Fic]—dc23
2014041581

FOR EMILIA, MY DOROTHY

PART I

PROLOGUE

00:00

He had always wondered what it would feel like.

Would it hurt?

Would he know what was happening?

Ironically, Dr. Banks could have explained—in minute detail—the science behind the procedure. He could have listed every single step required to destroy a human body cell by cell in one place, and then reverse the process in another. And yet—until now—he'd have been unable to answer these most simple of questions.

So far—he was discovering—it didn't hurt at all. And yes, he knew exactly what was happening, though his thoughts were disconnected and transitory—clear for a brief moment before being snatched back into the folds of a dreamlike fog.

The gentle tingling of pins and needles in his legs became noticeable only when it began to contract, pooling in strength as the area of focus narrowed in at the center of his left shinbone and then started to move upward. His kneecap began to vibrate.

A familiar checklist appeared in Dr. Banks's mind. *The beginning of Stage Eight,* he thought—the reconstruction of detail. It was almost over.

The sensation—now a deep shiver—began to travel slowly around his body—a body that, at this moment, only half existed.

It was uncomfortable, but not painful.

Dr. Banks felt the vibrations move up his spine, climbing his vertebrae one by one, like rungs of a ladder. On reaching the base of his neck, the shiver began to spread out across his shoulders, and a wave of overwhelming panic engulfed him.

Something was very wrong.

Before Dr. Banks could work out what that something was, the fear was gone and the thought vanished from his consciousness.

The sensation continued to travel upward as his body was rebuilt piece by piece: his jaw, lips, cheeks, then nose.

Another wave of anxiety hit him: there was something he was forgetting. Something urgent.

His left eyelid twitched. Orange-white rectangles appeared, trapped behind his eyelids. His vision was returning. The rectangles bounced in and out of sight as his eyelids began to twitch with increasing violence and then, with the immediacy of somebody clicking their fingers, everything stopped. The humming surrounding him disappeared and the vibrations ceased.

His eyes snapped open.

Dr. Banks lay completely still on what felt like a padded table, staring upward and waiting as his eyes adjusted to the low ultraviolet light. His sight sharpened, and the black lines separating the dark gray ceiling tiles above him came into focus, but his head still felt as if it were stuffed full of cotton wool. It was the same confusion and grogginess he felt when his alarm clock woke him from a deep sleep. Except that he was almost certain he wasn't asleep. And he definitely wasn't at home in his bed. From what he could see, by flicking his eyes around the enclosed space, he appeared to be in a small square room with plain black walls. There were no pictures, no signs. Nothing except the table he was lying on and now, himself.

And . . . And . . . What *was* that?

Dr. Banks stared at a turquoise leather handbag sitting in the corner of the room and wondered if he was imagining things.

He squeezed his eyes closed and opened them again. It was still there.

Where was he?

The humming sound suddenly reappeared and the shivering feeling returned, deeper this time, on the exact same spot on either side of his body—just below his elbows. He turned his attention to his right hand.

It was only then that he noticed it wasn't there. Yet.

Dr. Banks stared at his elbow—the point at which his arm currently stopped—and watched as his lower arm began to slowly materialize. Atom to atom, molecule to molecule, linking together like tiny building bricks until the arm began to taper for his wrist and then widen again for his palm, then fingers.

Finally the sensation ceased. He lifted his newly formed hand to his face and bent each finger in turn, then ran his eyes over the deeply etched lines on his palm and down to his wrist. A wrist, he realized in horror, that looked very different from how it should look.

And *that* was when he remembered.

His mind suddenly clear, Dr. Banks felt his heart rate shoot up and his breathing quicken.

Without thinking about what he was doing, he raised his other hand and began to frantically press on both sides of his right wrist.

"Parker!" he cried. "Emma!"

Nothing. He sat bolt upright on the table and pressed down harder.

"Answer me!"

He was still calling out, his face now dripping with sweat, when the wall in front of him slid open with a loud *whoosh*, and a blinding white light flooded the room.

For a moment, as his eyes adjusted to the light, Dr. Banks continued to press down on his wrist and shout, panic overriding any sense of logic. It was only when the view of the adjoining room came into focus that he stopped.

The first thing Dr. Banks saw—before the people dressed

in purple or the view from the window in the background—was the sign on the wall.

Three letters made of solid gold.

Three letters that speared him with the greatest terror he had ever felt.

SIX.

CHAPTER ONE

71:38

Parker had been a student at River Creek Middle School in Upstate New York for only five days, but he already knew that he hated it. It wasn't just that he missed his school and friends back in England, or the farmhouse he had grown up in, or even that he had been forced to move less than an hour away from where his mother had died. Mostly, he thought, as he sat at his desk listening to the whispers around him, it was that he had never felt so alone.

Parker watched as Jenna skipped to the front of the class. She twirled around, sending her two brown plaits flying out on either side of her head, then looked at her friend in the front row and giggled.

"Whenever you're ready," said Mrs. Ford.

Mrs. Ford clasped her hands and leaned over her desk, beaming as if *this* was the presentation she had been waiting for. It would have been more believable if she hadn't done exactly the same before every one of the twenty-two presentations that Parker and his classmates had already sat through.

He wondered if Mrs. Ford would perform the same gesture for the twenty-third presentation: his. He was hoping not to find out, at least not today.

Jenna gave a small cough, giggled again, then began to read from the single handwritten piece of paper in her hand.

"The person I admire most is Missy May. . . ."

At the mention of another celebrity's name, Parker's heart sank. He looked up at the clock. Eight minutes left.

"I think she's an amazing singer and role model for girls my age. Her songs are amazing and she never stops smiling, even though she has to smile for photographers all day. . . ."

Parker's eyes followed the red second hand as it moved, painfully slowly, around the face of the clock.

"My favorite song is 'Happy La La Land.' The lyrics are amazing. . . ."

If Jenna could just keep repeating the word *amazing* for five more minutes, thought Parker, he would be able to go home and rewrite his presentation before their next class.

The funny thing was, of all the assignments he had been given so far, this one had been the one he had been least bothered about. Back at his old school in England, he had been assigned the exact same piece of work. Parker had written down as much of his previous talk as he could remember, added a few extra details to bring it up-to-date, put it in his bag, and thought nothing more of it. But now almost the entire class had delivered their presentations, and so far every single one had been about a celebrity. He knew it was a petty thing to worry about, and it wouldn't have bothered him back in his old school, but it was just that after having been completely ignored the entire week, he didn't want the first time he drew attention to himself to be for the wrong reason.

"And that is why I admire the *amazing* Missy May. Thank you for listening."

Parker's head snapped up. She was *finished*? *That can't have been more than two minutes,* he thought. He looked up at the clock and saw that he was right.

"Great job, Jenna. Maybe a little short on time and facts but excellent delivery," said Mrs. Ford. Jenna grinned and skipped back to her seat and to a smattering of weary clapping.

"We have time for one more."

Oh no, thought Parker. He bowed his head low and slid down as far into his chair as he could without falling to the floor.

There was a brief pause, and then he heard Mrs. Ford asking somebody what was the name of the new boy at the back. There was no answer.

From the corner of his eye he saw Mrs. Ford making her way toward him. He waited until she stopped at his desk and only then, reluctantly, did Parker look up.

"Parker? It's your turn," said Mrs. Ford.

Parker hesitated. He wondered whether if he explained that he really didn't want to do it, she would let him off.

Before he had a chance to ask, however, Mrs. Ford leaned down.

"Did you do the assignment?"

Parker nodded. "But, I, um—I don't think I properly understood what we were meant to do. Would it be okay if I did it next week?"

Mrs. Ford didn't seem to have heard him, and then he realized why: she was too busy reading the paper on his desk. He quickly put his hand out to cover it, but it was too late.

"I don't see what the problem is; it looks wonderful!"

Parker could feel the eyes of the whole class on him. He lowered his voice.

"It's not about a famous person."

Mrs. Ford gave a small laugh. "Oh, honey, that's absolutely fine. Now come on, up you get."

Parker grimaced. He slid the paper off his desk and walked slowly to face the class. For the first time during class, the room was completely silent. Everybody, Parker realized with a sinking feeling, was watching him attentively—curious to find out about the new student, he supposed.

Mrs. Ford was already back at her chair, hands clasped and smiling once again. She gave him a nod, and Parker, shoulders hunched and looking down, began to talk.

"The person I admire most is my father—"

"A little louder, Parker. We can't hear a word you're saying," interrupted Mrs. Ford.

Parker took a deep breath and started again, still looking down, but this time in a louder voice.

"The person I admire most is my father, Dr. Geoffrey Banks. . . ."

As soon as he said it, a wave of muffled laughter traveled across the class.

"The reason I chose my father . . ."

There was some more stifled giggling. Parker clenched his jaw and looked over at Mrs. Ford.

"You're doing fine," she said, glaring at somebody sitting in the last row.

"The reason is that not only has he brought up my sister and me on his own for the last three years, but also that he has done this while working on some of the most important research that's going on right now in the science world. My father . . ."

There was another wave of muffled laughter, and Parker felt his whole body tense. He turned to Mrs. Ford, who motioned for him to keep going.

He took a deep breath but didn't look up. *It's just a few minutes,* he told himself, *then you can forget this whole thing.*

"My father is a molecular biophysicist," continued Parker. "While still a student at Cambridge University, my father and mother, who was also a scientist, were on a team that worked on sequencing DNA. DNA is the molecule that instructs each cell in an organism to tell it what to do and can . . ."

As Parker began to explain what DNA was, he saw a girl at the side rolling her eyes in boredom, and another one smirking. He turned and saw a boy—Aaron, if he remembered correctly—leaning over and whispering something to the boy sitting next to him. They were both grinning.

In that moment, Parker decided he didn't even care about the grade he got for this. He just wanted it to be over. He looked back at his sheet and ran his finger down the page until he got to the final paragraph.

"My father's work has influenced everything from DNA testing to cloning. I admire him very much—as a person and for his work—and, because of his influence, I also hope to be a scientist one day. Thank you."

Parker was already halfway back to his desk before most people realized that he had finished. There was no applause.

Red-faced, Parker sat down. He folded his arms and didn't look up, even when Mrs. Ford thanked him for his brief but interesting presentation. He felt like such an idiot. If only he'd chosen an astronaut or someone who everyone knew, he thought. And yet, feeling his embarrassment begin to turn to anger . . . It hadn't actually been *that* bad. Sure, he'd chosen his dad, but his dad had an interesting job. In his opinion, choosing Missy May was far worse. It was only when the bell went and everybody jumped out of their seats and started to rush past him to the door that he realized they hadn't been laughing at his choice of subject.

"Farth-uhhh," he heard somebody say in a mock English

accent. Everybody around him started laughing. A couple of other people—Parker didn't look up to see who—repeated it.

"Farth-uhhh!"

Parker felt his face burning as he realized they weren't laughing at *what* he'd said but at *how* he'd said it. Right now, even though he'd chosen him for his presentation, Parker hated his dad for making them move here.

CHAPTER TWO

71:15

Parker would have stayed in the classroom for the entire lunch break had Mrs. Ford not insisted on escorting him to the cafeteria. As they walked, Parker kept his head down and listened in silence as Mrs. Ford did her best to offer him some words of comfort.

"Just remember," said Mrs. Ford as they hovered by the cafeteria entrance, "the first week is always the hardest."

"I know. Thanks," mumbled Parker. There was an awkward pause as he waited for her to leave.

"Do you want me to go in with you?" asked Mrs. Ford finally.

Parker's head snapped up. "No. I'm fine."

Before she had a chance to insist, Parker quickly walked away.

The lunch line was long, and as Parker waited and did his best to ignore the whispers of a group of students from his English class ahead of him, the now-familiar pangs of missing England bubbled deeply in his gut. He had hoped, over the first two weeks after his arrival, that those pangs would disappear once he started school. Unfortunately, he thought miserably, the exact opposite had turned out to be true. He paid for his lunch, tray in hand, and caught sight of his sister waving him over.

Despite how he felt, it was true that he wasn't completely alone. He did have his dad and sister, yes, but he couldn't talk about his loneliness with either of them. Since starting his new job, his father had been so stressed and overworked that he no longer had any time to spend with them. And Emma, well, he'd always been the one to watch out for her. Anyway, even if he were to confide in her, he already knew exactly what she would say:

Of course you'll make friends. Stop being such a pessimist.

She *would* say this though because, being ten, she was two years younger than he was and because, unlike him, she had settled into their new American life with annoying ease. It was also because she had only recently learned the word *pessimist* and liked to drop it into conversation as much as possible. In Parker's opinion, however, there was a big difference between being a pessimist and a realist. A pessimist expected the worst at all times. A realist expected the worst only with good reason. He was a realist.

Emma waved again, thinking Parker hadn't seen her. She was sitting at a table surrounded by her new friends: all girls, all ten years old. Even if this hadn't bothered him—which it did—the table was packed anyway. Emma, having apparently already taken this into account, pointed to a two-inch gap between the two girls opposite her. Thankfully, Parker had already spotted an empty table a bit farther along, and he motioned over to it with his head. Emma didn't seem bothered. She shrugged and turned to her friends.

"He doesn't want to be seen hanging out with us," she signed, smiling.

"I don't blame him," signed her friend, opposite.

He heard them all laugh as he walked over to the table and sat down.

Emma was deaf. She had been born with a damaged auditory nerve that meant she couldn't hear any sounds at all. This was the reason that their father had enrolled them here at River Creek instead of at the middle school closer to their new home: this one had a deaf unit attached and would allow Parker to keep an eye on his sister. Emma had objected, arguing that she was now old enough to take care of herself. Their father hadn't agreed. As it turned out, Parker thought as he unwrapped his sandwich, she had been right, Emma wasn't the one that their father had needed to worry about.

"Mind if we sit here?"

Parker looked up and saw three girls standing next to him. He recognized them all from his English class that morning. Becky, the one with the long red hair and freckles, had been at the front, giggling when he'd been talking. Next to her was Jenna, the Missy May fan. He couldn't remember the third one's name. This was the first time any of them had spoken to him.

Parker hesitated before deciding that it would only cause him more problems if he refused.

"No, go ahead," he mumbled.

"Thanks," said Becky. She placed a tray next to Parker's and climbed over the bench. Jenna and the other girl sat down opposite him and started talking between themselves.

"I'm not saying I don't like her, but I don't think her last album was the best one."

"Are you *crazy*? Did you actually listen to it?"

"Yeah. I just didn't like it that much."

"Fine, but you're wrong. 'Lipstick Your Love Away' already won a ton of awards."

"That doesn't mean . . ."

I really *need to get out of here,* thought Parker. He picked up his sandwich and took as big a bite as he could manage, gulping it down with a large swig of orange juice. Before he had swallowed properly, he was already taking another bite. He was about to wash it down with another gulp of juice when Becky, sitting next to him, interrupted him.

"Are you from England?"

The two other girls stopped talking to listen.

Parker, his cheeks stuffed so full of food that he looked like a hamster, nodded.

"Where?"

Parker couldn't answer, at least not without spitting his half-chewed sandwich out onto the table. The prolonged silence grew awkward as he tried to chew his food as quickly as possible while the three girls stared at him. Finally Parker swallowed.

"A place called Kent. It's near London," he said at last.

As soon as he spoke, the girl next to Jenna giggled. Parker's jaw tightened. *Here we go again,* he thought. Here, however, unlike in class, he didn't have to stick around to be laughed at. He picked up his cup, took another swig of juice, and looked down at his half-eaten sandwich. He would have to leave it unfinished. He took ahold of his tray and was about to stand up when Jenna interrupted him.

"Your accent is—"

"Really funny. Yeah, I know," said Parker.

"No!" said Jenna. "It's awesome!"

Parker rolled his eyes. "Yeah, right."

"It is!" agreed the girl next to her. "It's cool. Say something else."

Parker narrowed his eyes. "Like what?"

"Say 'egg,'" said Jenna.

Parker looked confused. "Egg."

Jenna looked disappointed. "Oh, it's kind of the same."

The girls went quiet and, seeing an opportunity to escape, he went to stand up again.

"I know! Water!" said Jenna. "Say that!"

Parker hesitated and looked at Jenna. She was smiling with what looked like genuine interest.

He decided to give her the benefit of the doubt. "Water," he said finally.

The girls giggled again but, Parker realized with some surprise, they didn't appear to be laughing at him. He allowed himself a small smile. Maybe it wasn't all that bad, he thought.

For the next few minutes the girls quizzed him about life in England.

"Does it always rain?"

"Have you been to Buckingham Palace?"

"Did you wear a uniform at your old school?"

"Is it weird driving on the wrong side of the road?"

Parker answered their questions, and the girls listened to him, completely fascinated. As he loosened up, he began to wonder if he might have been overreacting about the incident earlier. No sooner had he thought that than a group of boys from his year came over and sat down at the other end of the table.

"Hey, Aaron!" called Jenna.

"What?" asked Aaron.

"Listen to this. He . . . What's your name again?"

"Parker."

"Yeah. Parker sounds like Shakespeare or something. Say 'water' again, Parker."

Parker looked over at the group of boys staring at him.

"I really don't want to," he mumbled.

"Oh, come on! *Please?*"

Parker hesitated. *They're just interested,* he told himself. No harm.

"Water," he finally said with a shrug.

The boys didn't react.

"Isn't it cute?" asked Jenna.

Parker tensed. *Cute?* He felt himself turning red.

Aaron shrugged. "It's just a stupid accent."

Jenna flicked her head in disgust, and her plaits flew behind her. "You're just jealous."

Aaron's jaw clenched. "You're such a loser, Jenna."

"Whatever, Aaron. At least *I* don't sound like . . ."

There was a pause as Jenna searched for the right insult. "A donkey."

Everyone burst out laughing, and Parker, horrified at the way the conversation had suddenly turned, decided that this might be a good moment to leave. He stood up.

"Don't let him bother you," said Becky, turning to face him. "He's always like that."

Parker looked over to see Aaron glaring at Jenna.

"Actually," said Parker, "I have to go. I, uh, have to get something from the library."

"Oh, okay. Sure," said Becky.

Parker stood up and grabbed his tray, Becky and the girl opposite waved, and Parker nodded back. Jenna was too involved in her staring match with Aaron to notice him hurrying off.

What was that all about? he thought as he cleared his lunch off into the trash. He put the empty tray on top of one of the lunch carts and was about to walk away when he felt a tap on his shoulder. He turned.

"Hey," said Aaron, with a nod.

Parker nodded back, his mind racing to assess the situation. Was Aaron planning to start a fight? Though they were the same age and looked similar (well, they were both the same build and had brown eyes and messy short brown hair), Aaron was a couple of inches taller than he was. He was also on the wrestling team. Parker straightened and pushed his shoulders back.

"What do you want?" asked Parker.

"I just wanted to say I'm sorry," said Aaron.

Parker hadn't expected that.

"Those girls are just idiots," continued Aaron. "Your accent is cool."

Parker stared at him for a moment as he thought about how Aaron had been whispering and laughing during his presentation. Was he being sincere now? Parker had no idea.

"Um, okay. Thanks," said Parker.

"What was the word they were getting you to say?" asked Aaron.

Oh, right, thought Parker, his eyes narrowing. It was obvious where this was going.

"I'm not stupid," he said. "I have to go."

He turned to leave, but Aaron stopped him with a hand on his arm.

"Oh, come on," said Aaron.

Parker paused and stared at Aaron.

"Seriously, I'm really sorry," said Aaron. "It wasn't about you. It's just Jenna—she drives me nuts." He couldn't be sure, but Aaron did seem to look genuinely apologetic. Parker didn't reply but he didn't leave, either.

And to be fair, thought Parker, Jenna *was* kind of annoying.

"I shouldn't have said anything about your accent," continued Aaron. "I just came over to apologize."

"Okay. Well, thanks," said Parker, shrugging.

Aaron looked relieved. He smiled. "So, what was the word they were getting you to say?"

He hesitated for a moment and then decided to give Aaron the benefit of the doubt. "Water?" he asked.

Aaron's smile widened into an unpleasant grin. "Sure," he replied.

In Parker's mind, the events of the next few seconds felt like they played out in slow motion:

Aaron swinging his right arm out from behind his back.

Parker looking down and seeing the full cup of water in Aaron's hand.

Parker realizing what was about to happen.

Parker also realizing that it was too late to do anything about it.

Parker's eyes following the arc of Aaron's arm as the contents of the cup were flung forward, directly into his face.

Someone screamed.

Parker stood, frozen, his mouth open in shock as the water ran down his face. In front of him, Aaron burst into laughter just as a voice from behind called out.

"Aaron, are you *crazy*?!"

Parker turned and saw Becky running toward them, her face red with what looked like a mixture of concern and fury.

"I was just kidding," said Aaron, a wide grin still on his face. "It was a joke. No hard feelings, right?" he said, turning to Parker. He gave Parker a playful punch on the arm.

Parker looked down at where the punch had landed and then slowly up to Aaron as his shock began to turn to anger. His hand began to curl up into a fist. In twelve years, he had never once punched anybody but, he thought, if there was going to be a first time . . .

Aaron looked down at Parker's fist and the smile vanished.

"Whoa! Calm down. It was just a joke. Don't get so weird about it."

Parker's mouth dropped open. He could hardly believe what he was hearing. He had done nothing to this boy. Nothing! Now Aaron had thrown water in his face and *he* had the nerve to call *him* weird.

It was the last straw.

"Weird?" he shouted. Aaron jumped back in surprise. "You

think *I'm* the one being weird? What is wrong with you? All I said was 'water' . . ."

As soon as Parker said the word, Aaron's eyes turned to the cart next to him. In that split second, Parker knew exactly what Aaron was going to do. As Aaron grabbed another cup and swung it in Parker's direction, Parker was already jumping out of the way. He was quick enough to avoid a second soaking but, in his haste, he forgot about the pool of spilt water already at his feet.

Parker's eyes widened in shock as he felt his foot slip out from under him. There was nothing he could do to stop it. With every person in the cafeteria watching, Parker flew up into the air and then, with an enormous thud, he landed on the floor faceup.

This time, nobody laughed. Not even Aaron. There was complete silence. If there was any pain, Parker's body hadn't yet registered it. Too shocked to move, he lay on the floor as water seeped in through his clothes, wishing only that he could close his eyes and make everything disappear.

And then Parker's wrist began to vibrate.

Parker knew exactly why it was happening, and he knew, even before she forced her way through the crowd, that the cause of it was his sister.

Emma was *not* going to see him like this.

The thought sent a jolt of furious determination through him. He jumped up and found himself once again face-to-face with a now nervous-looking Aaron. Maybe it was the expression on Parker's face—thunderous, his jaw clenched tight—or maybe it was the fact that his little prank had suddenly turned more serious than he had expected.

"Hey," said Aaron, holding his hands up. "I'm sor—"

Parker didn't want to hear it. Before Aaron had a chance to react, Parker rushed forward and slammed into him. Aaron stumbled backward into the crowd that had gathered. He may have fallen, but Parker didn't turn to see. Instead he grabbed his now wet schoolbag by his feet and then, with his wrist still vibrating, Parker ran out of the cafeteria.

CHAPTER THREE

70:31

As Parker raced the corridors of his school, sweating, frantically searching for somewhere to disappear to, his father—in complete contrast—was sitting utterly still at the desk of his laboratory, his eyes fixed on the equally static page of numbers lying on the desk in front of him.

Where am I going wrong? he thought, his frustration building.

Dr. Banks squinted, and the stark, sharp black numbers dissolved into a pool of gray haze. When his eyes refocused, the small illogical part of his mind—the part that he relied on only in desperation—was disappointed to find that the numbers had not somehow managed to rearrange themselves into a different conclusion. Everything that Dr. Banks had always loved about numbers—their certainty, their total reliability—was what he hated them for now. No matter how much he wanted it, deep down he knew that there was nothing he could do; the numbers would not be changing, and the rat lying on the counter behind him would not be coming back to life.

"Dr. Banks?"

Lina's voice was hesitant—not because she was worried about how he might react to being interrupted, but because she seemed to have an uncanny ability to understand the way he worked. Though only a year out of graduate school, she was possibly the most competent and intuitive of any assistant that Dr. Banks had ever had. And, though she had been his assistant for only three weeks, he already trusted her completely. It was a good thing, too—there was no way he was going to be able to carry out what he needed to do without being able to confide in her.

Dr. Banks looked up and saw that Lina's eyes were fixed on the rat behind him.

"I'm sorry," she said.

"I just don't know what I'm overlooking," said Dr. Banks. "It shouldn't be this hard."

"That's what people have been saying for thirty years," replied Lina.

"I know," said Dr. Banks, "but those people didn't have as much to lose as I do."

Lina didn't say anything. She walked over to the lifeless body of the rat, picked it up carefully, and gently stroked its head.

"Do you want me to get you another?" she asked.

Dr. Banks shook his head. "Maybe later. I can't bring myself to do that again right now."

Lina nodded. She, like him, hated this part of the job. In

the past some of Dr. Banks's colleagues had teased him for being too soft about testing procedures on animals.

A small sacrifice for the greater good, they'd said.

And, with regard to the majority of the work that Dr. Banks had carried out over the course of his career, this may have been true. Nevertheless—perhaps influenced by his wife and now his daughter—the taking of a life, even a rat's, was not something that had ever sat easily with him. So much so that, as soon as he had enough authority to demand it, Dr. Banks had refused to work with any more living animals. This, for the first time in years, was the exception—and only because he had truly believed that he would not be doing any killing. Unfortunately, it turned out that his perception of his own ability had been misguided.

Lina gently placed the rat into a small white plastic box and then turned to face Dr. Banks.

"I came in to let you know that the shipments go out this afternoon. I'm going to go to the terminal in about an hour."

"What did you tell them?" asked Dr. Banks.

"Just that you're very particular about who handles your work and you want me to ensure it gets sent fine. They all think that everybody who works in this department is odd anyway, so nobody questioned it."

Dr. Banks shrugged. "Better odd than suspicious, I suppose. Good work."

He leaned down, reached into the open briefcase at his feet, and pulled out a small black memory stick. As Lina looked, he opened the long desk drawer and pulled out a small bottle of Wite-Out. Then, on the body of the memory stick, he began to carefully brush a simple outline of a diamond with a smiley face inside it. When he had finished, he replaced the lid of the Wite-Out bottle and blew on the glistening white lines.

"It'll need a bit longer to dry," he said as he carefully handed the stick to Lina.

"Is it . . ." Lina paused, as if unsure whether to finish the question.

"Yes?"

"Is it the letter you told me about?"

"Yes," replied Dr. Banks. He bit his lip. "But also, I asked Parker and Emma to write letters too."

"They know?" asked Lina.

"No, they don't know. I told them it was for something else."

Lina nodded. "So I just put it with the others?" she asked. She was looking at the memory stick.

"Yes. But it really shouldn't arouse any suspicion, even if they were to look at its contents—I disguised it all well enough." He gave a small laugh. "I can't tell you how long it took—Emma got a bit carried away."

"You should have asked me—you have enough to think about. I can do it next time, if you'd like."

Dr. Banks considered the offer for a moment.

"It's just that . . . ," he began.

Lina raised her hand to stop him. "No need to explain. I completely understand. I'm sorry—forget I mentioned it."

Dr. Banks pursed his lips in a tight smile. "Don't apologize, Lina. Perhaps I'm being too hasty—it *would* be helpful."

"All you have to do is ask," replied Lina.

"I'll have to show you the code, but it's very simple."

"I'm sure I can pick it up."

"I have no doubt," said Dr. Banks. "And you . . . well, you wouldn't say anything, not to anybody?"

"Of course not."

There was a pause, and Lina, perhaps sensing it was time for her to leave, picked up the plastic box containing the dead rat and crossed the room without another word. She was about to turn the handle of the door when Dr. Banks interrupted her.

"Is it wrong to do this?" he asked.

Lina stopped and turned to face him. She shook her head. "No. I don't think so."

"If Parker and Emma knew, they'd never forgive me."

"They would if they knew why you were doing it."

Dr. Banks gave Lina a grateful smile, then turned his attention back to the page of numbers.

He hoped she was right.

CHAPTER FOUR

70:15

With the door closed, the technology storeroom—the room
that Parker had decided to hide in—was almost pitch-black
but for a tiny sliver of light sneaking its way in through a thin
vent high up on the wall. Parker sat on the worn carpet-tiled
floor with his back against the far wall and his knees pulled up
to his chest. He was well hidden—tucked in behind a wooden
cart that was missing a wheel and surrounded by crates overflowing with tangled cables and broken keyboards. Even
if somebody were to walk in, which seemed unlikely given
how the room seemed only to serve as a dumping ground for
defective equipment, they wouldn't have seen him. It would
have been the perfect place for Parker to forget about the
outside world—if only for a moment—had it not been for the
persistent vibration in his left arm.

Effie could be so annoying.

Parker looked down at the two tiny dots of orange light on
either side of his wrist. This was Effie—rather, E. F. E., "Ears
for Emma," a device his father had invented not long after

Emma was diagnosed as being deaf. Effie translated electrical impulses created by thoughts into audible speech for Parker and his parents to hear through an implanted microphone, and into subtitles that Emma could read using specially designed glasses.

In short, Effie was much like a cell phone, only that it transmitted thoughts instead of voices.

The light on the left of Parker's wrist was the link to his father, the one on the right—the one that had been flashing almost continuously since he'd run out of the cafeteria—the link to Emma. There had once been another light in the center of the two, but that had turned off the day his mother flew out of range on her business trip. She had been due to return four days later, but just a few hours before she should have been boarding her flight, they had received the call about her accident. Her light had never come back on.

As far as Parker was aware, only three people in the world now knew about Effie. His parents had asked him and Emma to keep it a secret and, though he had to admit that there'd been a couple of times he'd considered telling his friends, in all it really hadn't been too difficult. Both Parker and his sister enjoyed what they liked to think of as their secret superpower, even though they rarely used it for anything very important. (Notable exception: the time Parker saved his sister's life by warning her about a speeding car. He liked to remind Emma of that.) It also helped that nobody had ever asked them any awkward questions about it. This was because in daylight Effie's lights looked like nothing more than tiny marks on the skin, and in darkness she and Parker wore watches or long sleeves to hide the faint glow. Nevertheless, over the four years that they had been using it, both Parker and Emma had questioned their father about the reasons for keeping his invention a secret. After all, if Effie could allow Emma to communicate with her family and vice versa, then surely it could help other families in their same situation.

Every time they had brought it up, however, Parker's father said the same thing: that there were people in the world who would always find a way to turn an invention for good into one for evil. Until he could make sure Effie could be used only for what he intended it to be used for, it was to remain a secret. Before their mother died, his father had been working on doing just this. After she died, he had never discussed working on it again. For the time being at least, Effie was their family secret.

Parker's wrist started vibrating again. He pressed down on the flashing light until it stopped.

Their father had implanted the device into Emma and Parker on the first day of their summer vacation, just a week after Emma had turned six. Parker could remember many things about that day—his picture of a space shuttle framed on the wall of his mother's office, her white lab coat draped over the back of her tall-backed chair, the smell of antiseptic— but he couldn't remember the procedure itself. It had been done under local anesthetic administered by his mother, so perhaps the absence of pain had lessened the memory's impact.

He did—not surprisingly—recall in vivid detail the moment he had used Effie for the first time. His mother had knelt at his side and shown him how to call Emma by pressing down on the light on the right side of his wrist. In response, Emma's arm had started to vibrate. She had jumped in surprise, and his father, kneeling next to her, had smiled and, with his hand over hers, had pressed down on the flashing light on her wrist.

"Think of something to say to your sister, Parker. Nothing too complicated, so that she can read it easily."

In time, Parker would come to realize the significance of this moment—the first-ever thought-to-thought transmission—and would wish his first words had been more fitting of the occasion. As it was, he had simply relayed the first thing that had come to mind.

Your glasses are a funny color.

Emma's eyes had lit up in amazement as Parker's thought had been translated into subtitles that had scrolled—imperceptibly to anybody else—across the right lens of her new lime green glasses. There'd been a brief pause as she'd slowly read what Parker had said. She'd looked up at Parker, grinned, and her thought had been translated almost instantaneously into a very slightly robotic voice inside Parker's head.

Not as funny as your face, she had replied.

Parker's thoughts were interrupted by his wrist vibrating once more. He had tried hanging up the call a few times, but Emma just kept calling back. She wasn't going to give up. Finally Parker sighed and pressed down quickly on his sister's light to answer.

I don't want to talk, he said. Well, he didn't say it; he thought it. For Parker and Emma though, thinking via Effie was as natural as it was for others to open their mouths to speak.

Where are you?

I'm fine. Don't worry. I just want to be by myself for a while.

What happened? Are you okay?

I said I don't want to talk about it.

Just tell me what happened.

I'm going now.

But, Parker—

Parker pressed the light on his wrist and Emma's voice cut off before she could finish her sentence. There was nothing she could do to help. That was the thing about Emma; she wanted to help everyone. Victims of disasters, starving children, injured animals, and now him. His father said that she was just like their mother. He meant it in a good way. If anybody asked their father about his children, he would tell them (to Parker's and Emma's embarrassment) that Parker was going to grow up to be a Nobel Prize—winning scientist, and Emma, well, she was going to save the world. *Good for her,* thought Parker, but she wasn't going to start by saving him. Not today. Right now all he wanted to do was hide.

Parker—his eyes adjusting to the dim lighting—unzipped his backpack and pulled out a bright yellow Walkman that had once belonged to his dad. Emma had found it in the attic of their old house when they'd been packing for their move, and neither she nor Parker had had a clue as to what it was. Their dad had been shocked, and even more so when he'd pulled out a cassette tape with a tangled loop of brown plastic ribbon hanging out and neither of his children had looked any more the wiser. Mumbling something about getting old, their dad had left and returned some time later, triumphantly holding a pencil, a pack of batteries, and a set of headphones.

Parker had watched as his father had put the pencil into one of the holes of the cassette then had turned it slowly, causing the ribbon to wind back into its housing. Turning it upside down to show Parker that the ribbon had now become taut, Parker's father had then placed the cassette into the Walkman and pressed play, only to find that it didn't work. He'd shaken it, replaced the batteries with another set, pressed all the buttons with increasing frustration, and finally banged it against the wall before giving up. There was, he'd said, too much packing to do to be wasting time fixing junk.

Parker, however, was not so easily deterred—it was exactly the kind of challenge that he loved. That night, after hours spent carefully dismantling the Walkman, locating the problem, and then rebuilding it, Parker had lain on his bed and listened to the mixtape his dad had made while at university. The next day, Parker had rummaged around in the attic and found three more cassettes. It was one of these—another homemade collection of songs with the words *ROAD TRIP* scrawled in thick black marker on the front sticker—that he pulled out now. Parker clicked the cassette into place, closed the cover, put on the headphones, and pressed firmly down on the play button. He leaned back against the wall, closed his eyes, and allowed his thoughts to be washed away by the music.

Three songs into side B of the cassette, the lights above Parker began to flicker on. Startled, he bolted upright and, with a swift yank, pulled the headphones from his ears.

Clunk. Rattle. Clunk.

It sounded like somebody was rummaging through a box. *Of all the days to pick,* thought Parker, cursing his bad luck. He held his breath and waited, hoping that whoever it was would find whatever it was they were looking for quickly and leave.

A few seconds later the noise stopped. Parker waited— every part of his body frozen in high alert, but instead of hearing the door opening, as he'd hoped, he heard the sound of something—a crate maybe—being moved not too far from where he was sitting. As quietly as possible, Parker scooted over to his left until he found a small gap between the crates and the cart. He leaned forward and, with his eye pressed to the gap, looked out onto the room.

Parker saw him straightaway. In the center of the room,

leaning over a box with his back to Parker, was a boy wearing black trousers and a short-sleeved blue-and-white-checked shirt. He guessed that the boy was maybe his age and could see the brown skin of his arm but, other than that, Parker couldn't make out much more from where he was sitting.

Parker stayed still and kept watching as the boy gave up on the box, stood, and turned to his left to survey the line of boxes against the wall. Now that he could see the boy properly, with his closely shaved black hair and thick black-framed glasses—Parker realized that he knew him. He was almost certain they were in the same grade, and he was trying to work out what classes they shared when, in a decision that took him completely by surprise, the boy suddenly turned on his heels and began to walk toward him.

Parker ducked down and listened as the boxes in front of him were opened one by one in turn. Finally Parker heard the sound of a box being opened in front of the cart he was hiding behind, and he realized that the game was up—he was going to have to do something. Without enough time to think of a better plan, Parker reached into one of the boxes next to him and grabbed the first thing that came to hand.

"Found it!" he said as he jumped up and found himself face-to-face with the boy standing only a couple of feet in front of him.

"Aaaargh!"

The boy screamed then did a strange whole-body wobble before staggering backward to the floor, holding both hands in front of his face for protection. In spite of himself, the reaction was so comical that Parker had to laugh.

"I'm really sorry," said Parker, pushing the crates out of his way and stepping out from behind the cart. "Did I scare you?"

The boy stared at him from behind his black-rimmed glasses, the whites of his eyes large and brilliant against his skin. "No," he answered as he stood up. "I always scream when I meet people."

Parker gave a small laugh, but the boy didn't smile back.

"Why were you hiding?" asked the boy. His voice was still weak from shock.

"I wasn't hiding," Parker said, too quickly. "I was looking for something." As proof, he held up the object he'd grabbed, before realizing what it was.

The boy tipped his head to the side and his eyes narrowed. "Why were you looking for a broken mouse?"

Parker looked at the dangling computer mouse in his hand and winced. He answered with the first thing that came to mind.

"I collect them."

The boy considered this for a moment, then—with a look that said he was satisfied with the answer—shrugged and nodded, as if collecting broken mice were the most normal thing in the world.

"Okay," he said.

"Well," said Parker, eager to get away, "sorry again for scaring you. I'm going now."

The boy didn't respond. He also didn't move from his spot. Feeling awkward, Parker walked back to his hiding place, stuffed the Walkman quickly into his schoolbag, and then stepped back out. The boy was still standing there, watching him.

"How could you look for something in the dark?" he asked as Parker emerged. "The lights were off when I came in."

"I don't think they were," said Parker. He placed the broken mouse on the cart to put his backpack on.

"No," said the boy. "They were definitely off. I specifically remember turning the switch on, which means you had to be in the dark."

"Okay," said Parker. "Maybe. I don't remember."

"You don't remember whether you were standing in a dark room?" asked the boy.

Parker breathed out loudly. "Wow," he said, "you ask a lot of questions. Look, I'm going. Sorry again for jumping out at you."

Parker nodded good-bye and turned to walk away. He was at the door, about to turn the handle, when the boy called out to him.

"Hey!"

Parker took a breath and looked back. "Yes?"

"You forgot your mouse."

"Oh," said Parker. He walked back and held his hand out, but the boy didn't offer it forward.

"Why would you want this mouse? IBM made millions of these. They came as standard with any desktop computer."

The boy was beginning to really irritate him. "That one's European," said Parker. "They only made a few of them in 1994. Okay?"

The boy raised a single eyebrow. "Really?" he said, nodding over to the wall. "Then that box must be worth millions."

Parker turned his head and saw a huge white opaque crate overflowing with identical mice. He winced.

"You weren't really looking for this, were you?" asked the boy.

Parker turned back to the boy. "No, okay, Sherlock? I wasn't. Keep the mouse," he said.

The boy didn't seem in the slightest bit bothered at Parker's obvious irritation. "I think you were hiding," he said.

"I'm going," said Parker. He turned.

"Was it because of that thing in the cafeteria?"

Parker stopped and threw his hands up in the air in frustration. "You know about that?"

The boy nodded.

"Then why were you asking me all those stupid questions if you already knew?"

The boy looked hurt. "I didn't know. That's why I was asking."

Parker glared at him. "Well, now you've worked it out. Great. Can I go now?"

"You're annoyed."

"I'm not annoyed," said Parker. He was very annoyed.

The boy pursed his lips tightly in thought. Then, as if

having come to a decision, he held his arm out to offer a handshake.

"I'm Michael."

Parker shook his hand quickly. "I'm Parker. I've got—"

"I know. You're in my art class."

As soon as he said it, Parker remembered. Michael was perhaps the only boy worse at art than he was.

"I'm sorry, I didn't mean to get you angry," said Michael.

Parker stiffened. "I'm not angry—I'm just not in the mood for talking. Can I go now?"

"You shouldn't let Aaron get to you," said Michael, ignoring Parker's question. "He's weak. All bullies are. They need to bully other people to feel better about themselves. You did the right thing and you should feel good about that."

Parker pretended to think about this for a moment. "Okay," he said finally. "Good pep talk. Thanks. I'll keep that in mind."

"I don't let it bother me."

"You don't let what bother you?" asked Parker.

"When Aaron and his friends take my money and stuff. I just remind myself that it's evidence of their weakness. One day, I'll be—"

"What?" interrupted Parker. "You *let* them take your money?"

"I don't let them. I just don't *not* let them."

"That's exactly the same thing. Don't do that. Just tell them to get lost. Or tell a teacher or something."

Michael shrugged. "It's no big deal, seriously. I can get more money, but I only have one face."

Parker tried to work out the logic in that before deciding that there was none. "You don't have to choose between getting beaten up or giving them money. There are other options, you know. How long have they been taking your money?"

Michael looked down at the floor. "Since I started here. In September."

"You're new? Where were you before?"

"Homeschooled."

"Ahh," said Parker, nodding slowly. "That explains it."

"That explains what?" It was Michael's turn to sound defensive.

"No. I mean, there's nothing wrong with being homeschooled. It's just you're probably not used to standing up for yourself."

"What, like you did today?"

"That's different. It took me by surprise. It won't happen again."

"What are you going to do?"

"I haven't decided yet. Something."

"You could just pay them to leave you alone."

"I'm not . . . oh," said Parker, realizing that Michael was smiling. "Very funny. Seriously though, don't give them any more money."

Michael shrugged and nodded. "I won't," he said.

Something occurred to Parker. "Is that why you're here? Are you hiding?"

Michael looked offended. "No. I don't skip classes. I have computer class, and the teacher asked me to help retrieve the data from this."

For the first time, Parker noticed that Michael was holding a hard drive.

"It failed?"

"Yeah, completely. I've tried everything. I think I'm just going to rebuild it from scratch."

"Freeze it."

"Eh?"

"It might not work, but if you've tried everything else, it's worth a go. Stick it in a bag and put it in the freezer, then try it again as soon as you get it out."

"Cool. How do you know that?" asked Michael.

The next thing Parker knew, he'd spent twenty minutes talking to Michael about computers. Michael, it turned out, was something of a genius when it came to programming but not quite as much of an expert on hardware. It was the exact opposite of Parker who, at the age of seven, had found he had a knack for anything mechanical after pushing his father's computer off his desk whilst climbing over it and managing to piece it all back together. He had done it so quickly and so well that his parents had never suspected a thing. The respect between Parker and Michael, therefore, was mutual. And, despite first impressions, it turned out that—though slightly awkward and somewhat lacking a sense of humor—Michael was actually pretty good company. Best of all, he didn't mention Parker's English accent. Not once.

Michael looked up at the clock on the wall. "I need to go and ask Mr. Nowak if I can take this hard drive home over the weekend. Want to come?"

Parker was quick to say yes. He followed Michael out of the room and, as he switched the light off, he smiled.

CHAPTER FIVE

68:29

Mr. Nowak, the computer teacher, was at his desk when Parker and Michael walked into the computer lab. Unlike his old school, this lab had plenty of computers, each one housed in its own private booth. The class should have been in full swing, but there was clearly no teaching happening today. Instead Mr. Nowak was holding his cell phone with both hands and had his feet up on his desk, the soles of his tatty brown leather shoes on display.

"Hold on," said Mr. Nowak without looking up. "I've been trying to get past this level for days. Just two more clowns and . . ."

His voice trailed off as the game drew him back in. Parker and Michael stood and watched, slightly perplexed, as Mr. Nowak tapped on his phone furiously with his lips pursed until, after a minute or so, he let out a sudden yelp of joy.

"Yes!" he said, his hand shooting up in the direction of Michael. It took Michael a moment to realize that he was being expected to high-five his teacher and, when he did so, he half missed and the moment of celebration seemed to fizzle out.

"What's up?" asked Mr. Nowak.

Before Michael had finished asking if he could take the hard drive home, Mr. Nowak had nodded his approval. It was possible that he would have objected had Michael told him about his plans to freeze it, but Parker suspected that he was one of those teachers who would say yes to anything, as long as it didn't involve him actually having to do any work—especially on a Friday afternoon.

"I want to show you something," said Michael, leaving Mr. Nowak to get back to his game. He began to lead Parker over to a vacant booth in the far corner when Parker realized that he was in a room surrounded by people in his grade. He didn't want to make it too obvious that he was looking but, from taking quick glances around him, he wasn't able to find Aaron, Becky, or anybody else directly involved in the cafeteria incident. Even if they were there, Parker told himself, they were unlikely to notice him—everyone he could see had headphones on and was too busy playing games to notice. He assumed that Michael was going to do the same—maybe show him a cheat he'd found on a game or something—but it soon became obvious that Michael had something else he wanted to share with him.

"I finally cracked this yesterday," said Michael in a hushed voice as he typed furiously on the keyboard.

Curious, Parker rolled his chair in closer. For a moment it wasn't clear what Michael was doing. Parker didn't recognize the program, and Michael was typing so fast and jumping so quickly from one screen to the next that it was impossible to read anything. Finally, after a couple of minutes, Michael pushed his chair back slightly and pointed. Parker leaned forward and read the words on the screen.

BANKS, PARKER.

It took Parker a moment to work out why he was seeing his name. When he realized, his head snapped around to Michael in surprise.

"You hacked into the school server?"

Michael nodded with an embarrassed smile, and Parker could tell, though he was doing his best to hide it, that Michael was feeling rather pleased with himself.

"What are they?" asked Parker, running his finger over the line of letters next to his name.

"Your grades." said Michael.

"Cool," said Parker, reading the marks. They were good—excellent in the cases of science and math—with just one exception. Parker winced.

"Better than my mark," said Michael on seeing what Parker was looking at.

"How do you get worse than a fail at art?"

"Unmarkable."

"Oh," said Parker. Then something occurred to him. "Did you change it?"

"Did I change what?" asked Michael.

"Did you change your grade?"

Michael raised his eyebrows and his mouth dropped open in horror.

"No!"

"You should do it," said Parker, as the potential of what Michael could do started to dawn on him. "And change mine, too, while you're at it. But don't make it too obvious—maybe just a C."

Michael eyes widened even farther, and he looked around to make sure that nobody had heard. *"That's cheating!"* he whispered.

Parker was confused. "Why else would you hack into the system if that wasn't what you were going to do?"

Michael shrugged. "I don't know. I just wanted to find out if I could."

"And that's it?" asked Parker.

"Yeah. Why, is that bad?"

Parker shook his head, slightly confused. "No, it's good, obviously—just seems a bit of a waste."

Michael considered this for a moment and then sheepishly closed the program.

"I do cheat sometimes," said Michael defensively. Parker could tell he was embarrassed.

"It's okay—I wasn't saying you should cheat."

Michael opened up a car game.

"Look, I can get unlimited money."

"Really?" asked Parker. "I thought they'd made that game cheat-proof."

"No," said Michael, getting excited again. "If you just open this, then press *f*, space . . ."

Parker and Michael spent the rest of the afternoon buying every expensive car modification in the game and laughing as they easily outran every other online player. By the time the end-of-school bell rang, Parker felt like maybe he'd just made his first friend since arriving at River Creek. Michael, it seemed, felt the same.

"You want to come play at my house tomorrow?" asked Michael as they walked down the corridor to their lockers.

"Only if you don't say 'play.'"

"What then?" asked Michael.

"Hang out."

"Okay. Do you want to come to my house and hang out tomorrow? Bring your bike, if you have one."

Parker was just about to respond when he saw Emma walking down the corridor toward them. She waved, and Parker stopped to wait for her.

"Who's that?" asked Michael, slowing down next to him.

"Emma. My sister."

"She's pretty."

Parker recoiled in disgust. "She's ten. And she's my sister."

Michael shrugged. "She's still pretty."

Parker looked at Michael like he might be crazy.

Emma waved as she approached. Before Parker could introduce them, Michael stepped out in front of him and offered his hand to Emma.

"Hi, I'm Michael. I'm in your brother's art class."

Emma smiled, shook his hand, and then turned to Parker. *"He doesn't know?"* she signed to Parker.

Parker shook his head. He turned to Michael. "She's deaf."

"Oh," said Michael.

The reaction of people finding out that Emma was deaf was always different. Most of the time people took it well, though they often had a tendency to then just ignore Emma, which annoyed them both. Sometimes—rarely—people would look horrified and make their excuses, and sometimes—as Michael did now—they would start to shout.

"NICE TO MEET YOU!"

"Deaf," said Parker. "As in she can't hear anything. She can lip-read though."

"Oh yeah, right. How do I do the sign for 'nice to meet you'?"

Parker showed him, and Emma, still smiling, waited patiently as Michael got Parker to demonstrate it three times before turning to Emma and repeating it.

"Nice to meet you, too," signed Emma.

Michael paused for a moment in thought and then turned to face Emma. He slowly pointed to her, then to himself, and then made a triangular shape with his arms above his head. Parker watched—half confused, half amused—as Michael then proceeded to do an elaborate mime that looked like he was pulling something as he ran furiously on the spot with his arms out.

Emma turned to Parker and shrugged.

"What are you trying to say?" asked Parker.

"It's a bike. I'm riding a bike. Wasn't it obvious?"

Both Parker and Emma shook their heads, and Michael sighed.

He turned to Emma and mouthed his words slowly. "Do you want to come to my house tomorrow and ride bikes?"

Emma hesitated and Parker stepped in. "Emma doesn't have a bike. She got a goat instead."

"What?" asked Michael.

"Yeah, my dad offered to get us a bike each when we got here, but Emma said she'd rather use the money to buy a goat in Africa. My sister's a bit strange."

Emma signed to Parker.

"She says one goat can provide enough income to feed a family of four."

"That's really nice," said Michael slowly to Emma. "I have enough bikes—you can use one of mine."

"How many bikes do you have?" asked Parker.

Michael shrugged. "A few. Anyway, do you want to come or not?"

Parker looked at Emma and she nodded. "Sure," said Parker. "I think my dad can drop us off, but I have to check with him first."

Michael grinned. He swung his backpack to the floor and unzipped it, then scrambled around until he found a pen and a scrap piece of paper on which he wrote his name, address, and phone number.

"Here," said Michael, handing Parker the piece of paper. "You can get your mom to call if you want."

"Not my mum, my dad."

"Your dad then. Come at eleven? Or whatever time you want. You can stay all day if you want to."

"Okay," said Parker. "I'll call you later and let you know."

"Call you later about what?" said a voice behind them.

Parker turned and found Aaron standing behind him with his arms crossed. He was alone.

"None of your business," said Parker.

Aaron repeated Parker's words in a terrible English accent, and Parker narrowed his eyes at him.

"That's not even a good impression."

"That's not even a good impression," repeated Aaron in the same voice.

Parker stared at Aaron. "What's wrong with you?"

"What's wrong with *you*?" responded Aaron in his normal voice.

Michael pulled on Parker's sleeve. "Just leave it," said Michael quietly.

"Yeah, listen to four-eyes," said Aaron.

"Leave him alone," said Parker.

"Or what?" asked Aaron. He lifted his chin and pulled his

shoulders back. Aaron, it was obvious, was looking for a fight. Maybe it was the humiliation of earlier, or maybe it was that his sister and new friend, not to mention the other students in the corridor, were watching, but whichever it was, Parker was not ready to back down.

"Or you'll regret it," said Parker, taking a step forward. His heart began to thump loudly, but he clenched his jaw and narrowed his eyes, determined not to let Aaron see any fear.

"The only person who's going to regret this is you," said Aaron. He reached out with both hands and gave Parker a small push.

Parker took a step back. He clenched his fists and went to take a step forward when the sound of running footsteps behind him made him turn. Parker watched, shock quickly turning to horror, as his little sister ran in front of him and then, taking Aaron by complete surprise, karate-chopped him in the face.

"Ah!" shouted Aaron, clutching his nose as he doubled over.

Parker stepped forward to grab Emma, but he was too late; she ran behind Aaron and jumped on his back.

Parker and Michael watched, frozen, as Emma wrapped one hand around Aaron's neck and, with the other, began to pull on Aaron's hair.

Aaron shouted out in pain and tried to slap his hands behind him, but Emma refused to let go.

"Get off him!" shouted Parker. But Emma wasn't looking

at him to be able to lip-read what he was saying, and she was definitely not going to be turning Effie on. Parker ran around, grabbed Emma's waist, and pulled her off Aaron's back. He turned her around to face him.

"What are you doing?"

But Emma didn't respond; she was looking at something just past his shoulder, her eyes widening. Parker snapped his head around to see Aaron's fist heading directly toward his sister. Instinctively, Parker leaned forward and pushed Emma out of the way, putting his own face in line with the punch.

Smack.

The fist caught the side of Parker's nose and right eye socket with such force that his neck snapped back. Disorientated, Parker staggered to the floor.

"Aaron Knoll!"

Parker looked up, his hand pressed flat against his right eye, and saw the vice principal, Mr. Andrews, taking long strides toward them.

"What do you think you're doing?" shouted Mr. Andrews. When he reached them, he turned first to Parker, who was rubbing his face.

"Are you okay?"

Parker nodded.

"Go to the nurse's office and get it checked out. Do you know where it is?"

Parker nodded again. He didn't, but he had no intention of going.

"And as for you," said Mr. Andrews, turning his attention to Aaron.

"She hit me first!" said Aaron. Aaron pointed at Emma.

Everybody looked over at Emma, who shrugged and widened her eyes with a look of complete innocence. Parker had seen this look many times before and it always worked on his father, just as it did now on Mr. Andrews.

Mr. Andrews turned to Aaron and shook his head. "Always with the excuses, Aaron. This is the third time this week. How many times do I have to tell you that violence is *never* the answer?"

Aaron—his face scrunched up in silent fury—didn't respond.

"To my office," ordered Mr. Andrews.

Aaron didn't move.

"Now."

Aaron cursed under his breath.

"Next time fight your own battles," he whispered to Parker as Mr. Andrews grabbed Aaron by his arm.

Parker watched as Aaron was led down the corridor. Around him, the audience that had gathered to watch the fight began to move again. Parker looked at Michael, who was frozen to the spot, looking like he might pass out. Parker opened his mouth to say something when Emma appeared in front of him. She tried to move Parker's hand to look at his face.

Parker flinched away from her and turned to Michael. "I'll

call you later," he said abruptly before storming out of the school.

Parker was the first to board his school bus. He took a seat halfway up, placed his backpack on the seat next to him, and turned toward the window. Still furious, he didn't look around, even when he heard his backpack being lifted and then pushed under his feet.

There was a tap on his shoulder. Parker lowered his head. Another tap, hard enough to hurt. Parker still didn't look around but pressed down on his wrist. Emma answered immediately.

So you're not going to look at me? she asked.

No.

Do you want to talk?

No.

Do you hate me?

Parker didn't answer.

You do. You hate me. I was just trying to help.

I didn't need your help.

Does it hurt?

Yes.

I'm really sorry, Parker. Please don't be angry.

Parker didn't respond and was about to turn off Effie, when he heard the quiet sobs next him. He sighed and turned around to face his sister. Normally, they switched to signing when they faced each other in public, but the bus was moving now and the high-backed seats hid them both from view. He kept Effie on.

Stop crying.

I was just trying to help, said Emma. There were tears rolling down her cheeks. She looked so desperate and sorry that Parker couldn't help but soften.

I know. But you shouldn't have done that. I look like an idiot now.

Emma read his words on her glasses and her forehead wrinkled in confusion.

Why?

Parker shook his head in exasperation. **Because it looks like I need my little sister to fight for me. And I don't.**

But you don't know karate. I've been watching videos.

Parker rolled his eyes. **Pulling someone's hair is not karate, Emma.**

But I did hit him. It was a good, right? You have to admit that.

That's not the point, Emma! You're my sister. And you're younger than me. And you're *not me*. It looks like I can't sort out my own problems.

Oh. I'm sorry, said Emma. She wiped her cheeks with the back of her hand. **I think I scared him though.**

Parker looked at his sister, with her blond bob, neon blue-and-pink jacket, and yellow jeans, and wondered if it was possible to look *less* intimidating.

I know you were just trying to help but, honestly, this is for me to sort out. And you could have been expelled for that—you shouldn't have hit him.

As he said this it occurred to Parker that he was being slightly hypocritical, but he decided there was no need to mention that he had considered doing the same.

I just don't understand why he was being so mean to you.

Parker sighed. **He's an idiot, okay. I'm fine and there's nothing you can do.** Then something occurred to him. **Except don't tell Dad what happened.**

Emma raised an eyebrow—a neat little trick that Parker, to his frustration, hadn't been able to master. **He's going to find out anyway. You skipped class. And you've got a black eye.**

I do? asked Parker. He put his hand up to his face and felt the swelling. **Well, maybe he'll find out, but he doesn't need to know what started it. Don't say anything about the cafeteria, and I'll think of something to explain the black eye. Okay?**

Emma didn't say anything, but Parker could tell by the way her lips were pursed that she wasn't convinced. He tried again.

Look, Emma, don't you think Dad has enough to worry about? It was one of those things, and I'm fine. He's stressed with his new job, and I don't want him to have to worry about me, too.

Emma bit her lip. **I hadn't thought of that. . . . Okay, I won't tell him.**

Promise?

I promise.

Thank you, said Parker, turning to the window.

But if it happens again, I'm going to tell him. I don't care what you say.

Parker shrugged. **Fine.** He switched off Effie. He'd deal with that matter if, or when, the time came.

Back at their house, Parker went straight to his room while Emma stayed downstairs watching television. By the time their father came home, two hours later than planned, Parker had taken a shower and changed into clean clothes. He felt better. Best of all, his father didn't seem to know anything about what had happened at school that day. If he had, Parker was sure he would have brought it up the moment he'd walked through the door. The only question that his father asked was about his eye, which was now a deep mottled purple and black and which Parker explained was an injury from gym class. His dad had seemed satisfied by the answer.

Relieved, Parker sat down to eat the lukewarm pizza their father had brought home with him. They all turned on Effie (one of its benefits was being able to eat and talk at the same time), and then, before either Parker or his father could say a word, Emma started the conversation in exactly the same way she did every night.

What did you do today? Emma asked her dad.

Their father looked up from his slice of pizza and smiled. **You know I can't talk about that.**

Please? Just a little clue?

Their dad shook his head. **Sorry.**

This was a new thing. In England their father had worked in scientific research for a university and had always been able to discuss what he was doing, even if neither of them understood a word of what he was saying. Back then Emma had never been interested. The moment he wasn't allowed to discuss his job, however, Emma had wanted to know everything. Parker, though just as curious, accepted the situation. He knew this much: that his father's work was some kind of collaboration between the governments of a number of countries and that, before accepting the job, he had been asked to sign a confidentiality agreement. Based on his previous work, Parker guessed it might have something to do with medical research, possibly cloning, but he understood that, for now anyway, his father couldn't talk about it. Unlike Emma, he didn't see any point in pushing the matter.

You can't tell us _anything_? Emma pleaded.

It's just boring government stuff. You'd be very disappointed if I told you.

Emma grinned. **Tell me and I'll tell you if you're right.**

Good try, kiddo. Now, why don't you two tell me about your day, he said, turning to Parker.

Parker tensed. **I can't. I signed a confidentiality**

agreement, he said with a shrug. He hoped he sounded less anxious saying this than he felt. He obviously did, as Parker's father laughed.

Very funny, he said. Then, to Parker's enormous relief, he turned to Emma. **And you, did you sign any confidentiality agreements today?**

Nope, said Emma. And off she went. Once Emma started talking or signing, nobody else ever got a word in edgewise. Sometimes this was annoying; today it was a relief.

Emma told her dad about the new sign language she was learning (Parker hadn't known that they used a different version here; apparently, even signing had an accent), and then—without a pause—about being picked to go to a swimming tournament the following Monday. Back in England, Emma had represented her county in swimming. The swimming coach had called her in that morning to tell her this was evidence enough of her abilities for her to earn a place on the school team without a trial. It was the first that Parker had heard of it—the incident with Aaron had probably distracted her, he guessed.

As Emma chattered away, Parker pressed down twice on his wrist. By doing this when a call on Effie was active, Parker could hear what his dad and sister were thinking, but they couldn't hear him. Two presses and they could hear him again. Keeping it pressed for two seconds hung up the call. It sounded complicated, but over the years, Parker could mute his thoughts midconversation and back again without a second thought.

Can we get some chickens?

Emma had moved on from telling them about her day without, Parker noted gratefully, a word about what had happened in the cafeteria or the fight that afternoon.

Chickens?

Yeah. Not many.

What's not many? Two?

Multiply by five, said Emma.

Ten! That's a lot of chickens, Emma.

Emma stuck out her bottom lip in a sulk. **You said I could get an animal when we got here. You promised.**

That has been the hardest thing for Emma, thought Parker: handing her collection of injured birds and animals over to their neighbors when they moved.

His father was obviously thinking the same thing. **Okay, fine. You can get some chickens as long as you take care of them.**

Emma nodded enthusiastically.

I mean it. I don't have time to be taking care of one chicken, let alone ten.

I'll do it all. Promise.

And where are you going to keep them? We'll have to get some cages.

Emma's eyes widened in horror. **No! They have to be able to roam free.**

I'm not sure that's a good idea. They could get lost. Or eaten.

Parker's going to make an alarm for me, to stop

other animals from getting in or out of our yard. And he said it won't hurt them.

Parker's dad turned to him. **Can you do that?**

Parker nodded. **I think so. I just need a few bits from the hardware store.**

Okay. We'll get them on Sunday. After we visit your mother's . . .

There was a pause. Parker's dad didn't like to say *grave*. And it wasn't a grave anyway, though Parker didn't know what to call it either.

After we visit your mother.

You're not working? asked Parker and Emma at the same time.

No. I have a very important meeting tomorrow, but after that things should get quieter.

What's the meeting about? asked Emma.

Their dad shook his head. **Nothing interesting. But it is important, and I have a lot to do before it. In fact, if it's okay with the two of you, I might go in for a couple of hours later.**

What, tonight? asked Parker.

It's just for a bit. I'll do as much as I can here, but there are some things I have to do in the lab. He looked up at the both of them and rubbed his forehead as if in pain. **I'm so sorry. I know I haven't been around much. I'll make it up to you this weekend. We'll celebrate the end of your first week at school properly. We can . . .**

Parker could see how bad his dad felt. **It's okay, Dad,** he said, **we understand. Anyway, we've been invited to my friend Michael's house tomorrow. Can we go?**

Oh. Well, great! I'm glad you're making friends. Parker's father paused. **Except I don't know if I can drop you off. Can I talk to his parents?**

Parker walked over to the side table and picked up the piece of paper that Michael had given him.

Parker and Emma watched as their father called the number and asked if he was speaking to Michael's mother. There was a short conversation and, before Parker could ask if he could pass the phone to him to speak to Michael, his father had hung up.

His parents are working away, but that was the housekeeper.

Housekeeper? Parker turned to Emma, and they both shrugged at each other in surprise. Michael hadn't said anything about a housekeeper.

Anyway, she sounds very nice, continued his father. **She said that they can send a car to pick you both up and drop you home later.**

Really? asked Parker.

Apparently so. If there's any problem at all, call me at the office. I'll step outside when I can and call you on Effie to make sure you got there fine.

Parker nodded. Effie needed a good signal to work. The building his father worked in received no signal at all.

Emma jumped out of her seat and wrapped her arms around their father's neck.

I love you, Daddy.

Parker's dad smiled. **I love you too. I'm very lucky to have you both.**

He undid Emma's arms from around his neck and stood up.

If you need anything in the night—anything at all— you can call the office. I'll be back before you wake up.

When are you going to sleep? asked Emma.

I'll be fine. Can I leave you two to tidy everything away and get ready for bed?

Parker nodded, and their father gave them each a kiss on the head. He picked up his bulging briefcase.

I'll come say good night in a bit, he said, walking out. Before he had even left the room, Parker's dad had turned Effie off. Parker guessed it was because his mind was already back on his work.

That night Parker lay in his bed thinking about everything that had happened at school. No matter which way he thought about it, he couldn't see how the situation in the cafeteria could have turned out any different. Whether today or any other day, Parker would have had to speak in front of the class at some point. His classmates would always have picked up on his accent and teased him about it.

Parker wondered, as he often did, if it might have been

different had his mother been here. It was an easy question to answer. Parker already knew that, if his mother were still here, they wouldn't have moved. She had loved their house far too much to ever consider leaving it.

Parker pressed down on his wrist.

I wish you were here, Mum, he thought.

There was no answer, of course—there never was—but Parker liked to imagine she was listening anyway. He had never told his dad or his sister that he did this. In fact, he was the only one of the three who didn't talk about their mother all the time. Emma was always asking what their mother would have done or said in every situation, and Parker's dad would only talk about her in the present tense. It annoyed Parker sometimes—the fact that his dad did this—but he guessed it was just his way of coping. Emma's was to ask questions, and his was to talk to his mother via Effie. In a way, none of them had ever let her go.

He leaned over the side of his bed and turned off his bed-side lamp.

"Good night, Mum," he said. He pressed down on the middle of his wrist once more and fell asleep.

CHAPTER SIX

48:10

At precisely eleven o'clock the next morning, a long black car with tinted windows pulled up outside Parker's house. Both Parker and Emma stared out the window by the door as the driver, an older man in full uniform, including hat, stepped out and made his way to their front door.

"Wow," said Parker as he put his coat on.

"His parents must be millionaires," signed Emma.

Parker nodded in agreement and picked up the bike that was resting on the wall. He wheeled it out behind Emma and turned to lock the door.

"Are you Parker and Emma?" asked the driver.

"Yes," said Parker. "Hi."

"Hi, I'm Brendan. I'm here to take you to Michael's house. Let me take that for you."

Parker thanked him as he handed his bike over. He followed the driver to the car.

"I'll put this in the trunk," said Brendan, opening the passenger door. "Make yourselves comfortable."

Parker climbed in behind Emma and ran his hand along the sleek gray leather interior.

"Can you believe this?" signed Parker as he slid in beside Emma and put on his seat belt.

Emma giggled and pointed to the television screen in front of them.

"You can turn it on if you'd like; the remote is in the pocket next to your seat."

Parker looked up and saw that Brendan was watching them in the rearview mirror.

"Thanks," said Parker, picking up the remote.

"Right. You both have everything you need?"

Parker nodded.

"Good. Sit back and enjoy. We'll be there in approximately twenty minutes."

With that, a wall of black glass rolled up behind the driver's seat and the engine started up.

It was raining when they arrived, but neither the downpour nor the gray skies did anything to lessen the impressiveness of where Michael lived. Parker and Emma, both now ignoring the television screen, peered out the window and watched as the car rolled slowly along the driveway, past tennis courts, a golf course, a swimming pool with a waterfall and slides, and acres of landscaped gardens.

"Did he tell you it was going to be like this?" signed Emma.

Parker shook his head. *"I had no idea. He didn't say a thing,"* he signed back.

"I wonder what his house . . ."

Emma's question was answered before she had a chance to finish asking it. Michael's house—though it wasn't a house like any Parker had ever seen—was a wide curved structure of glass and wood that rose from the ground like a snake emerging from its underground lair, and wound three quarters of the way around a lake. The movement of the rain running down the glass panels coupled with the reflection of the rippling waters of the lake made the entire structure appear as if it were moving, alive under the elements. Parker and Emma, transfixed in open-mouthed amazement, watched as Brendan drove slowly around the lake before coming to a stop under a glass canopy that curved out over the driveway. There, standing by a set of open glass doors, was Michael, waving enthusiastically.

"Hi!" said Michael, opening the passenger door before Brendan had even turned the engine off.

"Wow," said Parker, climbing out of the car. "You didn't tell me you lived in a mansion."

"Oh, it's not really a mansion. But thanks," said Michael dismissively. He smiled at Emma as she climbed out behind Parker and pressed down on her wrist, a frown on her face.

It's a bit much, she said via Effie.

Parker narrowed his eyes at his sister.

"Emma says she loves it," he said to Michael.

Michael looked at them both in turn. "But she didn't sign anything."

It was only then that Parker realized his error. He hesitated. "I can kind of tell what she's thinking."

"How?"

Parker was beginning to realize that Michael was not somebody to let anything get past him. "I just can. It's a deaf thing—we're close."

"Oh, like twins?"

Parker nodded and Michael shrugged.

"Neat. Come on, let's go inside."

Parker waited for Michael to walk ahead of him. He turned to Emma and gave his brow a theatrical wipe with the back of his hand.

Close call, he said on Effie. **Turn it off?**

Emma nodded and pressed down on her wrist to hang up their call.

The inside of Michael's house was as spectacular as—if not more so than—the outside. Parker was sure that Michael must have known how impressive his house was to his visitors and yet, as they made their way along the building, he played it down to such an extent that Parker started to wonder whether he was too modest to make a fuss or so accustomed to this lifestyle that he saw nothing out of the ordinary about it. He didn't know Michael well enough yet to know which one it was.

Parker looked up at the hexagonal panes of glass that formed the dome of the living room, hypnotized by the movement of the raindrops racing down all around them. "Why can't I hear anything?"

"I think they're double-paned or something."

"How do they clean them?" signed Emma. Parker translated.

"Window cleaners," said Michael. "Obviously."

"Doesn't it get hot?"

"Not really," said Michael. He pressed a switch on the wall, and every one of the glass panes turned from clear to opaque, enclosing the three of them in a dull gray dome.

"Unbelievable," said Parker slowly.

"Not really. It's not that big a deal—it's actually pretty simple technology. Anyway, come on. Let's go up to my room," said Michael. He switched the panes back to clear and walked off before Parker or Emma had a chance to ask another question.

Parker shouldn't really have been surprised by Michael's bedroom, and yet he was. For one thing, it was by far the biggest bedroom that Parker had ever seen. It was so large, in fact, that *bedroom* didn't seem an adequate description of it, although it did contain a set of bunk beds built into a deep recess in one of the walls. The room was teardrop-shaped with a long wall of glass that curved around the widest section of the space. At the far end—where the teardrop ended, a spiral glass staircase led up to a mezzanine floor that looked out over where they stood.

A friend of Parker's parents had once mentioned over dinner (back when his mother had been alive and they'd still invited people around for dinner) that if you want to know what a person is really like, take a look at their bedroom. It was an observation that had stuck with Parker (that same day he had quietly taken down all the posters of his once-favorite cartoon astronaut), and he thought of that observation now as he looked around Michael's room. It was immaculate. There was not so much as a pen out of place. This was in stark contrast to Parker's own bedroom; his idea of tidying up was to push everything into a corner or, for special occasions, under the bed and into the wardrobe. Parker wondered if the room looked like this only because Michael had a housekeeper to tidy up after him, but this question was answered when Michael picked up Parker's jacket from where Parker had thrown it on the bed and hung it in a hidden wardrobe behind the wall by the door.

The other thing that struck Parker about Michael's room was that it wouldn't have been at all obvious—had he not known it was Michael's—what the age of the person was to whom it belonged. Action figures sat neatly on a shelf alongside academic-looking textbooks. Colorful robots adorned the bedsheets, and a blue teddy lay on a pillow whilst, directly opposite, a bank of the most sophisticated and up-to-date computer equipment lined the long curved desk that had been built to fit against the glass wall.

"The rain is supposed to let up in an hour, according to the weather reports," said Michael, interrupting Parker's thoughts. "We can play—I mean hang out—in here until lunch, if that's okay, then go out after we eat."

Michael opened a drawer at the desk nearest to where he was standing and took out a remote control. He pressed a button, and the smooth white wall that curved under the overhanging gallery swooshed open to reveal shelf after shelf lined with toys.

For a moment Parker and Emma stood side by side, staring.

Michael turned to Emma. "You can play with anything you want," he said.

"Wow, you have a lot of toys, Michael," signed Emma, and Parker translated.

"I . . . um . . ."

Parker looked over at Michael and saw that he was biting his lip.

"I . . . didn't ask for them—my parents just buy this stuff for me," replied Michael.

Emma smirked. *"Lucky you,"* she signed.

"But," added Michael quickly, grasping her meaning, "I'm thinking of giving most of them away."

"Really?" asked Parker. "Why?"

"Um . . . I don't really play with them all. I was thinking of giving them to a hospital or something."

"Ah, that's so nice, Michael!" she signed, smiling, and Michael smiled back.

She didn't seem to realize, as Parker did, that Michael was obviously saying this to impress her. As his sister skipped over to the toys and pulled out a long drawer that turned out to be filled to the brim with thousands of plastic building bricks, Parker turned and followed Michael over to the long desk.

"Are you really going to give them all away?" asked Parker.

"Yeah," replied Michael. "I was thinking I had too many anyway."

"So you're not doing it because of her?" asked Parker, nodding in Emma's direction.

"No!" said Michael slightly too emphatically. He didn't look at Parker.

"Hmm," said Parker.

Michael didn't say anything as he knelt down and turned on two of the computers.

"So what do your parents do?" asked Parker, changing the subject.

"My mom's an aviation safety engineer, and my dad has a software company."

"What kind of software?"

"Games, mostly," said Michael as he pulled out a pair of headphones and handed them to Parker. "Clown Apocalypse is one of them."

Parker's head snapped around in disbelief.

"No. Way."

Clown Apocalypse was not only Mr. Nowak's favorite

game—it was also the most downloaded game in history. "No wonder you have all this stuff."

"They're never home, so they pretty much buy me whatever I want. I think it's a guilt thing," explained Michael. He sounded embarrassed. He took a seat in a leather office chair and pushed an identical one next to him in Parker's direction.

"My dad just buys ice cream when he feels guilty about working too much. I think I need to have a talk with him," said Parker, smiling as he sat down.

Michael didn't reply. Instead he turned on the two screens in front of them, handed Parker a pair of headphones, and started up a computer game—the third installment of the car game they had been playing the day before.

"I thought this wasn't coming out until next month," said Parker.

"Perks of having a dad who owns a gaming company," said Michael.

Parker grinned. He turned, saw that Emma was busy exploring Michael's collection of toys, and picked up his headphones.

"Right," he said, choosing his car, "let's do this. I hope you're a good loser."

"I wouldn't know," said Michael, with a straight face. "I never lose."

Michael put his headphones on, and Parker turned back to his screen, but not before catching the sight of Michael's mouth curling up into a smile.

* * * * * *

Parker would have stayed at the computer all day—and he suspected Michael would have been happy to do the same—had it not been for the housekeeper, Hilda—a stern-looking woman with an efficient tone of voice—coming into the room to call them down for lunch. Parker, Michael, and Emma followed her down to the kitchen to find three bowls of steaming spaghetti Bolognese and warm freshly baked bread waiting for them. By the time they finished eating, the weather had cleared and the sun was shining—exactly as Michael had predicted.

"Let's get our bikes. We can ride up to the tree house," said Michael, leading them out of the main building and into a glass-covered walkway that branched in opposite directions ahead of them. They took the left path, which led to a set of elevator doors.

"Where does this go?" asked Parker.

"The basement," said Michael as they stepped inside. He turned his back to Parker and pressed the button marked B. Parker looked over at Emma to give her an isn't-this-amazing? look, but she was too busy staring at the sleek leather-padded walls of the elevator. Her face was scrunched up in thought.

Parker pressed down on his wrist.

Without looking down at her arm, she pressed down on her wrist to answer.

You okay? he said.

Emma looked over at him and gave a small shake of her

head. **I'm just trying to work out how many schools could have been built in Africa with the money they spent on this house.**

Lighten up, Emma. Seriously, it's annoying. You can't think like that about everything.

Yes, I can, replied Emma as the elevator came to a smooth stop.

Ding.

The doors opened and Michael stepped out.

Just try to enjoy it, said Parker.

Emma gave a small shrug and rolled her eyes. **Fine,** she said. She turned off Effie and stepped out in front of Parker as the lights in the room flickered on.

Without waiting for them, Michael began to cross the space. Parker and Emma followed slowly behind, surveying the room as they walked. It was, other than the curved ceiling, much like a regular garage—only at least twenty times bigger. In stark contrast to the rest of the house, this floor, being underground, had no windows and therefore received no natural light. Instead stark white light shone down from the spotlights that ran the length of the room and bounced off the smooth gray floor and white walls, giving the space a clinical feel. At the other end of the room, opposite an open archway that Parker guessed led outside, three vehicles were parked side by side: the one that had picked them up that morning, a shiny red sports car, and a golf cart. Beyond that, a line of bikes hung from a rack mounted on the wall. Other than that, the room was empty. Parker's eyes scanned the floor as he crossed it and found nothing—not a single leaf, nor a speck of dirt.

"How long have you lived here?" asked Parker.

"I don't know—about five years maybe. Why?"

"It's just so"—Parker searched for the right word—"tidy."

"It's called minimalist."

"It's definitely that. Don't you ever just feel like—I don't know—throwing paint around or something?"

"Er, no. Why? Is that what you do in your house?"

"No, of course not. It's . . . oh, never mind. Hey, there's my bike!"

Brendan had hung Parker's bike on the first slot of the rack. Next to it was the only bike that looked as if it had been used recently—a state-of-the-art mountain bike with mud-covered wheels.

"That must really bother you," said Parker, grinning as he reached out and spun the wheel of the bike. A smattering of dried mud fell to the floor and Parker flinched.

"I'm really sorry," he said. He bent down and began to brush the mud into his hand.

Michael gave Parker a quizzical look. "It's okay—I don't have a phobia about dirt or anything. You can leave it there."

"Oh, okay. Good," said Parker, brushing his hands and letting the dirt fall to the floor once more.

"Though we will have to get the room disinfected now."

"Seriously?"

"No, of course not. You're kind of weird, Parker."

Parker raised his hands and brushed the remainder of the dirt on his palm in the direction of Michael, whose knee-jerk reaction was to jump back.

"Takes one to know one," said Parker.

He smiled as Emma tapped him on the shoulder.

"They all look too big for me," signed Emma.

Parker looked along the bike rack and saw that Emma was right. "Which one can Emma use?" he asked Michael. "I think they're all too big. She can use mine if you don't have one for her."

"No, no, it's fine. I've got one for her," said Michael. He waved Emma over and pointed to a spot behind the golf cart. Leaving Emma to it, Parker turned his attention back to his own bike. He lifted it up off the rack and was about to swing his leg over to mount it when he heard a loud gasp. Parker turned and saw Michael standing by the golf cart, biting his thumb nervously.

Parker quickly rested his bike against the wall and hurried over.

Emma, Parker found, was standing next to a purple bike that was exactly the right size for her. Even if it hadn't had a large red bow tied to the handlebars, Parker would have guessed anyway—from the gleaming paintwork and spotless tires—that it was brand-new.

Emma ran her hands over the bow and turned to Parker with a confused look on her face.

"*Is it a gift?*" she signed. Parker translated the question to Michael.

"Yes, but it's not from me."

"You *bought* my sister a bike?"

Michael looked embarrassed. "I already said: it's not from me."

Parker shook his head, not knowing what to make of the situation, just as Emma found the tag hanging from the handlebars. Parker watched as she turned it over, then, upon reading what was written on it, let out a small laugh.

Parker walked over, leaving Michael standing by the cart, and looked at the tag that Emma was now holding out for him to read.

To Emma, from Gary the Goat.

Parker read it again to check that he had read it correctly. He looked over at Michael. "*Seriously?* Gary?"

"That's a very popular goat name in Africa," said Michael, shrugging. "Is it okay?" he asked Emma.

Emma considered her answer for a moment and Parker winced. He knew exactly what Emma was going to say—she was going to tell Michael to take it back. He was just wondering whether this was going to make the rest of the day awkward when, to both Parker's and Michael's surprise, she broke out into a run and threw her arms around Michael. Michael stood stiffly, his arms by his sides, until she let go.

"*I love it,*" she signed.

"It's no big deal," mumbled Michael. He turned and lifted

his bike off the rack, then looked at Emma and Parker. "Shall we go?" he asked. He pedaled off and disappeared up the ramp before Parker or Emma could answer.

Parker was still shaking his head in disbelief as he picked up his own bike. He pressed down on his wrist.

Think of how many goats that bike's worth, said Parker.

Oh, lighten up, Parker, said Emma as she cycled past him with a wide grin on her face.

CHAPTER SEVEN

45:10

At two o'clock that afternoon, at the precise moment that Parker and Emma encountered a tree house larger than most people's homes, Parker's father, Dr. Geoffrey Banks, was preparing for possibly the most important moment in his career. Whether it would be his greatest moment, or his worst, was still very much of an unknown. Dr. Banks wiped the sweat from his brow. If successful, he and, more important, his children, would be rewarded with the greatest gift imaginable. If it failed, he would almost certainly lose his job. Or worse.

"They're waiting, Dr. Banks."

Dr. Banks looked up and saw Lina standing at the door of his office. The expression on her face was easy to read.

"You have nothing to be scared about, Lina; they're not going to blame you. I'll make sure of it," he said, standing up.

"I'm not worried about myself," she replied in a quiet voice.

"It could work—have you considered that?" said Dr. Banks with more confidence than he felt. "In three weeks we've got it up to a seventy percent success rate. Chances are, it will work."

"And if it doesn't?"

Dr. Banks didn't answer. Instead he took a deep breath, did the top button of his lab coat, and stood up straight. He forced a smile onto his face.

"Right, Miss Chan, let's get this over and done with. Lead the way to my execution."

It was supposed to be a joke, but Lina didn't laugh.

Bowveld was waiting in the corridor by the doors of Laboratory One. He also wore a white lab coat, which, in case anybody should need reminding, had his name and title embroidered across the upper left: *Dr. Warren Bowveld III, Director*. Everything about him, from his helmet of dyed black hair to his snakeskin loafers and oversize gold watch, suggested a man determined to impress his power upon the world.

Dr. Banks turned to Lina. "You go ahead," he said in a low voice. "Double-check everything."

Lina nodded and walked quickly past the director with her head held down. The director acknowledged her only by stepping aside to let her through. He waited until the doors had closed behind her before speaking.

"Are you ready?" asked Bowveld.

Dr. Banks refused to use the title Doctor in front of his boss's name. He did this mainly because it irked Bowveld when he did that, but also because Dr. Banks had learned before starting the job that Bowveld had never earned the title—it was just something he'd added to his name to make himself sound more competent than he was.

"You know the answer to that," replied Dr. Banks.

Bowveld glared his disapproval. "Do I need to remind you of the importance of today?"

"No, you do not," replied Dr. Banks. He could feel the anger rising inside him. He stopped, took a deep breath, and reminded himself that, though he had no choice about working for this man, he didn't have to give him the satisfaction of letting him know how much he resented it.

"However," Dr. Banks continued, his voice now more controlled, "that doesn't change the fact that I've only had three weeks to try to solve a problem that nobody has managed to solve in over thirty years."

Bowveld lifted his finger and, with a deep scowl, pointed it slowly at Dr. Banks.

"*You* were the one who said you could do this."

"And I can," replied Dr. Banks. "I'm almost there. But I need more than three weeks."

"Well, you don't have it. Your demonstration *must* be successful. This entire company, not to mention the Bowveld family name, is on the line. . . ."

But Bowveld's reputation wasn't the only thing at stake. He had in his power something that was far more important to Dr. Banks. It was what had forced Dr. Banks to come to work here, to move to a new country, and to uproot his children. There were only three things that mattered in Dr. Banks's life, and Bowveld held the fate of one—if not all—in his hand. The director wasn't going to let him forget it.

Slowly, Bowveld leaned down so his mouth was next to Dr. Banks's ear, and in a hissed whisper Bowveld pulled out the ace he kept up his sleeve.

"I'm sure your wife would like to see her children again, Dr. Banks."

The words cut through Dr. Banks like a knife. It didn't matter that he had heard them before, or that they haunted him every second of every day; the impact of them never lessened. Dr. Banks stepped back and met the director's eyes.

"I'll do my best," he said finally.

The director smiled like a predator savoring his helpless prey, and his brilliant white teeth sparkled.

"Yes, you will," he said.

There was nothing more to say and both men knew it. Bowveld turned and opened the doors to the laboratory, leaving Dr. Banks still trying to regain his composure.

It was showtime.

CHAPTER EIGHT

45:04

Laboratory One, the largest of the ten laboratories housed deep underground below the headquarters building of Avecto Enterprises, was quiet as Dr. Banks walked in behind Bowveld. Seated in silence in rows behind the wall of safety glass were some of the most important and influential people in the world. Dr. Banks didn't allow himself a closer look; his nerves were frayed enough as it was.

Bowveld picked up the microphone waiting for him on the side counter and then, as they had agreed, he took center stage, and Dr. Banks joined Lina at the other side of the room.

"Everything ready?" whispered Dr. Banks.

Lina nodded as Bowveld turned on the microphone and tapped it three times.

Boom. Boom. Boom.

"It's going to be okay," said Dr. Banks, as much to himself as to Lina.

Lina opened her mouth to reply but was interrupted by

Bowveld's voice, forceful and full of confidence, reverberating around the room.

"Good afternoon to you all," said Bowveld, "and welcome to the heart of Avecto Enterprises. Before we begin, I'd first like to thank you for taking the time out of your very busy schedules to come here today. We are honored by your presence. I know that many of you have engagements to attend, so today's presentation will be quick but will, I am sure, put your minds at ease. Afterward, there will be a question and answer session. Before we begin, though, I'd first like to say a few words. I'll keep it brief, which, as you all know, will be something of a challenge for me."

Bowveld guffawed at his own joke.

Dr. Banks turned to Lina and rolled his eyes. For the first time that day, Lina smiled.

"As you should all be aware from your monthly updates, work on SIX is progressing well. Only last week we sent parts to build ten new cranes. All damage from the sandstorm has been repaired, and we are working flat-out to ensure that we are back on schedule within the month. At this time, I'm delighted to announce that Great Bowveld—from which all central operations will run—is now completed. The progress of your own nations is also advancing well, as you will know from your individual reports. After almost twenty-five years of planning, preparation, and hard work, we can see the finishing line. Your new lives—*our* new lives—are within reach. No more red tape! No more having to bend over backward to please the common man! An existence of luxury and comfort await those who have earned it: you. We did our best here, but sometimes the courage is needed to say, 'This didn't work; let's start again.' You here today are the courageous ones, and for that, you will be greatly rewarded. SIX is our opportunity to correct the mistakes that have been made here on Earth. Many tools are needed to build a house but only one to build paradise: hindsight. As the motto of SIX proudly states, 'Practice Made Perfect.'"

Bowveld stopped, his face suddenly serious. He ran his hand through his hair. It sprang straight back up again.

"And now I'd like to address the reason you are all here today. I know many of you have concerns about the fact that you have not been able to visit SIX to see the progress for yourselves. I have been just as frustrated as all of you, I assure you. Avection, our patented form of teleportation, was first developed thirty-three years ago and yet, despite all the time that has passed, the ability to perform a second avection without any glitches has proved considerably more difficult than any of us could have imagined. Six months ago, we all sat together in a crisis meeting, and I promised you that I would solve the issue by today. As always, as you will see in just a moment, I have kept my word. The first return visits to SIX will be available to you next month, when you will finally be able to see the beauty, and wisdom, of your investments. And the man who has made this all possible, the man who finally got things moving—excuse the pun—is this man: Dr. Geoffrey Banks."

Bowveld motioned to the side of the room. All eyes turned to Dr. Banks who, at the mention of his name, straightened and gave a tight smile.

"Dr. Banks," continued Bowveld, "has been at the helm of some of the most influential and—"

"Can you get on with it?" called out a man's voice from the crowd.

Bowveld stopped abruptly. He looked around and, upon seeing the man who had spoken, visibly faltered.

"Oh. Yes, of course, Your Highness. My apologies." He turned to Dr. Banks and nodded for him to begin. Then, without waiting for a response, he walked around the safety wall to his seat at the center of the front row.

Once seated, Bowveld pressed a button next to a small microphone on his armrest, and the loudspeaker clicked on. Bowveld leaned over to speak.

"Dr. Banks, you may proceed."

For the briefest of moments, Dr. Banks wondered what would happen if he simply turned around and walked out. The consequences would be bad—undoubtedly so—but perhaps not as bad as if this demonstration failed. And then the image of Sarah, his wife, came to mind, and all his indecision disappeared. He had a responsibility to her, and to Parker and Emma. He had decided, when he had found out that his wife was still alive, that he wouldn't tell his children; it just wasn't fair to offer them that hope. They had already lost their mother once. Losing her a second time—strong as they both were—would destroy them. Until he was certain that they would see her again, there was simply no way that he could tell them. He hoped that time would come soon, which meant, unfortunately, walking out was not an option.

Dr. Banks gave a solemn nod in the direction of the audience. With Lina behind him, he walked over to the white metal box on the far left of the room and did his best to ignore the stares coming at him from the sea of white coats behind the safety glass.

The box was humming softly. Identical in appearance to the box at the other end of the room, the Avectrons looked not unlike large washing machines, except that each of these two machines came with a fifty-million-dollar price tag. It was a drop in the ocean compared to the amount of money invested elsewhere and that amounted to—literally—billions of dollars' worth of expectation resting on Dr. Banks's shoulders. He could feel every one of them.

"I checked everything," said Lina in a quiet voice, though nobody could hear them from this side of the safety glass.

He was sure she was right, but just in case, Dr. Banks ran his eyes over the numbers on the control panel one more time. Everything was in order.

"You checked the harness?" asked Dr. Banks.

Lina nodded. "She's in there and ready to go."

"Good." He turned to face Lina. "Thank you. I'll take it from here."

"Good luck," she whispered.

Lina stepped aside and Dr. Banks, with his back turned to the audience, took a deep breath and knelt down.

"Dr. Banks will now open the Avectron."

Dr. Banks flinched at the sound of the voice. He had forgotten that Bowveld would be commentating. He reached over, turned the heavy metal handle, and pulled the door open.

As soon as the pig saw him, she started squealing.

"Shhh," whispered Dr. Banks, "it's okay. You're going to be just fine."

"Ladies and gentlemen," announced Bowveld, "I'd like you to meet Polly."

There were a couple of small laughs from the audience and a light ripple of clapping.

The pig dangled helplessly from a harness. As Dr. Banks reached in to check the tension of the harness, she started to squeal louder.

"As you can see, she's quite the talker," joked Bowveld.

Dr. Banks pulled on one of the straps and thought of Emma. *How she would disapprove of what I am doing,* he thought. If—*if*—the pig survived, he resolved to bring it home to her to keep.

"She'll take very good care of you," he said, stroking the pig.

Calmed by the soothing voice, the pig soon quieted, and the room turned silent once more, heavy with the air of expectation.

Dr. Banks gave the pig a final pat on the head. "You're all good to go, Polly," he said as he pulled his hand away. "See you on the other side."

Polly stared at Dr. Banks but didn't make another sound as he closed the door and turned the handle all the way around.

Click.

"Polly is now ready for her first avection," announced Bowveld. "In order to demonstrate firsthand how quick and painless avection is, we have placed cameras inside the Avectrons."

On cue Lina pressed down on one of the buttons of the remote control she was holding, and the large white screen on the back wall of the laboratory came to life. Slowly, the image of the pig dangling under the dull purple glow of the Avectron's lights appeared above a flurry of constantly changing numbers and a continuous green line that spiked sharply every time the pig moved.

The entire room, Dr. Banks included, turned to the screen and watched as the pig wriggled about, desperately trying to squirm her way out of her harness.

Dr. Banks leaned over to the Avectron and pressed a button.

"The Avectron will now fill with the smell of lavender," said Bowveld. "We wanted to make the process of avection as comfortable and pleasant as possible. Lavender—our extensive research determined—proved to have the most calming qualities of any scent. If you have a preference, however, you may, of course, choose another scent for your own journeys."

Dr. Banks turned and, for the first time, allowed himself a good look at the audience. He spotted, amongst many other familiar faces, a past president, two members of the British cabinet, and a very well-known business magnate. Every one of them was staring intently at the screen, watching with considerable self-interest as the scent of the lavender began to take effect.

Dr. Banks joined the audience in watching as the pig began to calm. The green line jumped a couple more times until it finally evened out, barring only the tiny fluctuations for the movement of the pig's breathing.

"Polly, I believe, is now ready for her trip to the other side of the room. Is that correct, Dr. Banks?"

Dr. Banks nodded.

"Good. Then we may begin. Initiate scanning."

Three weeks earlier, this part of the process would have required Dr. Banks to input long lines of complicated code. Now all he had to do was to press down on the glowing red button. It was just one of the things that Dr. Banks had done to improve the process, not that anyone was going to be giving him any credit for it.

Inside the pig's compartment, a green light began to sweep the box.

"The pig is now being scanned and its exact data is being recorded. This analysis will include the harness, which, in the case of yourselves, would be your clothes. We have done this so that you will be dressed exactly as you left. There will be no need to parade around naked upon your arrival to SIX, you'll be pleased to hear." Bowveld laughed, then stopped abruptly when he realized that he was the only one amused by his comment.

He cleared his throat. "Dr. Banks, are we ready?"

Dr. Banks waited a few moments until the red button started flashing. He nodded.

"And off we go," announced Bowveld. "Begin first avection."

Everybody watched as Dr. Banks pressed down on the button.

There was a loud beep, and then the Avectron began to hum.

Polly looked around her enclosed space as the humming grew louder and louder and then, after only three minutes . . .

BOOM!

Everyone except for Dr. Banks and Lina jumped. On the screen, the green line went flat and the portion of the screen showing the dangling pig turned black.

The Avectron was empty.

There were a few murmurs in the crowd as Dr. Banks walked over to the second Avectron on the opposite side of the room. Dr. Banks knelt down, and everybody in the room, once again completely silent, watched as he reached out, pulled down on the handle, and opened the front of the machine.

There was a loud squeal.

"Ladies and gentlemen," announced Bowveld, "Polly has arrived."

As if to emphasize the point, Polly—still dangling, though a few feet away from where she had been only moments earlier—started to squeal louder. Dr. Banks saw a few smiles in the audience. There was, however, no applause—they had all seen this part of the demonstration before. It was the next part that they were all waiting for.

Dr. Banks reached into the Avectron and gently stroked the back of the pig again as Lina switched on the cameras in the machine. Polly, who had immediately calmed on being comforted by Dr. Banks, appeared once more on the screen, bathed in the dull purple of the ultraviolet lights and hanging limply in midair.

Knowing that it wouldn't benefit any of them to delay the next part of the presentation, least of all the pig, Dr. Banks reached under Polly's harness to check that it hadn't lost any tension following the first avection.

"We're nearly done, Polly," said Dr. Banks as he withdrew his hand and closed the door for a second time. He stood up.

"Are we ready for the second avection?" asked Bowveld.

Dr. Banks hesitated as his heart suddenly began to race faster.

"Dr. Banks?" asked Bowveld. His voice was calm but controlled. Dr. Banks could hear the effort the director was making not to lose his temper in front of the investors.

Dr. Banks turned, and for a brief but almost imperceptible moment, the two men's eyes met. It was long enough for Dr. Banks to clearly read the message behind the director's narrowed eyes: *Do this or suffer the consequences.*

Dr. Banks slowly nodded, and the director, visibly relieved, leaned into his microphone as Dr. Banks pressed down on the glowing red button a second time.

"For your security," explained Bowveld as the green light began to sweep the inside of the Avectron, "the scanning process is performed for every teleportation. This ensures that everything about you—from the way your shoelace has been tied to the exact placement of each strand of your hair, arrives at your destination *exactly* as it was on your departure."

There was silence as numbers poured across the screen. The sweeping green light switched off, and the red light began to flash.

It wasn't just the lives of the people here in the room that would change if this worked; it was also the lives of all their families and friends and of those they'd chosen to leave behind. The whole world would be different with the push of a button.

And all Dr. Banks had to do was press it.

"Begin the second avection," said Bowveld.

With his back to the audience, Dr. Banks took a deep breath and with his sleeve wiped the sweat now lining his brow. His hand trembling slightly, Dr. Banks reached out and pushed.

Beep.

The humming started up again. Dr. Banks held his breath, and then he did something he had never done in his entire career: he crossed his fingers.

Please work, he thought as the humming grew louder in volume. One minute passed. Two minutes. Then . . .

BOOM!

The green line went flat. The numbers stopped rolling. The pig disappeared from the screen.

It was done.

This time there was no commentary from Bowveld, only a heavy silence that followed Dr. Banks as he walked back over to the first Avectron.

Lina was standing next to it, ashen-faced and visibly trembling. Neither of them spoke. Dr. Banks knelt down to face the front of the machine and, as he did so, he saw that Lina was also crossing her fingers.

This is it, thought Dr. Banks as he turned the handle and pulled back on it slightly. Then, with the door slightly ajar so that only he would be able to see, Dr. Banks peered around into the Avectron. Polly blinked back at Dr. Banks. And then she opened her mouth and began to squeal.

"Eeeeeeeek!"

Upon hearing the pig, the entire room erupted into thunderous applause.

"Yes!" shouted somebody from the crowd.

"Bravo!"

"Turn the screen on, Miss Chan!" said the director, his voice ecstatic. "Show us the pig!"

The audience joined in. "Show us the pig! Show us the pig!"

Lina picked up the remote control next to her, then hesitated. She looked down at Dr. Banks's crouched figure.

"Did it really work?" she whispered.

In response Dr. Banks opened the door a little farther, just enough for her to see. Lina, on seeing the pig, gasped, and Dr. Banks's face broke out into a wide grin.

The audience continued to chant.

"Show us the pig!"

Dr. Banks stood up as Lina pressed down on the remote control and the image of the pig appeared up on the screen.

There, hanging docile in her harness, was Polly the pig, looking quite content and—more important—intact. Aside from the fact that she looked purple from the ultraviolet lights, she looked exactly like a regular pig. Four legs, check. Snout where it was supposed to be, check. The pig was fine.

The pig was fine!

The room erupted into thunderous applause and loud cheering.

Dr. Banks turned to Lina.

"It worked," he said in disbelief.

Lina stared at him, as if still trying to process what had happened, and then she burst out laughing.

"We did it!" she shouted, and flung her arms around Dr. Banks in celebration.

* * * * * *

The entire room was still hugging, cheering, and clapping as Bowveld strode out from behind the safety glass and picked up the microphone.

Dr. Banks looked at the director, who, with a wide grin on his face, gave him a thumbs-up in approval.

And then it hit him.

Sarah was going to come back. His wife was coming home! His children were going to see their mother again!

His eyes filled with tears as Bowveld turned on the microphone and addressed the audience again.

"Ladies and gentlemen, you'd better start packing! We are going to SIX!"

Loud whoops and cheers filled the room, and then a voice called out through the crowd.

"We want Polly!"

Bowveld gave a booming laugh. "Yes, of course!" he replied. "Dr. Banks, let the guest of honor out for her victory lap!"

Dr. Banks bent over and reached in. He pulled down on the hanging belt until the pig was standing on the floor of the dark enclosure, and then he opened the buckle. The harness fell off the pig but, though free to move, she remained still.

"Come, Polly," said Dr. Banks gently.

Lina's hand appeared, holding a carrot, and Dr. Banks took it from her. He held it out.

"It's okay," he said gently. "You're safe."

Polly wriggled her snout a few times, gave a low grunt, and then, slowly, she edged forward and emerged from the darkness of the Avectron.

Only then, under the bright unforgiving lights of the laboratory, did it become evident that something was very wrong.

Everybody in the room, Dr. Banks included, gasped.

The avection had failed.

The pig was white.

Polly, completely ignorant of the fuss she was causing, grunted as if to say, *Give me that carrot.*

The pig was not just a slightly paler version of pink—she was white. Pure white. And her eyes, brown at the start of the presentation, were now pink. Under the ultraviolet lights of the Avectron it had been impossible to tell, but now there was no doubt—the pig had lost all her pigmentation. It would have been funny had the consequences of it not been so terrible.

"Please calm down," said Bowveld, though clearly panicking himself. "It's just a small glitch."

"A small glitch?" shouted someone in the audience.

"Yes," replied the director, trying to sound breezy. It wasn't working. "Easily fixed. Isn't that right, Dr. Banks?"

Dr. Banks nodded robotically.

Someone in the audience—a woman Dr. Banks didn't recognize—realized that they all had microphones on their armrests and turned hers on. Her voice, tight with anger, came through the loudspeaker.

"Bowveld," she said, "do you think there is a single person here who would allow themselves to be teleported anywhere without a one-hundred-percent guarantee that the process was safe—"

"It's just a slight loss of pigmentation," interrupted Dr. Banks, leaning into Bowveld's microphone.

"I'm quite happy with the pigmentation I have, thank you very much," replied the lady. "And who knows what might go wrong next time?"

There were shouts of agreement from the crowd, and Bowveld motioned for them all to calm down.

"The process will be perfected before we would ever allow anybody to be avected. And that will happen by next month, I guarantee it."

"I don't believe you!" shouted someone from the back of the room.

The prime minister of a European country, seated in the front row, turned on his microphone.

"Warren," he said, then paused as he waited for silence from the audience. "I think I speak for us all when I say that this is what you Americans would call the last straw."

"But—" said Bowveld.

"Let me finish!" interrupted the man. "You have had your say, and now it is our turn.

"We have invested millions—no, *billions*—into this venture," continued the man. "Money that we could be using to solve global warming, famine, housing crises, and who knows what else, is being given to you. We will not be made fools of any longer."

"But you have seen the teleportation for yourselves!"

"Yes—and that has been enough for us to invest in your company for over thirty years. But now we have to ask, where is this utopia you promised us? Does it, I think we are all beginning to wonder, even exist?"

Wade Huckley—a wealthy Texan entrepreneur well-known as much for hosting a popular talk show as for his considerable wealth—joined in. "If we find you've been pulling a fast one on us, Warren, you're going to be moving into a cell quicker than a striped lizard on hot asphalt."

"I am not lying!" insisted Bowveld, his voice desperate and pleading. "*Please*. I can prove it to you. Another month. Just one more month."

There was no answer. Instead Wade Huckley switched off his microphone and turned to the people behind him. Dr. Banks and Bowveld stood rigid in silence as the group whispered amongst themselves. Finally there were a few nods, and Huckley turned back to his microphone and flicked it on again.

"You have one month, to the day."

Bowveld closed his eyes and breathed deeply in relief.

"Thank you," he said. "Thank you so much. I won't let you down."

Dr. Banks gritted his teeth. One month? It might be possible—but he couldn't make any guarantees.

"There are conditions," continued Huckley. "You don't see another penny from any one of us until you can prove that the process is safe and nobody here is going to be coming back with five eyes or a leg sticking out of his head."

"Yes, yes," agreed Bowveld.

"Good. The demonstration needs to be completely successful."

"It will be," said Bowveld.

"We need to discuss this," whispered Dr. Banks. Bowveld ignored him.

"And, to give you a little incentive, we've decided we want to see a person being teleported."

There was a pause.

"You."

Dr. Banks's eyes widened.

"Excuse me?" whispered Bowveld.

"We want *you* to teleport yourself to SIX and back again. While we watch."

Bowveld, his mouth open, began to splutter. "I . . . I . . . I . . ."

"Good. That's what I thought. One month. Now, if you don't mind, I have some business to attend to."

Huckley stood up and strode over to the exit. The rest of the audience stood up silently and followed him.

Bowveld turned to Lina. "Leave," he said. Lina hesitated and looked over at Dr. Banks, who nodded. She walked out.

Bowveld waited until the room was clear then slowly

approached Dr. Banks. Bowveld's eyes were almost popping out of their sockets, and his usually orange skin had turned a mottled mix of purple and scarlet. Dr. Banks wondered if he was about to get punched.

"*You . . . you . . .*" spluttered Bowveld. "*I'm going to . . .*"

Dr. Banks watched as the director struggled to get his words out.

"We'll get it done," said Dr. Banks. There was no panic in his voice—there was no time for that now. His mind was focused. "I need two more assistants," he added.

"What you *need* is to fix this mess," said Bowveld. He took a deep breath.

"I'm not going to argue with you," said Dr. Banks. "The situation is as it is and arguing about it is not going to solve anything. Now, if you'll excuse me, I have a lot of work to do."

Bowveld didn't respond. Instead he turned abruptly and began to pace the room. Dr. Banks saw his opportunity to leave.

"Come on, Polly," he said.

The pig didn't look up from the bag of carrots that Lina had forgotten to take with her.

Dr. Banks looked at Bowveld, who was still deep in thought, and decided to just leave. Polly was content enough; he would return for her once the director had left the room. He walked over to the door.

"I thought seeing your wife again would be incentive enough," called Bowveld, just as Dr. Banks was about to step out.

Dr. Banks turned. *"Excuse me?"*

The director strode over, his eyes fixed intently on Dr. Banks. "I said, I thought seeing your wife again—"

"I heard what you said," interrupted Dr. Banks. "I'm just not sure I understand what you mean. If you are suggesting that . . ."

"Do you know what my grandfather used to say, Dr. Banks?"

A ripple of anger ran through Dr. Banks. "With the greatest respect, *Dr.* Bowveld, I couldn't give a rat's ear what your grandfather used to say."

"He used to say," continued Bowveld, "that the word *impossible* was invented for the lazy man."

As the words sank in, Dr. Banks felt his body begin to shake with rage.

"How dare you?" he said.

Bowveld looked down at his hand and checked his fingernails.

"He was a very wise man, my grandfather," he said, without looking up.

Dr. Banks clasped his hands tightly in an attempt to stop himself from using them to punch Bowveld.

"I've had *three weeks*!" said Dr. Banks. "I have worked every waking hour for you since I got here and I have achieved more in this time than your entire company has managed to achieve in years. And now you *dare* to call me lazy? I think—"

"How old are your children, Dr. Banks?" interrupted Bowveld.

"What did you say?"

"Parker and Emily. Is that right?"

"Emma," corrected Dr. Banks, his voice slow and cautious.

"Emma," said Bowveld. He smiled. "Of course. Sweet little thing. You must love them both very much."

Dr. Banks felt his blood go cold. "What are you saying?

"I'm not saying anything, Dr. Banks."

Dr. Banks took a step forward so that he was face-to-face with the director.

"Are you threatening my children?"

Bowveld didn't flinch. "What I am doing, Dr. Banks, is *suggesting* that you solve this problem. The stakes are high for all of us. You'd do well to remember . . ."

As the director spoke, the meaning behind his words poured rage into Dr. Banks.

"Don't you dare bring my children into this," he said.

Bowveld watched as Dr. Banks's hand curled into a fist.

Bowveld looked down. "I don't think that would be a very good idea, Dr. Banks," he said calmly.

How could it be, thought Dr. Banks with furious disgust, that this pathetic man should hold such power over him? It was a power, however, that had its limits.

"Do not underestimate what a father will do to protect his children," said Dr. Banks as the director stood up. "Touch my children and I *will* kill you."

Bowveld's mouth curled into a smile. "And then what will you have? *Nothing*. The choice is yours, Dr. Banks; your wife and children. Or nothing." The smile disappeared. "The decision is in your hands."

Bowveld didn't wait for a response. Without so much as a backward glance, he walked away, leaving Dr. Banks alone in the room with his world crashing down around him.

CHAPTER NINE

39:05

Parker felt bad leaving Michael on his own, but Dr. Banks had called Hilda and arranged for him and Emma to be taken home by seven p.m.

"Have fun?" Dr. Banks asked as they both wheeled their bikes into the house. Parker noticed how pale his dad was. He looked exhausted, even more so than usual.

Parker nodded and Emma grinned, holding out her bike to show him.

Where did you get that from?

Michael gave it to me!

Parker's dad looked surprised but said nothing. Instead he waited until Emma had rested her bike against the wall and then went over to them both, arms outstretched, and swept them up into a hug.

I've missed you, he said, not letting go.

We've only been gone for the day, said Parker. He tried to pull away, but his dad's grip held firm.

It's been a long day, said his dad. He said this out loud, though it came through Effie also, and Parker heard the tightness in his voice.

Emma kept her arms tight around her father's waist. **What happened, Daddy?**

Dr. Banks didn't answer. He nestled his head between Parker's and Emma's.

Parker pulled back firmly and looked up at his dad. He saw his dad's eyes were glistening.

Dad, what's the matter? asked Parker.

Parker's dad hesitated.

Dad?

Emma was now staring up at him too. She looked scared. Parker's dad looked down and, upon seeing the expression on Emma's face, he shook himself.

I'm okay. I'm sorry. It just didn't go very well today. And I'm tired, that's all.

What were you doing? asked Emma.

For the first time, Parker's dad seemed to consider answering her before deciding against it.

I will tell you, but not today. He smiled and changed the subject. **I have a present for you.**

Emma's eyes widened. **Really?**

What about me? asked Parker.

For you, too—but more for Emma. You'll see what I mean. He turned to Emma. **She's waiting for you outside.**

She? repeated Emma slowly. She had a puzzled expression on her face, which changed suddenly as the meaning behind his choice of word began to dawn on her. Her mouth dropped open and she jumped up in delight. *She?*

Before their dad could say anything more, Emma was running to the back door. She flung it open and scanned the backyard, her eyes squinting to focus in the night's darkness. The moment she set her eyes on her gift, she froze. She snapped her head around to her dad, then back outside—as if she needed to check whether it was real—back to their dad with an incredulous look on her face, and then back outside again. Then she let out a piercing squeal.

Parker ran forward to see what it was. Surely, he thought as he stepped out into the night, Emma wouldn't be quite this surprised if his dad had gotten her a chicken, considering they'd discussed it the night before. Of course, she wasn't.

Parker stared at the white pig standing in the middle of their backyard—shining under the moonlight like a ghost ship at sea.

"You got us a *pig*?"

"I did. Her name's Polly. Do you like her?"

Parker's wide grin said it all. Leaving his dad in the doorway, Parker ran out to join Emma, who was sitting on the grass, stroking their new pet's snout.

Can she sleep inside? asked Emma, staring out the window.

Their dad glanced up from his laptop. **We are not having a pig living in the house,** he said.

Then why's Parker here? asked Emma.

Ha ha, said Parker.

Emma looked over at her dad and attempted her bottom-lip sulk. **But she looks so sad.**

How does a pig look sad? asked Parker. His dad and sister ignored him.

She looks delighted, said Parker's dad firmly. **She's been in a cage since she was born. I know it's not perfect but, for tonight, that kennel will feel like paradise to her. We'll get her a proper shed tomorrow and whatever else she needs.**

Were they going to kill her? asked Emma.

Parker's dad winced at the unexpected question. **No . . . ,** he said. **That wasn't the intention at all.**

I wonder what white bacon would taste like? asked Parker.

Emma wrinkled her nose in disgust. **That's not funny.**

Parker grinned. **I was just joking.**

Parker's father glanced up from his laptop. "Parker . . ." he warned.

"Sorry, Dad," said Parker.

His dad gave a small nod and turned back to his work. Parker pressed down on his father's light to stop him from listening in on the argument that he and Emma—who was now storming over in his direction—were clearly about to have.

So animal testing is a joke to you? asked Emma with her hands on her hips.

Parker shook his head in exasperation. **You're being oversensitive.**

Tell that to all the dead monkeys—I'm sure they'd find it hilarious.

I hear monkeys have a good sense of humor.

Not dead ones, answered Emma.

Well, they won't mind me joking about it then.

As soon as the words left Parker's mind, he regretted thinking them. He didn't think animal testing was funny—not in the slightest—it was just that when Emma got too serious about things—which was a *lot*—he sometimes couldn't help but make a joke about it. At times, however, like now, his jokes crossed the line.

Emma was staring at Parker. **What is *wrong* with you?** she asked finally.

Parker sighed. **I'm sorry—I didn't mean that. But you can't take every little thing wrong in the world so seriously.**

If everyone were as stupid as you, then nothing would ever get better.

Parker looked at his sister and saw tears forming.

Really, Emma, I'm sorry. You know I don't think it's okay to test on animals. And I like the pig—I shouldn't have made a joke about it.

And it was true, he thought, as Emma let out a loud *humph* and walked away; he was thrilled with the pig, even if he didn't jump up and down about it like his sister did. In fact, while Emma had been filling the kennel with blankets and teddy bears, he had spent the last two hours researching pig care.

"Dad, I can't find much about albino pigs," said Parker. "Was she born like that?"

Parker's dad pulled a slightly pained expression and looked over at Emma. "Do you mind if I don't answer that?"

"Did you know that you can teach them to sit?"

His father didn't look up. "I didn't," he mumbled.

Parker glanced over at the clock. His dad had barely looked up from his laptop all night.

"Dad, come watch television with us for a bit."

His father looked up and rubbed his eyes. "I'm sorry, Parker, I can't. I have so much to do."

"Can I help you?" asked Parker, walking over to the kitchen.

His dad breathed a deep sigh and closed his laptop.

"I wish you could," he said. He pressed down on his wrist. **Emma—come over here.**

What, Dad?

Here, he said, ripping out two sections of his lined note pad and handing one to each of them. **Go write your letters to your mum.**

Parker took the papers.

Do you really think she reads them? he asked.

Definitely, said his dad.

Parker knew his dad couldn't possibly know with any certainty whatsoever what his mother could or couldn't do. She was dead. He also knew that there wasn't any logic behind delivering the letters to the random location that they'd picked; if she was in heaven, and she could read a letter that they had dropped into a lake, then she could read it at their house.

Two weeks earlier, when his father first suggested writing the letters, Parker had been about to say this before he'd stopped himself. The fact that it made no sense was irrelevant. It was symbolic, a way of keeping her close to them all. And he was okay with that. He gave his dad a smile and took the papers up to his room.

What's in here? asked Parker's dad, bouncing the envelope in his hand as if he were weighing it. He looked concerned.

I wrote twelve pages, said Emma with a wide smile.

Twelve pages? What did you write? asked Parker as he handed his dad a flat envelope containing a single folded piece of paper. It seemed inadequate now next to Emma's effort.

I don't know—just girl stuff, really, answered Emma. **School, friends. And I told her about Polly, too, of course. Oh! And I told her about what's happening in the news—just the important stuff: the hurricane in the Philippines, the explosion in China—that kind of thing. I don't know if she'd keep up-to-date with that stuff in heaven. Did she watch the news, Daddy?**

Always, just like you, replied their father. He looked down at the envelopes, one in each hand, and considered his words. **Perhaps, Emma, you don't need to write all of that though. Couldn't you maybe get it down to two or three pages?**

Parker and Emma looked at each other in confusion.

Why? asked Emma.

Yeah, Dad. It's not like we have to pay extra postage, added Parker.

His dad gave an awkward laugh. **No, of course not. I don't know why I said that.** He placed the envelopes on the table. **Okay, go get ready for bed.**

Can I go say good night to Polly? asked Emma.

Yes, but don't stay too long. We have an early start.

Why?

I thought we could go to the lake before church tomorrow. Then we can go get the stuff for Polly, have lunch, and then I'll have to go back to work.

But you said you weren't working tomorrow, said Parker and Emma at the same time.

I know. But things have changed. I'm sorry. I'm going to have to go in, but I'll be home for dinner.

Emma looked upset. **You work too much,** she said.

Parker's dad clenched his jaw and swallowed.

I know it doesn't seem like it, said his dad finally, **but I'm doing this all for the two of you. It won't always be like this. I promise.** He gave Emma a kiss on the top of her head. **Go get ready for bed.**

*   *   *   *   *   *

Parker couldn't sleep that night. All the excitement of spending the day at Michael's house and even the arrival of their new pet had been canceled out by his father's sadness. He had seen his dad upset many times—too many times—over the last few years, but he hadn't seen him like this since just after his mother had died. Even then, in those awful days after they'd received the news, Parker had seen the effort his father had made to keep a brave face on for their sakes. But today was different. Today was the first time that he had seen his father unable, unwilling even, to make any attempt to snap out of his unhappiness. Nevertheless, Parker couldn't put his finger on why it was concerning him this much. It wasn't as if they had come home to find their father curled up in a ball, sobbing. In a way, though, this was worse. It was as if—Parker tried to think of how best to describe it—as if his father were broken. And the more that Parker thought about it, the more he came to realize that this wasn't something that had happened in one day; his father's downward spiral had begun not long after their move here. Was this, wondered Parker, the lowest point, or was there worse to come?

Eventually, after another hour of tossing and turning in his bed, Parker gave up his fight to sleep. The light from the hallway was glowing in a thin line at the bottom of his bedroom door. It was a sure sign that his dad hadn't gone to bed yet, though it was possible that he had just fallen asleep in front of the television. He did that sometimes. Parker threw back his bedcovers and stood up.

* * * * * *

The landing was silent. For a moment Parker wondered if his dad had gone to sleep and forgotten to turn off the light, but then he heard the faint yet unmistakable clinks of a teaspoon stirring liquid in a mug.

Parker padded down the carpeted stairs and into the kitchen. He wasn't being intentionally quiet and he certainly hadn't been intending to surprise his father, but that was exactly what he did.

The time between Parker walking into the room and his father realizing that he was there couldn't have been more than a few seconds. It was time enough, however, for Parker to see the letter to his mother sitting next to his father's laptop. The single page was folded open next to the envelope that Parker himself had sealed earlier. Emma's letter had also been opened, and the twelve pages, covered in her distinct colorful doodles, lay stacked one on top of the other in an untidy pile. Parker watched as his dad looked down at Parker's letter, then back to his laptop, as if he were typing it up.

"What are you doing?" whispered Parker.

At the sound of Parker's voice, his father's head snapped up, and his eyes almost popped out of their sockets. He looked down at the table and, on seeing how exposed the letters were, he grabbed the first thing he could find—a notebook—and slammed it down on top to hide them.

"What are you doing here?" asked his dad.

"Why are you reading my letter to mum?" whispered Parker. His voice was weak with shock.

"What do you mean? I was just working."

"I saw it. I saw Emma's letter. Why were you reading them?" He was distracted as he spoke, his thoughts on the contents of his letter—private stuff, stuff about his dad working too much, about how much he missed his mum, and, worst of all, about the fight with Aaron.

"I . . . um . . . I wasn't reading them . . . I was just . . ."

While Parker's dad stumbled on his words, Parker's mind raced to come up with his own explanation. He reached his conclusion before his dad could come up with any excuse that Parker would buy.

"You're *spying* on us?"

"No! I wasn't. I'm not . . . I . . ." Parker's dad stopped and put his head in his hands.

"Is this why you asked us to write them, so you could check up on us?" asked Parker. He could feel his voice getting louder the angrier he got.

"No, Parker, I didn't . . ."

"What do you think we're hiding?" continued Parker. His whole body began to shake in fury. "You could have just talked to us! Did you think of that?"

His dad bolted out of his chair. "Parker! Lower your voice! You'll wake up Emma. Let's sit down and talk about this."

"Wake up Emma?" shouted Parker, throwing his hands up in frustration, "*What* are you talking about?"

His dad rolled his eyes as he realized the stupidity of his comment.

"I wish she *could* hear this!" continued Parker.

"Parker, please . . ."

"She should know what you're doing," continued Parker, ignoring his dad. "She should know that it was all just a way for you to check up on us and that . . ."

Parker stopped as another thing occurred to him. "Why were you typing it up? *Were* you typing it up?"

There was a brief pause and then, in response, his father closed his eyes and dropped his head.

Parker felt a tear run down his cheek and he brushed it away quickly. "I don't understand," he whispered. "I don't understand why you'd do this."

"Parker," said his dad as he stood up. His voice was gentle. "I know you're upset. I understand. Just let me explain. Please."

Parker knew his father wasn't perfect. He understood that. He also knew that it wasn't in his father's nature to lie or be underhanded, which was why Parker had been so confused and upset by his father's betrayal. It was also why he accepted his father's hour-long rambling and cryptic explanation—an explanation so ridiculous that there could be only one reason for it: his father had lost his mind.

The anger was gone, mostly, replaced by a deep sense of concern. "So," said Parker slowly, as if he were talking to a young child, "you're typing up our letters because you want to have everything on a memory stick for mum in case she comes back. Is that what you're saying?"

His father pursed his lips and nodded.

"And you *really* think that? That mum might come back?"

Parker's dad gave a small shrug.

"After she died in a car crash?"

"I'm just saying that anything is possible."

Parker leaned forward on the sofa and tried to work out what was going on. He turned back to his dad.

"And you're not lying to me. You really weren't checking on us?"

"I swear to you, Parker," said his dad. He placed his hand on Parker's shoulder. "I trust you and Emma one hundred percent. With all my heart. I wasn't even thinking about the contents of the letters—I was just typing them up for your mum."

"But you know she's dead, right? We scattered her ashes."

"Yes. Well, sort of."

"Sort of what?"

"I don't know, Parker. It's complicated. I just think that maybe the end isn't always the end."

"Okay. But when you say that," continued Parker, still not sure if he was completely understanding what his father was saying, "do you mean it in an eternal-life-up-in-heaven way or in a she-might-actually-walk-through-that-door way?"

"Both, maybe. Who knows?"

Parker stared at his dad, examining his face for any signs that he was lying to him. He found none. His dad, the scientist. His dad who, up until this point, Parker had considered a rational human being.

"I think I should call a doctor," said Parker.

At the suggestion, his father bolted upright.

"No! Don't call anyone. I don't need a doctor."

"Dad, you're not well."

"I'm fine. I really am. I know how crazy this all sounds. I shouldn't have said anything. I'm just tired."

Tired. Of course! Suddenly it all made sense. Parker had once read about sleep deprivation as a form of torture and how it had the power to drive people mad—even kill them.

"Dad. You *have* to sleep."

His dad looked at him, and now all Parker could see were the deep gray bags under his father's eyes. His father nodded.

Parker stood, pulling his dad's arm. "Go to bed."

Parker's dad sighed and hauled himself up. Parker led the way out of the room and up the landing as his father followed and turned off the lights behind him. Parker turned to say good night.

"I'm really sorry I worried you tonight," said his dad before Parker could say anything. He put his arms out, and Parker let himself be pulled into a hug. "And I'm so sorry about the letters. I won't ever do that again."

Parker closed his eyes. "It's okay, Dad. I think I get why you did it now."

His dad let go. He reached out with his hand and pulled up Parker's chin to look him in the eyes.

"You and Emma are my world, Parker. I am so proud of you—of how strong you are, how kind, how responsible. I'm sorry I betrayed your trust."

Parker shifted uncomfortably at his father's show of sentimentality. He pursed his lips and smiled. "I guess you'll be wanting to talk to me about the thing at school, though."

Parker's dad smiled and shook his head. "No. But if you want to talk to me about it, I am always here for you."

"Okay."

"Really, Parker. I know I work a lot, but you and Emma are my number-one priority. All you have to do is say that you want to talk to me—about anything, no matter how small— and I'll drop everything. Do you understand?"

Parker nodded as his father put his hand up to his mouth to stifle a yawn.

"Get some sleep, Dad."

"I'm going, I'm going," said his dad, walking away. "Night, night."

"Night, Dad," said Parker as he closed his bedroom door and flopped onto his bed. He was asleep within minutes.

CHAPTER TEN

26:02

Parker's mother died at approximately six o'clock in the morning, when her rental car came off the highway, rolled down a steep slope, and crashed into a tree. The official report that his father had received had been unable to determine the exact cause of the accident, but the most plausible theory put forward was that she had swerved to avoid a deer and had lost control of the vehicle. There had been no witnesses—at least none who had come forward—and the first that anybody knew about the accident was that evening, when an eagle-eyed truck driver spotted the mangled wreck and called for help. The police had assured Parker's father that, even if she had been found earlier, her injuries had been instantly fatal—there was nothing that anyone could have done to save her.

Three years later, and a few days after arriving in the country, their father had taken them to visit the exact spot where their mother had died. His father had been there before, back when everything had happened, and he had warned them both that there was nothing to see. Nevertheless, Parker had been disappointed, if that was the right word. In his opinion, it was unfitting given its significance—a nondescript stretch of highway lacking a single identifiable feature other than the mile-marker sign on the side of the road.

That day, his father had parked on the hard shoulder with his hazards on so that Parker and Emma could leave the flowers that they had picked. A few minutes later a patrol car had pulled up and told them to move on. The cop had been ready to give them a ticket, until he heard why they were there, and then let them off with a warning. Nevertheless, they all agreed that it wasn't going to be a suitable place to visit regularly, and it was Emma who suggested finding another place, somewhere quiet where they could go and think about their mother. In the end they had picked Golden Hills State Park for two reasons: it was the nearest park to the actual spot where their mother had died, and it was on a lake. Their mother had loved the water.

So it was here, to the parking lot near the boat launch area, that Parker's father drove them to that Sunday morning.

As they pulled up into the parking lot, Emma turned to Parker for what must have been the tenth time on their journey and signed for him to turn Effie on.

"Don't feel like it," he signed back.

Under normal circumstances Emma would have been fine with that, except she could tell something was wrong;

neither Parker nor their dad had spoken barely a word since getting up.

Parker jumped out of the car as soon as it came to a stop and headed off by himself to the water. He turned and saw his dad watching him, a look of concern on his face.

Parker walked out on the rocky pier and sat down at the water's edge. He picked up a stone.

"Want to talk?" asked his dad, walking up behind him.

Parker shook his head.

"Are you still angry?"

He shook his head again. He wasn't, but he couldn't just forget what had happened. He also couldn't help but see this visit to the lake in a different light. It now seemed so pointless. His mother wasn't here, and she wasn't going to be reading anything that they had written. Whatever his dad might hope for, she was gone. She was never coming back.

His dad sat down next to him. Parker turned and saw the same heavy bags under his eyes that he'd had the night before. If anything, he looked worse.

"Did you sleep at all last night?" asked Parker.

"A bit," said his dad. He looked around and, on seeing Emma was content checking the squirrel's drey that she had found in a tree the week before, he turned back to Parker. "Are you okay?"

"I'm fine," said Parker.

His father said nothing. Instead he reached out and

rubbed Parker's back as if he knew Parker wasn't telling the truth. Parker, in response, felt his eyes fill up with tears.

"I hate it here, Dad," he said, his voice tight. "And I hate how you are since we got here. Why can't we go back?"

"We will."

Parker looked up in surprise. "What?"

His dad attempted a smile. "We will. I miss our family and friends too. I miss my work and I miss our house."

"Well, just . . . leave!" said Parker, shocked at the revelation. "It's just a job! With your—"

"It's not that easy, Parker," interrupted his dad. "My job here is complicated. I can't just walk out."

"Yes, you can! You just say 'I quit' and leave."

"I wish I could. I'm working on it."

"How long will that—"

"Emma!"

Parker jumped in surprise as his dad scrambled to his feet and broke into a run, his hand pressing down frantically on his wrist. Parker spun around and saw what his father was running toward: Emma looking up at two men talking to her. He leaped up and followed his father, who was still running at full speed across the grass.

"Leave her alone!" shouted his dad.

At the sound of the voice, the men looked up. The taller of the two, a man in a black coat and glasses, turned back to Emma and ruffled her hair. Then, calmly, both men turned and walked over to a silver car parked next to theirs just as his dad reached Emma. He grabbed her shoulders and raised her face to his to check she was okay, then looked over at the men, who were now getting into their car.

Seeing Parker had almost caught up, his dad pushed Emma in Parker's direction and ran toward the silver car. He was too late. The wheels screeched as the engine was revved, and then the car shot away, leaving a trail of smoking tarmac behind it.

Emma stared at Parker, a look of complete bemusement on her face.

"What happened?" signed Parker as his wrist began to vibrate.

"I don't know," answered Emma. *"I think . . ."*

They were interrupted by their father calling them on Effie.

What did they say to you? asked their father.

Even through Effie, their father's panic was palpable.

They just asked me the time, replied Emma.

His dad reached them and again grabbed Emma by the shoulders. **What else did they say?**

Nothing! Emma looked terrified. **They didn't say anything! They just asked the time and then you ran up.**

And that's it? asked their dad. Emma nodded.

Who are they, Dad? asked Parker.

His dad let go of Emma and sat down on a large rock next to him. **I don't know,** he mumbled. He ran his hand over his hair.

You don't know? asked Emma.

I just thought that . . .

What? asked Parker.

His father looked up and thought for a moment, then shook his head. **I just didn't know what they were doing, that's all.**

Dad! said Emma, **I'm not five. I'm not just going to follow strangers into their car. And you were right there.**

I know, I know. I'm sorry, said their dad. He put his head in his hands.

"What's the matter with him?" signed Emma.

Parker just shook his head. What could he say to her? That his father was losing his mind? He was quite certain of it now, but he wasn't sure it would help to upset Emma with that.

"He's tired," he signed back finally, just as his father looked up.

"Let's go," he said.

Parker nodded and their father stood up.

"But what about our letters?" signed Emma.

It was a muted ceremony. Their father handed Emma her letter, then turned to Parker and handed his over with what Parker read as a look of guilt. Parker took it, turned, and dropped it in the water, but not before noticing how expertly it had been sealed back up. Had he not found his father last night, Parker would never have suspected a thing.

He didn't bother to watch where it went. "Let's go," he said.

Emma, sitting cross-legged and watching her own letter float off into the distance, turned to Parker and their father with a look of utter confusion on her face.

"But . . ." she signed.

There must have been something in his and his father's expressions that told Emma that, for once, it was not worth arguing. With tears in her eyes—but not another word—she stood up. Their father put his arm around her, but she shook it away and walked off.

The silver car pulled up behind them as they exited the park. Parker would have been too lost in his thoughts to have noticed it had their own car not suddenly bolted forward as his father slammed his foot on the gas pedal.

"Dad!"

Parker's dad, his jaw clenched tightly, looked up at the rearview mirror and then, without saying anything, accelerated.

At the same time, Parker and Emma pulled out the straps of their seat belts and turned to look out the back window.

"Get your heads down!" shouted their father.

Parker pulled Emma down with him just as their father drove full speed into a bend. With the entire force of his body pressing into his seat belt, Parker strained his neck forward to get a view of what was happening from the side mirror.

The silver car was directly behind them.

For the first time, Parker began to wonder if maybe his dad wasn't going crazy after all.

He kept a silent watch on the side mirror as their car hurtled at top speed along the empty country road, the silver car in close pursuit. Parker glanced up and saw the lights of an intersection up ahead of them turning red.

"Dad!"

At the same time that Parker shouted, his dad cursed under his breath. Perhaps hoping that the lights would turn before they reached them, his dad kept his foot on the accelerator until the very last minute. Then, as Parker gripped tightly onto the seat, his father slammed his foot down on the brake and screeched to a full stop. Parker jumped around again to get a look at the two men in the car behind, half expecting one of them to be leaning out the window with a gun pointing in their direction. The reality, it turned out, was very different.

Parker stared at the men as they chatted to each other without the slightest look of agitation on their faces. The one in the passenger seat—the one who had ruffled Emma's hair—leaned forward and picked something up. A bottle of water. He handed it over to the driver, who took a sip of it just as the lights turned green. Perhaps unaware of how distracted the men in the car behind them appeared to be, their father slammed his foot back onto the accelerator, and their car shot forward again, straight through the intersection and up the long clear road ahead of them. Parker remained turned and watched as the silver car—still stationary—grew smaller with distance. At any point, thought Parker, the driver of the silver car was going to realize they were getting away and pick up the pursuit. Instead the car did the very opposite of what he thought it was going to do: it indicated and slowly turned left at the light. The chase—if that was what it had been—was over.

"They're gone, Dad," said Parker as he turned around.

His dad was looking in the rearview mirror, and Parker guessed—by the fact that his father had already begun to slow down—that he had also seen the car turn away. He looked as confused as Parker felt as he pulled the car to the side.

"Are you both okay?" he asked, turning around in his seat.

It was only then that they both realized Emma was crying.

"Three chocolate milk shakes," said his father.

"Great choice," replied the waitress. "Would you like something to eat, too?"

"No, thank you."

"Are you *sure*?" She was smiling. "You won't taste chicken wings better than ours." As if to prove her point, she motioned over to a sign with the words WORLD'S BEST CHICKEN WINGS shining in neon pink.

"Three milk shakes," said Parker's father. "That's all."

"They're very good," insisted the woman.

"I *said* three milk shakes. That's all. Now, if you wouldn't mind leaving us alone . . ."

Clearly taken aback by the curt response, their server

hesitated—as if wanting to give their father a piece of her mind—then looked at the two children: Emma with red eyes and Parker with a sullen face. She turned abruptly and left without another word.

As soon as she was out of sight, Parker felt his wrist vibrate, and both he and Emma—probably as reluctantly as each other—pressed down to answer.

We need to talk, said his father.

Neither Parker nor Emma responded.

I know you're both confused about what's going on.

Parker guessed that Emma was doing the same as he was; listening to their father with her thoughts muted.

Parker's father—probably realizing the same thing—sighed.

It's hard to explain everything, he continued. **You know that my work isn't something I can discuss. It's as much for your own protection as for mine.**

Parker looked up and pressed down on his wrist. **Why? Don't you trust us?**

Of course I trust you. I trust you both. There'll come a time—soon—when I can tell you more. I promise. In the meantime, I have to hold some things back from you both.

Did those men want to hurt me? asked Emma. It was the first time she had spoken since they'd left the park.

Parker's father considered the question for a moment. **I don't know,** he said finally.

Emma's eyes widened.

I don't think so, said his father, correcting himself. **I think they probably just wanted to give me a scare.**

The image of the man casually handing the driver a bottle of water as they chatted came into Parker's mind.

Or maybe they weren't doing anything at all, said Parker.

His father shrugged. **Possibly. The thing is . . .**

He stopped as the waitress returned and placed the milk shakes in front of each of them. She was no longer smiling.

The thing is, said their father, continuing his thought as they all took sips of their drinks, **the people I work for are very unhappy with me at the moment.**

Why? asked Parker.

Because they hired me to do something and I haven't managed to do it yet.

But you've only been there for three weeks! said Emma.

Parker's father gave a weak smile. **That's what I keep telling them.**

And they don't care? asked Parker.

His father shook his head. **My boss is not a reasonable man. That's probably the politest way I can put it.**

What's he going to do to you? asked Emma.

Nothing. It's going to be fine. I'll get the work that he wants me to do done and then I can leave.

He's just annoyed that it's taking me longer than he thought it would.

But you can do it?

Yes, I can do it. I'm nearly there. Like I said, I think today was just about giving me a bit of a scare. And it worked. But he needs me to get the job done and that's not going to happen if I were to leave. Do you understand that?

Parker and Emma nodded, though neither he nor Emma looked very convinced.

I know you're both going to worry about this—and that's why I didn't want to say anything, but nothing bad is going to happen and you don't need to worry—I'll take care of everything. I promise.

How long is it going to take?

A month. That's it. You'll have to put up with me working all hours for another month and then we're done. Okay?

Not really, thought Parker. Luckily, he had already pressed the mute button on Effie before the thought crossed his mind. He nodded and unmuted the call. **Okay, Dad.**

The waitress reappeared at their table. "Will you be wanting anything else?" she asked.

"No, thank you. Just the check," said their father with an apologetic smile. "We'll try the chicken wings next time."

The waitress narrowed her eyes at him, then turned on her heels and walked off to get the bill.

"Let's go home," said Parker's father.

"*I thought we were going to get the stuff for the alarm from the hardware store,*" signed Emma.

"Another time," said their father, standing up.

CHAPTER ELEVEN

03:20

Parker dragged himself out of bed on Monday morning with a heavy head and a tight knot in his stomach. The events of the previous day had been playing heavily on his mind, and he had struggled to sleep. When he had finally passed out—sometime in the early hours of the morning—his dreams had been filled with the sound of his mother calling for him, always just out of reach no matter how fast he tried to run. He had woken up in a cold sweat, exhausted, relieved only for a moment that it had been a dream before remembering that the nightmare wasn't over; he now had to go to school and face Aaron.

His father and sister were already having breakfast in the kitchen when Parker came in. Both were already dressed; Emma in an eye-watering mix of fluorescent pink and orange, and his dad in his usual white shirt and tie. His father's hair was wet from the shower, but he looked anything but refreshed; his face was gray and the deep bags under his eyes were just as heavy as they had been the day before. Parker guessed he wasn't the only one having trouble sleeping.

"I'm not feeling well," said Parker.

Parker's dad put down the cup of coffee in his hand and looked up. "What's the matter?"

Emma was standing at the kitchen counter behind his dad, staring at Parker. They didn't have Effie turned on, but Parker guessed by the look on her face that she had lip-read what he'd said. She raised her eyebrows at him, and Parker quickly looked away.

"I think I ate something bad. I was sick in the night."

"Why didn't you wake me up?"

"I didn't want to bother you. Can I stay home?"

His dad stood up and approached Parker. He put his hand on Parker's forehead, and Parker, already feeling guilty enough about lying, pulled back.

His father narrowed his eyes. "Are you really sick?"

Parker nodded as his wrist began to vibrate. Using Effie was such a normal occurrence in their house that his dad didn't notice Parker pressing down on his wrist to answer.

What are you going to do, stay home forever? asked Emma.

Just today, okay? I'll go in tomorrow.

Behind his dad, Parker saw Emma consider this and then, finally, she shrugged. Parker switched Effie off.

His dad stared at him a little longer. "If you're upset about yesterday . . ."

"I'm not! I'm just sick. Really."

"Parker, don't do this to me. Not today. I can't stay home."

"I don't need you to stay home. I'll be fine on my own."

His father was shaking his head before Parker had even finished speaking. "No way. I'm sorry. You're going to have to go in."

"But I'm sick!"

"I'm sorry. You're not staying home on your own." His dad paused. "Is this about the fight with the boy at school?"

Parker looked at his feet. "No. And you said you weren't going to talk about that."

"Okay. Fine. I understand it's hard, but you've only been there a week—it'll get easier. You have to go in. I'll give you a note to excuse you from gym, if you want."

Parker was furious. "I was *throwing up.*"

"I'm sorry—I'm not changing my mind."

"You're actually going to send me in to school throwing up?"

"You're not throwing up now. You'll be fine."

Parker willed himself to be sick right there at his father's feet, but unfortunately, nothing more than a gagging sound came out.

"Go and get dressed," said his father calmly. "You can rest when you get home."

Parker glared at his dad and then, realizing that nothing was going to change his mind, stormed off.

* * * * * *

Parker was still fuming when he arrived at school. As soon as the bus stopped, everybody jumped up except Parker. He felt a tap on his shoulder.

"Wish me luck!" signed Emma. She was standing up, her backpack already on her back.

Parker shrugged. "Why?"

Emma's mouth dropped open as if she couldn't believe he didn't know what she was talking about.

"The swimming tournament, Parker!"

"Oh, yeah," signed Parker, remembering. *"When do you leave?"*

"Now. It's for the whole day. I'm . . ."

She stopped upon spotting something outside of the window. *"Hey! There's Katie!"*

Emma leaned over Parker and signed for her friend to wait for her.

"I have to go!" she signed. *"See you later."*

"Okay," signed Parker. *"Good luck."*

Emma was already scrambling through the line of students waiting to get off the bus. *"Thanks!"* she signed, and then ran off. Parker leaned back in his seat. He was in no rush to leave.

Looking out the window, Parker watched as Emma darted across the asphalt to her friend. They hugged and ran over to the waiting bus at the entrance gates, holding hands and giggling with giddy excitement.

"You planning on staying here all day?" called the driver's voice from the front.

Parker looked around and saw that the bus was completely empty. Reluctantly he stood up and made his way to the front.

"Smile," said the driver brightly upon seeing Parker's glum face. "It might never happen."

Parker forced a half smile, which disappeared the moment he turned to go down the steps. As soon as both feet touched the ground, the driver closed the doors, leaving Parker to face the steady stream of students entering the school. He reached up and pulled his hood over his head.

"Fall asleep?"

Parker turned and saw Michael standing by the rear of the bus.

"Hey," said Parker glumly. "You just got in?"

"No. I was waiting for you," said Michael. He picked up his bag and walked over to Parker. "How's the eye?"

Parker reached up to his face. He had forgotten about his eye. "Fine," he said. "Want to skip school?"

The question took Parker by surprise as much as it did Michael.

"What?" asked Michael.

"I'm not staying," said Parker with growing certainty. "Want to come?"

"*Why?*"

"No reason. I just don't want to stay."

Michael hesitated. For a brief moment Parker wondered if Michael was actually considering the idea or just trying to work out how to say no. He suspected the latter, and he was right.

"I can't do it," said Michael finally. "My parents would kill me if they found out."

Parker thought about this for a moment, and then an idea came to him. "You can hack into the server and mark us in."

Michael's eyes widened. "Are you crazy?"

Parker thought about this for a moment. Was it crazy? The more he considered it, however, the better the idea seemed. Suddenly animated, he grabbed Michael by the sleeve and pulled him over to the front of the bus, away from earshot of other students.

"Nobody will know if you hack into the system," he said. "Just change it."

"What would we do?"

"I don't know. Go hang out somewhere."

Michael thought about this. "Well," he said with a shrug, "my parents *are* away. Hilda's off today and I could call Brendan—he wouldn't say anything."

"Great!" said Parker. "Come on, Michael! Just once. I've never done this either."

Michael was quiet as he considered what Parker was asking of him. In the end he shook his head. "I can't do it. I'm sorry. It's not right."

Parker sighed loudly with the frustration of having a perfectly good plan thwarted for the second time that day. He was about to ask Michael if he could just sign him in instead, when an unwelcome voice called out to them.

"I was looking for you two."

"I hate today," mumbled Parker as Aaron approached with a glowering look on his face. It was not unlike the one on Parker's own face.

"I thought you'd be suspended," said Parker dryly.

"Detention," answered Aaron. "And nice to know you care. All week. I figure you owe me three dollars for each day. That's twenty dollars and we call it quits."

"Fifteen dollars," said Parker.

"I'm not bargaining with you."

"No. I mean, three dollars a day times five is fifteen dollars."

Aaron looked down at his hand and bent each finger in turn. "Whatever," he said finally, turning back to Parker. "I want twenty dollars."

"Leave him alone," blurted Michael.

Both Parker and Aaron turned to Michael in surprise. Michael, in response, shrank back against the grill of the school bus. It was obvious that he was regretting speaking out.

"You ever fight your own battles?" Aaron asked Parker as he took a step toward Michael. Before Parker had a chance to respond, Aaron leaned forward so that his face was within inches of Michael's.

"Twenty dollars from him, and now twenty dollars from you, too."

"I don't have twenty dollars on me," said Michael. He was visibly shaking.

Aaron shrugged and reached up to Michael's face. Before either he or Parker had a chance to stop him, Aaron pulled Michael's glasses off.

"I'll take these instead, then," said Aaron. He folded them up and put them into his jacket pocket, all the while keeping his eyes on Michael.

"Give them back to him, Aaron," said Parker.

"Or what? You'll get your sister to hit me?"

Parker couldn't believe people this irritating existed in the world.

"What is wrong with you?" asked Parker. "Just give Michael his glasses back."

Aaron smiled and shrugged. He folded his arms.

"Fine," said Parker. He stepped forward, determined that one way or another he was going to get those glasses. His intentions were obvious; Aaron took a step back.

"Okay," said Aaron before Parker could get to him. He pulled out the glasses from his pocket and handed them to Michael.

Parker didn't show any reaction. Inside, however, he was shocked at how easily Aaron had backed down.

Michael took the glasses and put them on as Aaron leaned in and whispered loud enough for Parker to hear.

"I'll find you at lunch," he said. "And you'd better have my money. Or else."

"But I don't . . ."

Michael stopped midsentence as Aaron stormed off. He turned to Parker.

"Let's get out of here," he said. Then, without waiting for a response from Parker, he picked up his bag and walked straight out of the school gates without so much as a glance back.

Michael bit his lip in concentration as his fingers tapped away on his keyboard. Parker, standing behind him, said nothing in case he distracted him. It took no more than a few minutes before Michael raised his finger and dropped it down hard on the return key.

"Done."

"Really?"

Michael stared at the screen. "I can't believe I just did that."

Parker gave a small nervous laugh. "I can't believe it either." He puffed his cheeks out and exhaled loudly. "Wow."

Michael spun his chair around to face Parker. "I'll definitely be expelled if they find out," he said.

Parker's earlier bravado had all but disappeared as the reality of what they were doing had sunk in. "Can they trace it back to your computer?"

Michael looked at Parker as if he'd just asked him the most inane question he'd ever heard. "No way. If they do try to trace the source, they'll end up at an Internet cafe in Panama. I meant, if somebody says anything."

"I won't say anything. Brendan?"

Brendan had not said a word about coming to pick them up from a street corner two blocks away from their school, but, figured Parker, that didn't mean he approved.

Michael shook his head. "He'd never say anything to anybody. I trust him more than anyone I know."

"Okay, then we're probably fine," said Parker. He shrugged. "So . . . I guess we have a day off."

The two boys stared at each other, both unsure what to do next.

"Race you?" asked Michael finally.

"Good idea," said Parker, taking the seat next to Michael.

As they raced around the streets of a virtual Berlin, Parker struggled to keep his mind on the game. Guilt snaked its way through his guts: guilt for skipping class, guilt for the lies he would have to tell later, and guilt for bringing Michael into it. Not to mention the worry of being found out. And even if he did get away with it, Parker now realized that he would have to go back to school tomorrow and deal with what he had chosen not to deal with today anyway. Instead of it being a relief, Parker felt like he was just prolonging the agony and, though he didn't say anything, Parker suspected that Michael might be feeling the same.

At eleven, they went in search for food in the kitchen.

"Hilda will definitely know if we've touched anything in here," said Michael, staring at the fridge packed full of food.

"She'd tell?"

Michael nodded. "Definitely. She is *not* like Brendan. Hard to believe they're married."

Parker's eyes almost popped out of his head. "They're *married*?"

"Uh-huh."

Parker couldn't work out why Michael wasn't looking as panicked as he felt. "Michael! Brendan is obviously going to tell his wife that he picked us up. How could you not have thought of this?"

Michael shook his head. "It's fine, Parker, honestly. He won't tell her. They hate each other."

"Really? How long have they been married?"

"About thirty years. Dad said they've been like that as long as he's known them—she shouts at him and he says nothing. As long as Hilda doesn't find out, we're fine."

He walked over to the pantry and looked around whilst being careful not to touch anything. Finally he reached out to the back of a shelf and emerged with a plastic container half filled with crackers.

"I don't think she'll notice any of these missing," said Michael. He offered Parker the open box.

Parker reached in and was about to grab a handful when Michael stopped him.

"Maybe just four each. To be safe."

They ate the crackers in silence, leaning over the garbage can so as not to get any telltale crumbs on the floor. Their mouths tacky and dry, they then cupped water in their hands to drink from the sink, just in case Hilda counted glasses.

Parker wiped his wet hands on his jeans and turned to Michael.

"Shall we just go back?" he asked.

Michael sighed in relief. "*Yes!* You don't mind?"

Parker shook his head. "I don't think I'm cut out for a life of crime."

"Me neither."

Parker shook his head as Michael walked away to get his cell phone, surprised at the sense of relief he was feeling. Even the thought of having to deal with Aaron again didn't bother him anymore—after all, he'd proved that morning that it wasn't so difficult to stand up to him. As long as they could get back into school unnoticed, everything would return to normal.

And then his wrist began to vibrate.

Parker jumped in surprise and flipped his hand palm upward.

His father's light was flashing.

Parker felt the blood drain away from his head.

"Shall I bring your coat and bag down?" shouted Michael from halfway up the glass staircase.

Parker looked up, nodded mechanically, and then turned his attention back to his vibrating wrist with a growing sense of panic. His father *never* called during schooltime. Never. It could only mean one thing.

Parker gulped.

His father had found out.

Michael returned with jackets and bags a few minutes later.

"You okay?" he asked as he dropped Parker's bag at his feet.

Parker felt like throwing up.

"Parker?"

Parker lifted his head slowly and stared at Michael. He wanted to tell him—he needed another head to help him think—but there was no way he could do so without exposing Effie.

"Let's go," said Parker. He bent down—aware that Michael was staring at him—and picked up his bag with his vibrating arm. His father was not giving up.

If Brendan suspected anything was wrong when he arrived to collect the boys, he said nothing. Parker climbed in behind Michael and turned to face the window before Michael could engage him in conversation. Michael, it seemed, got the message and left Parker to his thoughts.

What am I going to do? thought Parker desperately as he tried to ignore the persistent vibration from Effie. His mind was spinning in panic and fear.

Parker took a deep breath and tried to reason with himself. *Maybe he'll understand,* he thought. It was possible. After all, his father knew that it had been a difficult week for him. He'd get into trouble—obviously—but maybe it wouldn't be as bad as he thought. Parker's stomach lurched.

Unless the school expelled him.

As much as he had hated his first week, the idea of getting expelled was terrifying. His father would definitely not forgive that. He looked over at Michael, who was staring glumly out the car window, and another thought—worse even than him getting expelled—came to him. If he had been found out, then so had Michael. If the school expelled him, they'd expel Michael.

And it would all be his fault.

As subtly as possible, Parker turned his arm and stared down at the faint flashing light. At some point, he realized with a deep sense of dread, he was going to have to answer.

He waited a few moments longer, in case an alternative occurred to him, but none came. Finally Parker came to the awful conclusion that ignoring his father's call was just delaying the inevitable. He squeezed his eyes shut, took a few deep breaths, and then, as if he were ripping a Band-Aid off, he reached over swiftly and pressed down on his father's light.

CHAPTER TWELVE

00:21

Parker!

Dad, I'm—

You have to listen to me!

I'm sorry, Dad—

I don't have time! Listen!

What?

You have to listen to me—Get your hands off me!

Dad?

Parker, I haven't got long—they're taking me in.

Taking you in where?!

Get Emma! Find a man called Solomon Gladstone.
Did you hear me?

Why—

Did you hear me?

Yes.

Solomon Gladstone. Say it.

Solomon Gladstone. Dad, what's—

Don't trust anybody except him. Tell him I've been

taken to SIX. Did you hear that, Parker? SIX. He can help you.

I don't—

Get that needle away from me!

Dad?!

Solomon Gladstone. Don't trust anybody else. You . . . you . . .

Dad?

Find him . . .

Where is he?

He's at the . . . the . . . I'm . . . I . . .

Dad? Dad!

The call went dead.

CHAPTER THIRTEEN

00:18

Bowveld stared down at the body of Dr. Banks, collapsed in a heap on the ground.

"Take him in."

Clay, the taller of the two men, nodded and placed the now empty syringe on the table next to him. He squatted down and wrapped his arms around the top half of Dr. Banks's body. The other man, Darin, grabbed Dr. Banks's feet, and then, without a word passing between them, the men stood up at the same time and carried the body in the direction of the Avection chamber.

Bowveld pressed the gold button at the entrance of the first capsule in the chamber's corridor, and the doors whooshed open to reveal a small black room containing only a single black padded leather table.

"Just lay him down on the bed," he said, stepping aside to let the men through.

The men, both now struggling with the dead weight they

were carrying, waddled into the center of the room. With a mumbled "one, two, three," Dr. Banks's body was lifted up and dumped unceremoniously onto the table—or bed, as Avecto Enterprises preferred it to be called.

"Should we secure him, sir?" asked Darin as he rearranged Dr. Banks's body so that it lay straight.

Bowveld waved his hand to dismiss the idea. "No need. By the time he wakes up, it'll be too late. Let's go."

The men nodded and walked out of the room. Bowveld took one last look at Dr. Banks's sleeping body and frowned.

"Don't let me down, Dr. Banks. I expect you back within the month," he muttered as he pressed down on the gold button once more.

The doors glided firmly closed.

It was only once they had gone through the procedure of locking the main doors of the Avection chamber and were halfway up the steps to the control room that Bowveld realized he had forgotten something very important.

"The purse!" he said, turning to Clay.

"Sir?"

"The purse for my sister, you idiot. Where is it?"

"I don't know, sir. You didn't tell me—"

"Is that it?" asked Darin, pointing to a fuchsia pink shopping bag sitting on one of the rows of leather seats in the waiting lounge below.

"Open up the chamber, Clay," said Bowveld as he rushed

down the stairs. Clay didn't move as he watched Bowveld reach into the bag and pull out an expensive-looking purple purse with a gold chain strap.

"Sir," said Clay, "couldn't we send it with the next shipment? We've already closed the doors."

Bowveld glared up in disgust at Clay's insolence. "My sister is not a patient woman. She expects her treats with every shipment and she's going to get them. Or I'll be the one paying for it. Understood?"

Clay knew better than to argue. "Of course, sir," he said. He came back down the stairs and took the bag from Bowveld.

There was plenty of space for the three men in the control room, but—partly for security, partly for discretion—Clay and Darin stood on either side of the doors as Bowveld strode up and down the control unit, filling the room with an uneasy tension. He muttered to himself as he tried to remember in what order Dr. Banks had told him to do everything. At the front of the room, a row of television screens were mounted side by side on the wall. Below each one hung a black plaque with the name of the capsule it pertained to printed in thick white lettering. Only one of the screens was on—the one labeled SAPPHIRE.

Bowveld glanced up at the live video feed of Dr. Banks lying still under the purple ultraviolet light of the room.

"Okay, I think I know what to do," said Bowveld, mostly to himself. He pressed his thumb down on the small square black scanner and waited until the machine came to life.

Bowveld withdrew his hand from the scanner and stepped over to the computer screen.

WELCOME, DIRECTOR BOWVELD.

PRESS 1 TO COMMENCE AVECTION.

PRESS 2 FOR LAST AVECTION DATA.

PRESS 3 FOR MORE OPTIONS.

Bowveld nodded and pressed down on the button marked 1.

FOR SECURITY PURPOSES, PLEASE RESCAN THUMBPRINT AND ENTER YOUR CLEARANCE CODE AT THE SAME TIME.

"Hmmm," said Bowveld as he reached out and placed his left thumb back on the scanner. With his right hand poised over the keypad, he turned his other wrist—carefully so as not to lose contact with the fingerprint scanner—and began to slowly read out the numbers written on his palm in blue ink.

"One . . . nine . . . I can't read that," he mumbled. He turned his hand some more, and the machine beeped.

DO NOT REMOVE THUMB UNTIL CLEARANCE CODE IS ACCEPTED.

"I know that!" shouted Bowveld at the computer screen

"Would you like me to read it out for you, sir?"

"Um. Yes," said Bowveld. "Good idea."

Bowveld placed his thumb back on the pad and, as Clay called them out, he typed each number in turn and then waited until the computer responded.

IDENTITY CONFIRMED.
BEGIN AVECTION?
PRESS 1 FOR YES. PRESS 2 TO RETURN TO MAIN MENU.

Bowveld smiled and stood up. He rubbed his hands together, then reached out and pressed 1.

SELECT CAPSULE FOR AVECTION.
1—SAPPHIRE. 2—DIAMOND. 3—TOPAZ. 4—RUBY.
5—EMERALD. 6—OPAL. 7—AMETHYST. 8—CARGO.

Bowveld pressed 1.

YOU HAVE SELECTED
1—SAPPHIRE.
IS THIS CORRECT?
PRESS 1 FOR YES. PRESS 2 FOR NO.

Bowveld turned to Clay and Darin and rolled his eyes. "Is this really necessary?" he asked. He pressed 1.

Bowveld waited.

AVECTION READY TO COMMENCE.

A green light in the center of the panel began to flash. Bowveld gave a wry smile.

"Good of Dr. Banks to make this so easy for me," he said.

He reached out and, with his hand hovering over the glowing button, looked up at the television screen.

"Bon voyage, Dr. Banks."

He slapped his hand down.

A loud beep sounded, followed by the sound of a woman's voice coming through the loudspeaker.

"*Avection commencing in ten seconds. . . .*"

Bowveld looked over at Clay and Darin and gave them a thumbs-up.

"*Nine . . . Eight . . . Seven . . . Six . . . Five . . .*"

Bowveld picked at his manicured nails impatiently.

"*Four . . . Three . . . Two . . . One . . . Avection initiated.*"

The image of Dr. Banks flickered briefly, and then the screen turned black.

He was gone.

PART II

CHAPTER FOURTEEN

"Pull over!" shouted Parker.

Brendan looked up at the rearview mirror.

"Everything okay?"

"Pull over!"

Brendan didn't ask again. He swerved to the side of the road and switched off the engine. Then he turned around in his seat, a look of concern on his face.

"I can trust you, right?" said Parker to Michael. He was shaking.

Michael looked over at Brendan, as if hoping he might give him an explanation.

"Can I trust you?" shouted Parker.

Michael snapped back around to face Parker and nodded quickly.

"And him?" asked Parker, looking over at Brendan.

"Yes," said Michael quickly. "With your life. Parker . . ."

"What's wrong?" asked Brendan.

"You can't tell anybody," pleaded Parker.

Brendan and Michael nodded.

"Anybody," repeated Parker. "I promised." There were tears in his eyes.

"Nobody's going to say anything," said Brendan. "Tell us what's wrong."

Parker nodded as he stared down at the single remaining light on his wrist. He had no choice. Despite what his father had asked of him, he knew he needed help. He opened his mouth to speak and then closed it again. He had no idea where to begin.

"Take your time, son," said Brendan.

Parker nodded again and wiped a tear from his cheek. Then he held up his wrist.

"And your sister?" asked Brendan after Parker had finally finished explaining everything. Parker was surprised at how easily both Brendan and Michael had accepted his explanation. The flashing wrist, he suspected, had helped. As crazy as his story sounded, the physical evidence was hard to ignore.

"She's at a swimming thing," said Parker. "She doesn't wear her glasses in the water, so she can't answer my call." He was hardly aware of Michael holding his arm and examining his wrist.

"I *knew* it wasn't just a twin thing," mumbled Michael to himself. "I knew it."

"Do you know where she is?" Brendan asked.

Parker shook his head.

"And you have no idea who this Solomon Gladstone is?"

Parker shook his head again. "I've never heard of him."

Brendan looked away. He removed his hat to reveal his thinning silvery-blond hair and rubbed his face in thought.

"You're going to tell someone, aren't you?" asked Parker.

Brendan turned back again but didn't say anything.

Parker leaned forward. His red eyes were wide and pleading. "You can't do that. *Please*. You promised!"

Brendan nodded slowly. "I know I did, son. But if this is true, then . . ."

"*True?* You don't believe me?"

"I'm not saying that," said Brendan, choosing his words carefully. "It's just not something you hear every day."

"My dad wouldn't lie."

"No, of course. I'm not saying that." Brendan thought for a moment. "Okay. So let's say it's true . . ."

"It is."

"And your dad has been taken somewhere and you've got nobody at home. No family to look after you. Then what am I supposed to do: leave two kids on their own?"

"They could stay at my house," said Michael.

"Your parents are going to ask questions," said Brendan.

"They don't have to know. They could stay in the tree house," said Michael.

"Really?" asked Parker.

Michael shrugged. "It's not like they're ever home anyway. What do you think, Brendan?"

Another pause. Longer this time. Parker felt like he was going to explode with frustration.

"I have to go find Solomon! My dad needs help. Just leave me back at my house if you don't believe me. I'll work something out."

Brendan shook his head and turned around. He started the car.

"We're going to your house," called Brendan as he pulled back out onto the road. "You can get what you need for you and your sister for a few days. You have a key?" He looked up at the rearview mirror. Parker nodded.

"Keep trying your sister. Tell her I'll pick her up from school when she gets back."

Parker nodded again.

"I'll help you as much as I can. And I won't say anything. But if nothing's happened in a few days, you're going to have to report it to the police."

"Okay," said Parker. His eyes began to fill up with tears again.

"It'll be all right, son," said Brendan, looking at Parker's reflection in the mirror. "We'll find him."

"I'll look up . . . Oh. My cell phone's out of battery. Brendan, can we use your phone?" asked Michael.

Without taking his eyes off the road, Brendan leaned over to the passenger seat and picked up what looked like a gray brick.

Michael took it and turned it over in his hand in horror. "When did you get this? 1965?"

"It does everything I need it to do," said Brendan.

"Does it have the Internet?" asked Michael. He pressed down randomly on some of the thick rubber buttons.

Parker sighed. "I don't think they had the Internet in the sixties."

Michael shook his head in disbelief and handed the phone back to Brendan. "We'll have to wait till we get mine back."

Deflated, both boys leaned back in their seats. They spent the rest of the journey to Parker's house in silence, with Parker trying Emma on Effie at regular intervals while Michael stared at Parker's wrist.

"What is *that*?" asked Brendan.

"I can't leave her," said Parker as he ushered Polly up his driveway. "Is it okay?"

Michael laughed and then stopped abruptly as he realized nobody else was finding the situation amusing. He shrugged apologetically. "It's a white pig."

Brendan sighed. "Come on then. It can sit in the back with the two of you. Give me that."

Brendan took the bulging backpack from Parker and put it in the trunk as Michael and Parker wrestled Polly up onto the backseat.

"Is your sister still not answering?" asked Brendan as he sat back in the driver's seat and closed his door.

"No," said Parker. "I think she's swimming all afternoon."

"Keep trying."

Parker and Michael left Brendan to deal with Polly and rushed inside Michael's house.

"I'm just glad his name isn't John Smith," said Michael as he ran over to his computer and turned it on.

Parker nodded in agreement and sat down at the neighboring computer. He turned it on.

"Come on, come on," urged Parker as the screen came to life.

Michael was already typing. *"S-o-l-u—"*

"O," corrected Parker. "Solomon is *S-o-l-o-m-o-n*."

Parker pulled up the Internet search engine on his computer and typed in the full name too.

The room was silent as they both scanned each page of results in turn, looking for anything that might be relevant. There was nothing about anybody named Solomon Gladstone, except a single profile of a teenager in South Africa.

"Do you think that's him?" asked Michael. They were both looking at the same page.

"It can't be," said Parker. "It says he's fourteen."

Parker bookmarked the page and began the search again. This time, he added *NY* after the name. Still nothing.

"I'll try searching for 'six, New York,'" said Michael. "Hmm . . . That's not going to work. 570,000,000 results."

Parker winced.

"Wait! I know!" said Parker. He was already typing. "Solomon. Gladstone. Avecto."

"What's Avecto?"

"The company my dad works for," said Parker. "I got it!"

Michael searched using the same words, as Parker clicked on the link.

"Cassandra's Army?" asked Parker as the page loaded up. "What's that?"

Michael was staring at the same page. "'The truth nobody wants to hear,'" he said, reading the slogan at the top.

Parker scrolled down the page of hundreds of forum entries. He read out some of the post headlines, mostly to himself as Michael was already looking at the same thing.

"'Lizards are running our government,'" read Parker. "'Anybody else found their cat has been fitted with a recording device?'"

"'Tinfoil *does* prevent alien abduction. Confirmed,'" continued Michael.

"Who *are* these people?" asked Parker as he scrolled down. He was getting the feeling that this was not going to be providing him with any of the answers he needed.

"They're all nuts," said Michael. "It's a conspiracy forum. Who's Cassandra?"

Parker continued to scroll down as he answered Michael. "From Greek mythology. She's the one who always told the truth and nobody believed her."

"Wow. Weird," said Michael. "Okay. This isn't going to work. Let's search for something else."

Parker shook his head. "I want to find what it says about

Solomon. There has to be something if it came up in the search."

He scrolled down farther.

> All new models of microwaves fitted with timed
> detonators.
> Reality shows are vehicles for government mind-
> control program.
> All twelve-year-olds have superpowers for one
> year only. Worldwide cover-up!
> Flood in Philippines was deliberate! Hollywood
> to blame!!!
> Utopian planet called SIX being constructed by
> Avecto Enterprises. Funded by the elite.

"Got it!" shouted Parker. Michael spun his chair around as Parker followed the link to the post. Parker bit his lip as they both began to read.

> There is a planet called SIX being prepared
> for the elite to escape to when Earth's natural
> resources run out.
> THIS IS 100 PERCENT TRUE!!!

Parker dropped his head in disappointment. "Oh no."

"It gets better," said Michael.

Parker could barely bring himself to read on.

It is being built by a company called Avecto Enterprises. (Look them up <u>here</u>. They say they are a telecommunications company. This is NOT TRUE.) It is being funded by the US government and other individual investors and countries in the West. Other countries definitely involved: United Kingdom, Austria, New Zealand, Ireland, Greece, Canada, Norway, Germany, France, Italy.

Billions of dollars have been sent to SIX. Funding has increased heavily in the last five years. I believe this is because they are planning to leave Earth soon.

READ THE NEWS!

Why do you think there are recessions happening? Where do you think all the money has disappeared to?

THE MONEY IS BEING SENT OVER TO SIX!!!!

Avecto Enterprises is run by Warren Bowveld. He is the one responsible for sourcing investment. The head of the program itself was a man called Solomon Gladstone. He disappeared three years ago.

When I tried to find out who replaced him, THEY TRIED TO KILL ME.

SPREAD THE WORD. KNOWLEDGE IS POWER.

Source: My dad worked for Avecto.

*   *   *   *   *   *

"I'll search again," said Michael.

"We can't ignore that!" said Parker.

"Yes, we can."

"*No*, we can't. I know it's crazy, but he says his name. *And* the company my dad works for."

"You really think your dad's been taken to another planet?"

"No, of course not. I'm just saying he knows about Solomon Gladstone. He might know where I can find him."

Parker clicked on the name of the person who had posted it. "Anteater," muttered Parker. "What kind of a name is that?"

"The name of a lunatic," replied Michael.

"Wow," said Parker, staring at Anteater's profile. On it was a list of his posts—all 2,623 of them.

"They all say the same thing," said Parker, scrolling down.

"E-mail address?"

Parker shook his head. "Nothing." He went back to the original post. "I'll leave him a message. What shall I write?"

"You need help."

Parker frowned.

"Okay, okay. Just ask him to e-mail you. Hold on . . ."

Michael picked up a pen and scrawled down an e-mail address. "Use this," he said. He slid the piece of paper over to Parker. "It's untraceable."

Parker nodded and began to write.

> *URGENT! Please contact me. I need*
> *more information. E-mail me at*
> *donteventhinkabouttryingtotracethis@grapevine.com.*

"Is that enough?"

Michael shrugged. "Probably. Maybe just add a line about believing him or something. Lie."

Parker nodded. He turned back to his computer to write, when a familiar sensation ran up his arm.

"Emma!" said Parker, turning his wrist to look down.

Michael looked impressed. "So cool," he muttered as Parker pressed down on her light.

Emma?

Parker! What happened to Dad?

Parker froze. **How do you know?**

They sent police to the swimming tournament to get me. They said Dad's been in an accident.

Parker felt himself turn pale. **Do not go with them, Emma.**

He turned to Michael. "They're trying to take Emma. Get Brendan."

Who's that? asked Emma.

I'm with Michael. Listen. Do not go anywhere with them, okay? They're lying. Just get away from them. We'll come get you.

What?

Dad was right about those men yesterday. He's been kidnapped. Get away from them now.

Emma was silent.

Emma! Did you hear me? I said whatever you do, do not go with them.

There was no response. Parker flipped his wrist around to check that the light was still on.

Emma?

When Emma finally replied, her voice was barely more than a whisper.

It's too late, Parker. I already did.

CHAPTER FIFTEEN

All his life Parker had been told to get an adult when help
was needed. Being bullied? Tell a teacher. Lost? Find a
policeman. He had been programmed to think, from day
one, that everything—from feeling unwell to opening an
oven door—required the help of a responsible adult. It had
been a while since he'd needed to ask for adult assistance
with oven-opening, but for the big things he had always had
his father to turn to. Until now. Now, for the first time in
his life, there was no adult to take charge of the situation.
Brendan would help—and he was grateful for that—but
how long would that help last? And anyway, Brendan could
only help with what Parker told him he needed to do. That
required a plan.

Emma. Listen to me.

Parker, I'm scared.

**Don't be scared. I'm going to come and get you. I
just need to know where you are. Look around you.
What do you see?**

Parker waited.

There's not much. We're driving past fields.

There must be something.

A barn. And a house.

Come on, Emma.

That's it!

Keep looking. Did the men say anything to you? Do you know where you're being taken?

No. They freaked out when they realized I was deaf, and then they started arguing with each other. I couldn't lip-read what they were saying.

But they're policemen? You're in a patrol car?

Emma's voice went quiet again. **No. It's a normal car.**

Okay. But they're wearing uniforms?

Emma?

No!

Parker could tell by the high-pitched voice coming through Effie that Emma was crying.

They had badges.

Badges? Emma!

They knew my name. They knew Dad's name. Even my teachers believed them. You would have gone with them too, wouldn't you?

Parker had to admit she had a point. **Fine, just—**

He was interrupted by Michael running back into the room. "Brendan's waiting in the car."

Parker nodded and jumped up. **We're going to come**

**get you. You just need to work out where you are. Do
you see anything?**

**Just houses. Nothing . . . wait! A dentist sign. It's
bright pink, in the shape of wings. It's called . . . the
Tooth Fairy.**

Parker ran back over to the computer.

"What are you doing?" asked Michael.

"Hold on . . . found it!" He searched frantically around the desk for something to write on. He picked up the thing nearest to him—a computer manual. He started to rip off the back cover.

"Um. Parker. Don't . . . ," said Michael.

Parker glared over as Michael ran to a drawer and pulled out a wad of fresh white paper. "Here. Use this."

Parker snatched the paper from him and grabbed a pen from a pen pot. He scribbled down the address, then folded the paper and stuffed it into his jacket pocket as he ran out of the room with Michael.

As Brendan drove them in the direction of the dental practice, Emma began to be able to offer them more information. Parker wrote down everything she said while Michael relayed it all to Brendan.

"They're not far," said Brendan. "We're fifteen minutes behind them."

Michael turned to Parker. "What are we going to do when we get there?"

Up until that point Michael had acted as if this was an elaborate game—a bit of an adventure. But now, for the first time, Parker saw fear in his eyes.

"I don't know," admitted Parker. He didn't. All he knew was that he had already lost his mum and his dad and he wasn't going to lose his sister, too. But that, Parker knew, was neither Brendan nor Michael's problem.

"If you want to," said Parker, "you can leave me there."

Brendan shook his head. "Don't be silly."

Parker didn't have a chance to thank him as he was interrupted by Emma's voice.

Shady Brook Lane, said Emma. Parker wrote it down and turned it to show Michael.

We're slowing down! We're here!

Where?

It's a house. Parker! Why are they taking me to a house?

The mailbox, Emma! What's the number on it?

1420.

Okay. Emma, calm down. This is what you're going to do . . .

Ideally, Effie would have been able to pick up on conversations happening around Emma. Were that possible, Emma, in a sense, would not have been deaf anymore. On the face of it, it seemed like a relatively easy problem to solve—certainly easier than inventing a thought-translating device—but it had turned out to be far more complex than their father had first imagined. Their father's attempts at an ear-implanted microphone had been uncomfortable and confusing, mostly because the microphone was unable to distinguish between voices and ambient noise. The result was a constant stream of gibberish racing across the lens of Emma's glasses, intermingled with whatever recognizable words the microphone picked up. Emma had hated it. She had found it too distracting and, anyway, as far as Emma was concerned, she did not need fixing. Effie was fine, and useful at home, but in the outside world Emma wore her badge of deafness with pride. She was unique and proud of it. Nobody Emma cared about had ever treated her like she had a disability, and she had never felt like she had one. So at her request the microphone had been discarded and the idea never pursued any further. This had never concerned Parker one way or another—right up until the moment his sister got kidnapped and he couldn't hear what was going on.

There was, however, a solution. By listening to a conversation—or lip-reading it, in Emma's case—and consciously repeating what you saw or heard, preceded by the name of whoever was speaking—the person on the other line of Effie could follow what was happening. It was this that Parker asked Emma to do as Brendan raced to reach her.

* * * * * *

I'm calling them Kermit and Piggy. Okay? said Emma, referring to the two men that had taken her.

Fine, said Parker. **Go.**

Piggy is waving me out. Parker, shall I go?

Parker nodded. **Just play along, Emma. We'll be there in a second.**

We're going up to the front door. We're waiting. . . . It's an old woman. She's hugging Kermit and Piggy. Okay. I can see them. I can lip-read. Ready?

Parker waited for Emma to translate.

Kermit: You look well, Mamma.

His mother? said Emma. Mamma Frog's kissing him.

Mamma Frog: Who's this?

Kermit: I need you to look after her for a while.

Mamma Frog: Is she yours?

Kermit: No, Mamma!

Mamma Frog: I don't know. You never tell me anything. Always sneaking around. You never call.

Kermit: I know, I know, Mamma.

Mamma Frog: What do you want me to do with her?

Kermit: Just look after her. Her dad's missing. He's a friend of mine. I'm taking care of her until we find him, Please, Mamma?

Mamma Frog: I don't see you for three months and now you show up on my doorstep with a kid for me to look after?

Kermit: Yes, Mamma. I'm sorry. I'll be back for her soon. Oh, and she's deaf.

Mamma Frog: Poor baby. Is she simple, too?

Simple? said Emma. **I'll give them simple.**

Emma . . . warned Parker. He knew what his sister's temper was like.

It's all right. I know. They're taking me inside.

Mamma Frog: Sit down and eat. I'll make you boys something.

Kermit: No, Mamma, we have to go.

Mamma Frog: Where are the child's things?

Kermit's pulling out some money.

Kermit: Here, get Francesca to buy her whatever she needs.

Kermit's going over to the kitchen.

Michael interrupted Parker.

"Ask her if they have any guns on them."

"Good point." **Emma. Do they have guns?**

Guns?

Guns. Can you see?

No. I can't see.

Maybe they're concealed. Look closely—

Hold on, interrupted Emma. **I have an idea.**

Emma! What are you doing?

Parker heard Emma wailing.

I'm crying. Hold on. I'm throwing myself on Piggy.

Emma wailed louder.

I can't feel anything round his waist, she said.

Parker couldn't help but smile. **What about Kermit?**

Yeah, he's coming over. Waaaaaahhhhhhhhh!

Parker winced. **What are you doing?**

He's trying to pull me away. I'm checking. Parker! I found a gun!

Just leave it, Emma!

It's okay. He's pushed me away. Oh, wait! His mum's seen it now. . . . She's screaming at him. . . . They're arguing. She's telling him to give her the gun. . . .

There was a brief pause.

She's taken the gun off him! said Emma. **She's asking Piggy if he has one. He's shaking his head. She's patting him to make sure. Wow, she is *really* angry. She's walking upstairs. I can't see what Kermit is saying—it looks like he's shouting at her but she's not listening. He's talking to Piggy.**

What's he saying?

That this job is turning out to be a pain.

Piggy: Why can't we just leave them somewhere?

Kermit: They don't want them getting the police involved. Two whining, crying kids on national television looking for their dad is going to get people asking questions. Look, the money's good. And we don't even have to do anything.

Piggy: Will the kid talk?

Kermit: She can't.

Piggy: She can probably write.

Emma was silent.

Emma! What's happening?

Kermit's writing me a note.

What does it say?

There was a long pause.

Where is Parker?

At the mention of his name, Parker froze. In all the excitement of listening to the conversation, Parker had forgotten—just for a moment—the brutal reality of their situation.

What shall I write?

Just say that I'm at school.

There was a pause. **Okay. He's writing something else. . . . He's not there. Where would he go?**

Look upset. Make it convincing. Write that you don't know. Ask him why you're there.

He's writing. . . . I'm friends with your dad. You stay here until he's better.

Ask him where Dad is.

He says that Dad's going to be okay. He'll take me to him soon. He's asking where I think you've gone again. Wait, I'm just going to cry louder—that seems to work. . . .

Parker waited.

Yep. He's walked away.

"We're here," called Brendan. Parker turned and looked out the window and saw the number on the mailbox—1420—as they drove by. It was hard to believe his sister was inside there.

Brendan kept going and stopped out of sight of the house. He turned to face Parker.

"I'm not sure about this," he said. "This doesn't feel right. We should call the police. They'll be able to help."

"No!" said Parker. "Please."

"We don't know anything about these people. If something happens to any of you, it'd be my fault."

Parker was regretting saying anything to Brendan. His dad had been right.

"What if they have guns?" continued Brendan.

Parker tensed. "They haven't." It was *almost* true.

Brendan sighed. "If Hilda found out . . ." He didn't finish his sentence.

"Just leave me here," said Parker. "I'll be fine."

He didn't know how true that was, but he also knew he had no option. He had to do this and no one—not Brendan, not anyone—was going to stop him.

"I can't do that." Brendan sighed. "We'll get your sister and then we can talk. First things first . . ."

Before Parker could ask what he was doing, Brendan was getting out of the car and opening the trunk.

"What's he getting?" asked Michael.

Parker shrugged. "No idea."

The trunk slammed shut, and Parker spun around as his door was opened.

"Here, take this," said Brendan. He handed Parker a license plate and slammed the door closed. Parker was too surprised to say anything. He took the plate and placed it between him and an equally shocked-looking Michael.

Brendan slid back into the driver's seat. "We need her outside. You think you can find a way to do that?"

The now unidentifiable car sat parked behind two cars not far up the street. Though it wasn't the best hiding place, they were counting on the two men not knowing that they would be following Emma. The three of them kept their heads down as Emma relayed the progress of their hastily drawn-up plan.

"She's crying," said Parker.

"She's good at that," commented Michael.

"You have no idea. If she wants something . . . Wait. I can't believe it! They're buying it!"

Parker listened as Emma pulled on Kermit's sleeve, crying for the teddy she'd dropped in the backseat. It was not, Parker thought in admiration, a trick he could have pulled off himself.

"Brendan. They're coming out."

He switched his attention back to Emma. **Emma, we're going to pull up and you have to jump in.**

Michael and Parker peeked out of the window as the front

door opened. Out came Emma, screaming and wailing and holding on to the arm of a goggle-eyed man. *Kermit had been a good choice of name,* thought Parker.

"She is doing a really good job," said Michael.

Parker noticed her glancing around to find them. If she did spot them, she didn't break from her performance.

"On the count of three," said Brendan. "I'm going to pull out slowly. They'll think I'm just a passing car. Open the door as we get there. Got it?"

Parker sat up as Brendan pulled out from the parking space. Kermit looked up but, just as they had all hoped, he seemed to think nothing of it. He opened the car door and leaned in. Brendan slammed his foot on the accelerator as Parker opened the door.

Kermit was the last to realize what was happening. It was only Piggy's shouts from the front door that alerted him. By then Emma was already sprinting away. Kermit reached into his pocket and let out a cry of frustration.

"My gun! Get my gun!"

Piggy was already running back into the house as Mamma Frog watched the events unfold with a look of utter shock on her face.

Quick, Emma! Faster!

Emma had not had far to run, but Kermit had the advantage of size. He ran forward and lunged in Emma's direction just as she hurled herself into the car. Parker grabbed her body and pulled, but she was not moving in.

"He's got her foot!" shouted Michael. He reached over Parker and grabbed Emma's arms.

"We've got her!" shouted Parker. "Drive!"

Without a word, Brendan accelerated forward gently. For a brief moment, with Emma staring up helplessly at them, Parker and Michael pulled with all their might until, at last, her foot slipped free. They pulled her in as Brendan accelerated away, the door still wide open. As Emma climbed over him, Parker looked around and saw Kermit holding her shoe and waving frantically back to the house. The last thing he saw before they turned a corner was Piggy running out holding the car keys and the gun.

Brendan slammed the brake. "Close the door!"

As soon as Parker did as he'd been told, Brendan slammed his foot down on the gas pedal again. This time he didn't hold back. Within five minutes they were back onto the busy highway. As Emma reassured Parker that she was okay, Brendan weaved in and out of the cars and then took the ramp two exits after the turning for Michael's house. They all watched behind them—Brendan in his rearview mirror—as they left the highway. Not a single car exited. They had gotten away.

Brendan burst out laughing and let out a loud whoop that made them all jump.

"Brendan?" asked Michael.

Brendan slammed his hands on the steering wheel. "That feels good! I needed that. How's she doing?"

"She's fine," answered Parker.

"Let's get you back to the house then," said Brendan. He let out another whoop.

"Fantastic," Parker muttered to himself.

Beside Parker, Emma and Michael were smiling. It seemed that everybody in the car was ecstatic, except for him. This, Parker knew, was only the beginning.

CHAPTER SIXTEEN

Technically Michael's tree house fit the description of *tree house*, insomuch as it sat in a tree, and it was a house. That was where the similarity between this place and any other tree house that Parker had ever seen in his life ended.

"There's a laptop in the drawer," said Michael. "I'll bring another one from my room later so we don't have to share. The bathroom works—the pipes run into the ground. Want me to show you how the TV works?"

Parker shook his head. He had too much to do. He looked over at Emma sitting on the sofa, looking pale as she processed everything that Parker had updated her on. "Maybe for her," he said. "Can you check your mail?" he asked.

"I've been checking the whole time. There's nothing."

Parker sighed. "Keep checking."

Parker spent the evening desperately searching for any more information about Solomon Gladstone. Apart from Anteater's posts, he could find nothing. He had never felt so frustrated. Emma had kept to herself since they'd got back. She had passed out a few hours earlier after checking on Polly, and Michael had left not long after, returning to the main house before Hilda got back so as not to raise suspicions. He'd remained in contact, however, sending Parker regularly updates via e-mail to tell him that Anteater hadn't responded yet. Eventually Michael had also gone to sleep, sending one final e-mail to let Parker know that he had convinced Hilda he was too sick to go to school the next day. Apparently, his performance had been more convincing than Parker's.

By midnight Parker could barely keep his eyes open any longer. He had achieved nothing and, as he closed the laptop and headed to bed, a terrifying thought occurred to him. What would happen if he never found Solomon? Would that mean his dad would never come back? And what would happen to him and Emma? Fortunately, the day's events had taken their toll, and exhaustion won over his worry. He fell into a deep sleep.

"He replied!"

Parker groaned and turned away.

"Parker! Wake up!"

Parker felt himself being shaken.

"Anteater wrote back!"

The mention of Anteater's name was like a bucket of water over his head. Parker bolted upright.

"What did he say?"

"He said he can't . . ."

"Read it!" Parker was already jumping up and pulling on his jeans.

Michael pulled out his cell phone and began to read. "Can't say anything on here. All correspondence being monitored. Meet me in the car lot of the Raw Meat Shack on Rochester Parkway at eleven a.m. on the dot."

Parker knew exactly where that was.

"That's around the corner from my house. He must know where I live."

Michael thought about this. "Maybe it's a coincidence?" he asked.

Parker could tell he was as unconvinced of this as Parker was.

"You think he traced your e-mail?"

Parker was starting to learn that Michael did not take kindly to having his computing skills questioned. "No way. Not possible."

"Then what do you suggest? You think that of all the places in the world he could be, he just happens to live next door to me?"

Michael thought about it for a moment and then his eyes lit up. "He must know about your dad! He must know you'd be looking for him. He probably works for the same company!"

Of course! It made perfect sense.

"What time is it?" he asked.

Michael checked his cell phone. "Eight thirty."

* * * * * *

Michael had to wait for Hilda to leave the house to run a quick errand before he was able to return to the tree house with breakfast.

"I told her being sick made me hungry," said Michael as he pulled out a mountain of toast and croissants from the bag he'd brought.

Michael and Emma, now awake, tucked into the spread but, despite the fact that he had barely eaten in the last twenty-four hours, Parker could only manage a few small bites.

"Checking the time won't make it go any faster," said Michael.

Parker looked up from Michael's cell phone and nodded. "I guess." He turned to Emma.

"I think you should stay here," he signed. *"It's safe. I'll let you know on Effie how it's going."*

Emma thought about it for a moment and then shrugged. *"Fine."*

"Oh, right. Good."

Parker had not expected her to agree so easily—she hated being excluded from anything. Then again, figured Parker, getting kidnapped and losing your father on the same day was likely to make anybody act strangely.

"You'll be safe," said Michael, speaking clearly in Emma's direction. "My dad has the whole place hooked up with every security feature possible. Anyone would think we kept gold bars here."

"You don't?" asked Parker.

Michael rolled his eyes.

* * * * * *

At ten o'clock Parker could wait no longer. Michael called Brendan, who drove up to the tree house to collect them.

"Bolt the door," said Parker as he climbed down the ladder.

Emma nodded. *"Please be careful, Parker,"* she signed.

"I will be," he said. He closed the hatch over his head and climbed down the rungs to the waiting car.

"Right then," said Brendan as he and Michael climbed in. "Where to?"

"Raw Meat Shack," said Michael. "We have to be there at eleven."

"We'll be early," said Brendan.

"That's fine," said Parker. "We can wait."

"Right you are, then," said Brendan as he pulled away.

They pulled into the Raw Meat Shack parking lot forty-five minutes early. It was empty, and a battered metal WE'RE CLOSED sign hung on the heavily padlocked doors. This was not a surprise; The Raw Meat Shack was not a breakfasting kind of place. Brendan pulled up at the space nearest the door and turned the engine off.

"What do you think he's going to say?" asked Michael.

"I don't know."

"What if he's completely nuts?"

"I don't care as long as he can tell me something that helps me find Solomon. Anything."

Parker picked up Michael's phone that was on the seat

between them and checked the time again. Forty-three minutes to go. Parker sighed. Two minutes later he looked at the time again.

"A watched pot never boils," said Brendan from behind his open newspaper. Parker knew he was right, and reluctantly he handed the phone back to Michael. He turned to look out the window, his knees jigging up and down impatiently.

Unable to help himself, Parker spent the next half hour ignoring Brendan's advice and checking Michael's phone constantly.

"I have to keep repeating the level every time you do that," said Michael. "You should get a watch."

"I will," mumbled Parker. He checked the time again. "Ten minutes," he said. Brendan nodded, and Parker turned to Michael to hand the phone back when it binged loudly.

"You've got an e-mail," said Parker. He read the name of the sender. "It's Anteater!"

Before Michael could check the phone himself, Parker pressed down on the e-mail icon. He read the e-mail out loud.

"'Hey, people of Avecto. Good try! I have nothing to say to any of you, so you can stop trying to find out what I know. You can follow me, threaten me, or even kill me, but one day soon the truth will come out. PS How's the work on SIX going? Yours (don't bother contacting me again), Anteater.'"

Parker turned to Michael with a look of utter confusion. "Is this from the same address?"

Michael grabbed the phone and ran through his e-mails. "No," he muttered. "Different e-mail."

The boys went silent, both trying to figure out what was going on. In the front Brendan whistled quietly to himself, oblivious to the confusion happening behind him.

"Okay. So first he e-mails us and tells us to meet him, and then he e-mails us to tell us not to. The guy really is nuts."

As Michael spoke, Parker's face turned pale.

"What's wrong?" asked Michael.

Parker didn't answer. His mind was racing through the logic of the explanation he had come up with.

"Parker?"

Parker lifted his head slowly and stared at Michael for a moment. His voice was barely a whisper when he finally spoke.

"We've been tricked."

"What?"

Parker could barely breathe. "It's a trick! It wasn't Anteater who e-mailed us this morning—it was the people who took my dad!" He leaned forward, and the red digital clock on the dashboard caught his eye. Four minutes to eleven. "Brendan, we need to go!"

Brendan threw his paper down in surprise.

"Get out of here!"

To his credit, Brendan didn't say a word. He leaned over, turned the key, and spun the wheel around.

"I don't get it," said Michael.

"That's how they knew I lived near here!" said Parker as the car zoomed across the lot. "Anybody could have checked the forum. Think about it!"

Michael stared at Parker as he processed what Parker was saying. His eyes widened.

"Ohhh."

"We need to get out of here, Brendan," said Parker.

"We're going, we're going," said Brendan, pulling out left onto the main road. He accelerated away.

He should have felt relieved as the red-bricked building of the Raw Meat Shack disappeared into the distance, but he felt nothing of the sort. His heart was pounding, and his mind was spinning with what-ifs.

"They wouldn't have let us get away a second time," mumbled Parker. "They might have killed us."

"Parker!"

Parker looked up and saw that Michael was turned in his seat, looking out the back window.

"Somebody's turning into the car lot. I don't think it's the car from yesterday," said Michael.

Parker spun around and peered out. He froze. Michael was right. It wasn't the car from yesterday—even at a distance he could tell it was the wrong color. This car was silver. Parker felt his stomach somersault as he realized he recognized it. It was the same car that had followed them to the lake on Sunday.

"They've parked," said Michael. "They didn't see us."

He turned back around and dropped into his seat.

"Wow! That was close," Michael said. He was laughing nervously. "You really think it wasn't him?"

Parker sat with his head in his hands. When he finally looked up, the expression on his face quickly wiped the smile from Michael's.

"E-mail him back. Tell him we're not with Avecto. Don't mention my dad's name! Ask him what he can tell me about Solomon Gladstone. Tell him I need to find him."

"What if this is another trick?"

"It's not," said Parker. Michael nodded in agreement. It wouldn't make sense if it was.

Michael started to tap away at his phone.

"Sent," he said, looking up.

They waited a few minutes in silence as Brendan took them on a long route home, just to be sure they weren't being followed.

"Has he replied yet?" asked Parker.

"No."

Another minute passed.

"And now?"

"No!"

Parker drummed his fingers on the armrest.

"Now?"

"No!"

Beep.

"I mean yes."

Parker leaned over and grabbed the phone.

"What did he say?" Michael asked.

Parker sighed deeply and read out the message. "'Leave me alone.'"

He let out a loud groan of frustration and turned back to the phone. He started typing.

"What are you writing?" asked Michael. Parker didn't respond until he'd finished the e-mail. He held it up for Michael to read.

"'Please. My dad has been taken to SIX. Before he was taken, he told me to find Solomon Gladstone. I need your help.'"

"I thought you weren't going to mention your dad?"

"What choice do I have, Michael? He's the only person who might be able to help me."

Michael shrugged, and Parker turned the phone back to face him. He clicked send. They spent the rest of the journey back to Michael's house staring at the phone in silence, Parker's thoughts broken only briefly to update Emma via Effie.

Did he answer yet? signed Emma as they climbed up into the tree house. Neither Parker nor Michael responded, but the answer was written clearly on their faces.

The three of them flopped down on the sofa and turned the television on. There was nothing more to do but wait.

CHAPTER SEVENTEEN

Anteater replied at twelve twenty-eight. Parker knew the precise time because he was staring at Michael's phone the exact moment it arrived. It was no coincidence—he had done nothing but stare at it since they'd got back to the tree house.

Emma, though she didn't hear the alert, didn't miss its arrival either, as both Michael and Parker leapt up off the sofa at the same time.

"What does it say?" asked Michael.

Parker switched on Effie so Emma could hear too. He read the e-mail to himself first, and Emma, who was listening in, heard it also. They both looked at each other in surprise, and their faces broke out into wide grins.

"Tell me what it says!" said Michael.

"Okay, okay. He says . . . 'This changes things. My dad was taken too. I will only talk face-to-face. Guessing you live somewhere around Avecto HQ. If so, I am at the Molten Comic Convention in Syracuse today and tomorrow. Let me know.'"

Parker rushed to press reply and, in his haste, dropped the phone.

Calm down! said Emma.

You calm down! said Parker as he picked the phone up off the floor.

That doesn't make any sense, grumbled Emma. Parker looked up and glared at her, then went back to typing the e-mail. He said nothing until he finished typing, and then he looked up at Michael.

"I'm going to Syracuse," said Parker. "Can I borrow some money?"

Emma had always insisted that it was possible to find the silver lining of any cloud—no matter how dark or ominous. Disasters raised awareness, injustices inspired collective action, deaths carried lessons that might save others, and also, as had happened with their family, made people stronger and closer than they might ever have been. The silver lining was not always easy to find for Parker, but in the case of the last few days it was clear as anything: Michael's friendship and Brendan's help.

He was grateful for everything that they had done already, but even more so when they both insisted they would not allow Parker to travel to Syracuse on his own. Somehow or other, Parker hoped he would have found a way to overcome every hurdle that had been put in his way since his father's disappearance, but there was no denying that having their help had made things considerably easier.

At last, thought Parker as he climbed into the car behind Michael and Emma, they were making progress. In less than two hours—Brendan's estimation—they would be in Syracuse and finally—*finally*—they would be able to get some answers. Anteater had given them precise instructions for when they got there. Until then there was nothing more he could do. He settled back in his seat and closed his eyes. He slept the whole way.

Parker had heard about comic conventions, and walked into the center expecting to find crowds of people dressed up as characters from sci-fi shows and comic books. He was not disappointed. Apart from the four of them, every single person in the ticket line was wearing a costume. Suddenly feeling very conspicuous for their lack of effort, Parker took the ticket that Brendan handed him and followed a group of three squealing teenage girls dressed as pink lizards into the main room. He led the way over to the side of the room, away from the steady stream of people entering, and looked around to get his bearings.

"Wow!" said Michael as the four of them stood side by side and took in their surroundings.

The vast space ahead of them was filled with hundreds of colorful stalls, around which swarmed crowds of equally colorful people moving in all directions. The noise of the place made it feel even more chaotic—the talking, shouting, loudspeaker announcements, and music pouring out of the different stalls each competed loudly for the attention of the people passing by.

Parker looked up at the white ceiling high above him. It was covered in a grid of metal beams from which hung bright spotlights and strobes that swirled around so that the entire space looked as if it were being attacked by thousands of multicolored lasers. It seemed to stretch interminably.

Emma nudged him and pointed to a full-size bright blue jet hanging from the roof in the distance. Parker nodded but didn't say anything—he was too busy working out where they were supposed to be going. He ran his eyes along the orange-and-white numbered signs marking the beginning of each row until he found what he was looking for.

"Let's go," he said, already walking.

At Parker's request, Brendan kept his distance in case he might unnerve Anteater. Brendan was not, however, going entirely unnoticed. As they made their way to the stall that Anteater had instructed them to go to, Brendan—in his suit and hat—was stopped a number of times by people wanting to compliment him on his likeness to Moldovan's Driver—a character none of them had ever heard of. Brendan corrected them the first couple of times until he gave up and instead started thanking them as he passed.

Parker pushed through the crowds until he reached the stall he was looking for: A46, a stall supplying costumes called Cloaks & Daggers. Parker made sure that Michael and Emma were behind him before he began to search the racks of shields, masks, swords, capes, and costumes for the disguises that Anteater had instructed them to wear. Not finding what he was looking for, he turned his attention to the hundreds of masks covering the back wall.

A young man wearing a faded lime-green T-shirt and a gold cape approached them. "What can I get you?" he asked.

Parker suddenly spotted them. He pointed up to the top row.

"Three frog masks please. The ones with the red crowns."

The man looked behind him and nodded his approval.

"Not sold one of those in a while. Fans of the Leapers, huh?"

"Yes, sir," answered Parker. He didn't have a clue who the Leapers were.

"Nice," said the man as he reached up and pulled the masks down. "Not many people have heard of them."

He handed them over to Parker. Michael—who had agreed to lend Parker whatever money they needed until they got their father back—handed over the cash.

"Need a bag?"

"No, thanks," said Parker. He waited until the man left them to talk to another customer before turning to Michael and Emma.

"Put them on," he said.

Michael was examining the large rubber mask. "Seriously, couldn't he have picked something cooler?"

"I like them," signed Emma. She gave a thumbs-up to Michael and then placed her mask over her head.

Parker shrugged. "I'd have worn a pink dress if it got my dad back."

"And I'd be waiting for you outside," said Michael. He sighed and put his mask on.

Parker took the phone out of his pocket—Michael had grown bored of passing it over every five minutes—and e-mailed Anteater to ask him what they should do next. The response was almost instantaneous.

"Hall Two. Second row from the back, other end from the doors," said Parker. He looked around.

Emma pulled his sleeve and pointed to a sign.

"Well spotted," said Parker. He checked behind him to make sure that Brendan knew they were leaving, and then stepped into the sea of people moving in the same direction.

They barely took ten paces before they came to a standstill. Parker tried to push through.

"Hey, kid, don't cut the line!" said a man in front of him. He was dressed—and painted—entirely in red.

"We're in a line? What for?" asked Parker.

"Trailer screening for *Return of the Amber Dawn Collective*. Hall Two."

Parker groaned. "Will it take long to get in?"

"Who knows? You just got to learn to love lines at these places." He wiped his sweaty forehead with the palm of his hand before remembering he had on a face full of makeup.

"Argh!" he cried, and turned to the purple woman next to him. "I *told* you I should have come as a gladiator."

The woman gave the man a sideways glance. "Quit complaining, Brian. I've just about had it with your whining today."

Red Brian huffed and turned his back to Parker. He pulled out a mirror and a tube of red face paint from his plastic carrier bag and began to carefully retouch his makeup.

Parker rolled his eyes at Michael and Emma, then remembered they couldn't see his face behind his mask.

"You should send him a message—tell him we're waiting to go in," said Michael.

"Good idea," said Parker. He took the cell phone out.

Michael grabbed Parker's arm. "Forget it," said Michael. "They're opening the doors."

No sooner had he spoken than the line swept forward in a rush of excitement, taking Parker, Michael, and Emma with it. As they neared the entrance of Hall 2, the crowds started to move faster, and Parker—to stop himself being from trampled on—was forced into a half run that he wasn't able to stop until they were through the doors and the crowds began to disperse in a frenzied rush to grab seats.

They hurried over to the second row from the back and took the seats by the aisle just in time. A few seconds later every seat had been taken and the doors were being closed, to the loud consternation of those who hadn't made it.

"I don't think Brendan got in," said Parker.

"He saw us," said Michael. "He'll wait outside. I wonder if Anteater made it?"

Parker shrugged and sat back in his seat. He tried not to make it too obvious as he cast his eyes around him and tried to spot Anteater. He could see Michael and Emma were doing the same. They all seemed to settle on the man in front of them for two reasons: he was sitting by himself, and he was wearing a set of green alien ears and a hat made of tinfoil. It was, thought Parker, *exactly* how he had imagined a member of Cassandra's Army would dress.

Michael nudged him. "Shall we say something?" he whispered.

Parker shrugged again just as the lights in the hall dimmed and a loud, thumping song started blaring through the surrounding loudspeakers.

"Keep looking straight ahead," whispered a woman's voice directly behind Parker. "Which one of you is Parker?"

Michael and Parker froze. Emma stayed staring intently at the man in front of them.

"Do you know Anteater?" whispered Parker.

"I am Anteater, numskull. And don't say my name out loud."

"Oh. Ohhhh," said Parker as he realized that Anteater had never actually said whether she was a man or a woman. "Sorry."

"Are you Parker?"

Parker nodded. "Yes."

"Keep your voice down! You didn't tell me you were kids."

Parker wasn't sure how to respond to that. He said nothing.

"Were you followed?"

Parker kept his eyes to the front. "No," he replied. "We checked."

"Okay, good. I can't take any risks. . . . Hey! Turn around, kid!"

Parker had been so distracted that he hadn't noticed that Emma was now facing the other way with a strange look of delighted shock on her face. He quickly unmuted Effie—having completely forgotten to do so earlier—but not before Emma had signed, *"I love it!"* in Anteater's direction.

Parker leaned over and grabbed Emma by the shoulder to spin her back around.

That's Anteater! It's a girl! said Parker.

Emma was looking straight ahead as she replied. ***Oh! Wow. Sorry. She's dressed as Dissenta! How cool is that?*** Dissenta—Warrior of Justice—was, unsurprisingly, Emma's favorite superhero. Emma had had three Dissenta-themed birthday parties in a row before their dad had finally insisted on a new theme the previous year.

"This isn't a joke," said Anteater. "I'll leave right now if you don't do what I tell you again."

"My sister's deaf," explained Parker. "She didn't know it was you."

There was a slight pause. "Right, well, I didn't know that. Sorry."

"That's okay."

"When did your dad get taken?"

"Monday morning. We need to find Solomon Gladstone."

"I can't help you with that. He disappeared three years ago."

Shocked, Parker snapped his head around and found himself face-to-face with a woman hidden under a green hood that obscured all but her mouth and the gold eye mask that she was wearing.

"But we came all the way here!"

"Turn around!"

Parker jumped back around. He was furious. "You said you could help us."

"I heard rumors. They say he was locked up in an asylum when he started objecting to the work they were doing. I don't know if that helps. What do you know about SIX?"

"Nothing. Just what you wrote."

"This might help."

Parker felt something being pushed into his shoulder. He reached up and took the object. It was only when he placed it on his lap that he was able to see what it was: a black memory stick.

"It's the best I can do," whispered Anteater. "Let me know how it goes."

"Your dad went missing too?" asked Parker.

"Yeah. His name was Thomas Green. He's not coming back—none of them are."

"What do you mean?"

"Once they're gone, they're gone. If your dad's already been sent, he's not coming back either."

"That's not very nice," Michael whispered loudly.

"Nothing about this is nice. It's just the truth."

Parker felt a hand squeeze his shoulder. "I hope you find him, kid. Keep in touch."

And with that she was gone. Parker, Michael, and Emma all turned and watched as the billowing green cloak hurried across the back of the room in the direction of the doors.

So that's that, thought Parker. He couldn't help but feel slightly disappointed as he watched Anteater talking to the two security guards at the closed doors. She must have been asking them to let her out, as one of them nodded and turned to open the door, only to be interrupted by a loud shout from the front of the room.

"Stop her!"

Parker and the entire audience in the hall turned their heads in the direction of the voice. Parker felt his heart jump at the sight of the two policemen by the steps of the stage, both pointing in Anteater's direction. He looked around and watched as Anteater reached forward to open the doors, but the security guard was having none of it. He pulled her away and closed the door as the two policemen ran up and threw Anteater to the floor.

Emma gasped and jumped up before Michael pulled her back down into her seat. The three of them watched in frozen panic as the policemen wrestled Anteater's arms behind her and cuffed her. And then the crowd began to cheer.

It took Parker a moment to realize what was happening.

"They think this is part of the show!" he said.

Michael's eyes widened as the excited crowd around them began to shout.

"Diss-en-ta! Diss-en-ta!"

The shouting turned frenzied as, just for a moment, Anteater managed to slip free and leapt up.

"Noooo!" screamed someone near the front, and everybody laughed as one of the cops lunged forward and brought Anteater back down to the floor.

As the air of excitement grew, the audience members began to jump up one by one from their seats until the entire room, except for Parker, Emma, and Michael, were on their feet. Parker moved desperately around in his seat trying to find a gap to look through. When he finally found one, he was not able to see much: just the head of one of the cops scanning the faces of the audience.

Parker ducked down in his seat. "I think they're looking for us!"

Michael and Emma both turned and looked at Parker in confusion and then panic. They ducked down in their seats too. For a moment none of them moved. Parker had a feeling that Michael and Emma were waiting for him to tell them what to do. The problem was, he had no idea.

"What's happening now?!" signed Emma.

Parker peered around and caught a glimpse of Anteater resisting wildly as the cops lifted her to her feet. Though they were both struggling to keep their grips, neither was looking at her. They were both staring intently at the audience. Parker realized that if the crowds were to sit down, they would be easily spotted. It was possible they weren't even looking for him, but it was not a risk Parker was prepared to take.

"Let's go!" said Parker.

With the crowds as cover, Parker slipped out into the aisle, followed by Michael and Emma, and ran forward to the fire exit near the stage.

"Justice for Dissenta!" shouted someone. The crowd changed their chant to join him. "Justice for Dissenta! Justice for Dissenta!"

Parker reached the exit and glanced around. Everybody was facing in the opposite direction, punching the air in unison as they chanted.

"Quick!" he said. He pushed down on the metal bar, and the door swung open. Parker rushed out into the busy corridor and waited for Emma and Michael to join him before slamming the door shut. The shouts of the crowd disappeared.

"We have to find Brendan!" said Michael.

Parker nodded and was about to break into a run when a thought occurred to him. He pressed the memory stick into Michael's hand.

"In case something happens to me," said Parker.

Michael looked like he was going to argue and then seemed to change his mind. He took the memory stick and stuffed it into his pocket. The three of them began to run.

"What was that?" asked Emma as she ran beside Parker.

"Not now," said Parker, whose only concern was getting out of the convention center unseen. He stopped abruptly at the end of the corridor and peered out across the main room. There was no sign of Anteater—just crowds of people milling around the stalls and, only a few feet away, Brendan—who appeared to be posing for pictures with an excited group of women in front of a poster of Moldovan's Driver. Parker had enough time to briefly acknowledge the uncanny similarity between the two before Michael grabbed his arm and pulled him back.

"They're coming out!" said Michael.

Parker leaned forward and watched the doors of Hall 2 opening. The shouts of the audience spilled out. Everybody in the main area stopped and turned to watch as Anteater was dragged, kicking and screaming, in the opposite direction.

Michael ripped off his frog mask and pushed it into Emma's hand.

"They're not looking for me," explained Michael as he ran forward. Parker watched Michael sprint over to Brendan and pull him by the arm. On seeing the panicked look on Michael's face, Brendan made his apologies and let Michael drag him away. Parker heard the disappointed moans from the line that had formed next to the poster.

"What's going to happen to her?" signed Emma as they ran to the parked car and climbed inside.

They had explained to Brendan what had happened as they'd run out, and he started the car immediately. He spun the car around and was already driving off before Parker had a chance to respond to Emma.

"I don't know," said Parker.

Michael was looking at his phone. "Shall we send her a message?"

"No!" said Parker. "No way. They'll see it."

"We can't just leave her," signed Emma.

"What are we supposed to do?" asked Parker. "We don't even know her real name."

"Green. Something Green," said Michael. He sighed. "It's not enough."

"She'll get in touch," said Brendan from the front. "Don't worry. She'll be fine."

Parker knew that there was no way that Brendan could be sure of that, but he also knew that there was nothing that they could do right now.

"We'll wait till tomorrow and send her a message. They might have let her go by then."

Nobody responded, and Parker wondered if they all thought this was as unlikely as he did.

CHAPTER EIGHTEEN

Hilda was waiting on the steps outside the driveway on their return. She looked furious.

"Where have you been?" she asked Michael as he stepped out of the car. "You're supposed to be sick." She turned to Parker and Emma. "And why are they here?"

Before Michael could answer her, Brendan, who was still riding high from his five minutes of fame, swept her up into his arms and planted a great big kiss on her lips.

"Brendan! What's got into you? Not in front of the children!"

Hilda pushed Brendan away, but she wasn't able to hide the smile on her face.

Brendan stepped back to admire his wife. "You look beautiful. Did you do something to your hair?"

Hilda blushed and ran her hand over her hair. "This? Nothing, really, I just put it . . ." She remembered she was supposed to be annoyed and, shaking her head, turned back to Michael. "What were you doing?"

Michael hesitated and Brendan jumped in.

"Their dad's been called away to work last minute. I said I'd pick them up from school and that they could stay here."

"Nobody said anything to me," said Hilda.

"Michael called me. They've got nowhere to go to. Just a few days."

Hilda shook her head despairingly. "I'll have to check with your parents, but I'm sure it'll be fine. I suppose you'll all want something to eat."

They all nodded enthusiastically.

"Lucky I made plenty then," she said. She walked back into the house, and Brendan turned to give them a thumbs-up before following her in.

The memory stick did not provide anything like the kind of information that Parker had been hoping for. Parker opened up file after file of scanned newspaper clippings and articles from the Web, all on much the same theme.

"'Market Crisis,'" read Parker. He closed it and opened up the next. "'Greek Bailout Denied.'"

And the next. "'Bankrupt Ireland.'"

And another. "'Global Warming Research Funding Slashed.'"

"It just goes on and on," said Parker. As Anteater had failed to name each file, however, Parker had no choice but to keep on opening each one in turn, in case one offered something different.

"'UK Economic Disaster. US Financial Crisis Worsens,'" continued Parker until, about halfway through, he finally found something. He turned and found that both Emma and Michael had lost interest and were both looking at Michael's computer, smiling.

"What are you doing?" asked Parker.

Michael and Emma turned to Parker, both with guilty looks on their faces. Behind them, a video clip of a kangaroo doing a backflip was playing on a loop.

Parker was not amused. "This is serious!" he said. "I'm trying to find our dad!"

Michael and Emma both dropped their heads. "Sorry," mumbled Michael.

Parker shook his head and turned back to the computer. "I found this."

Michael and Emma gathered around him and read the photographed clipping; it was from a local newspaper appealing for any information on Solomon Gladstone.

"It doesn't help," said Michael.

"It's got a phone number to call. That's something. Shall I try it?"

Michael and Emma nodded, and Parker reached out and picked up Michael's cell phone.

"Wait!" said Michael. He grabbed the phone from Parker and tapped it a few times before handing it back.

"I turned off caller ID," said Michael. "Just in case."

"Good idea," said Parker. He turned to the screen and started to tap in the telephone number.

"Wait!" said Michael again.

"What now?" asked Parker.

"Disguise your voice."

"Why?"

"You have an English accent. And you're obviously a kid. If you're calling the wrong person, they're going to put two and two together."

Parker sighed but nodded. Michael had a point.

"I can't do accents though," said Parker.

Michael was running over to a closet on the other side of the room. "You don't have to," he said as he rifled through one of the drawers. He pulled out a small yellow megaphone and ran back over.

"What's this?" asked Parker, turning the object over in his hand.

"It's a voice changer," said Michael. He leaned over and switched it on. "Try it. Say something."

Parker lifted the voice changer up to his mouth and spoke hesitantly. *"Myyyy naaaame isss . . ."*

The voice came out as a piercing alien squeal.

Emma laughed at Michael's and Parker's horrified reactions. Michael took it from Parker and adjusted the dial.

"Okay. That should be better."

Parker tried it again.

"My name is Parker."

This time the voice sounded deep and robotic. It could almost pass as a grown man's voice, albeit a deeply menacing one.

"That'll do," said Parker. He pressed call and waited.

The phone rang and rang until, finally, someone answered.

"Hello?" said an old lady's voice.

"Hello. Can I speak to Solomon Gladstone, please?" said Parker into the voice changer.

"Say that again, dear. I'm a little hard of hearing."

"Solomon Gladstone," boomed Parker.

"Benjamin Gladstone?"

"No! So-lo-mon Gladstone."

"Oh! Solomon Gladstone!"

The old woman paused.

"Never heard of him."

Parker sighed. He pursed his lips and shook his head at Emma and Michael.

"One moment. Bert! Do you know a Solomon Gladstone?"

"Who's asking?"

"I don't know. Hold on. Who's asking?"

"A friend," said Parker.

"He says he's a friend!"

"Never heard of him!" shouted the old man. "Do they mean Harry Gladstone?"

Parker perked up.

"Do you mean Harry Gladstone?" repeated the old lady.

"Um. Yes?"

"Ah. I'm sorry, dear. Harry Gladstone died two years ago," said the old woman.

"Did he have any family?"

"Bert! Did he have any family?"

"Well, how am I supposed to know? I think he had a brother."

"We don't really know, dear. He might have had a brother. People come and go around here all the time. That's the problem with living in a retirement village. . . ."

"Okay. Thank you."

"I've had to find three new bridge partners in the last year, if you can believe that."

"Okay," tried Parker again. "Thanks anyway."

"I'm sorry about your friend Harry—I hope I haven't upset you."

"No. It's fine."

"Pardon?"

"I said, 'it's fine'! Thank you!"

"Thank you, dear. It was lovely chatting with you."

The old woman put the phone down, and Parker let out a groan of frustration.

Emma put her hand on his shoulder and unmuted Effie.

Don't worry, Parker. It's going to be fine. We'll find him.

Parker nodded, more in appreciation of her concern than in agreement. The amount of time that had passed and the lack of information they had gathered were beginning to weigh down on Parker, but for once he didn't feel the need to inject his reality onto her optimism, however misguided he was beginning to think it was.

"I'll keep checking," mumbled Parker. He turned to the

screen and continued to run through the files—all back on the theme of recession—until he reached the final one. It was, he noticed as he clicked on it, the only one that was a different file type. A spreadsheet opened up.

Michael and Emma—who had not left his side this time, probably for fear of being told off by Parker—leaned in to read. The spreadsheet was titled "Personnel List: Avecto."

Parker perked up and scrolled down.

"It must be old," said Parker. "Dad isn't on it."

Solomon Gladstone, however, was. Alongside his name and date of birth was an address—not too far from the Avecto headquarters where his father had worked—and a phone number.

"I might as well try it," said Parker. He picked up the phone and took the voice changer from Michael. He dialed the number and waited as the phone began to ring.

"No answer," said Parker finally. He paused for a moment and tried again. "Still no answer," he said. He dropped his head.

"Try again in a bit," signed Emma. *"They're probably at work."*

Parker shook his head. "I'll just keep trying." He rang again. This time someone answered the phone after the first ring.

"I'm busy. What do you want?" shouted a woman as Parker scrambled to grab the voice changer from the desk. In the background he heard a baby crying.

"Could I speak to Solomon Gladstone, please?"

"No. He doesn't live here. Okay. Bye."

"Please!" he shouted, forgetting about the voice changer.

For a moment Parker wasn't sure if the woman had hung up.

"Why?"

"Please, I just need to find him. I need his help."

"How old are you?"

"Twelve," answered Parker. He realized how upset he sounded, but he couldn't help himself.

"Solomon Gladstone used to own this house," said the woman. Her voice was gentler. "It was repossessed three years ago. We bought it from the bank."

"Do you know where he is now?"

"I'm so sorry. I don't know anything. We never got a forwarding address for him."

Parker gulped. "Okay, thank you," he mumbled. He hung up and muted Effie so that Emma couldn't hear him. "We're never going to find him," he muttered with his head down.

"Don't say that!" said Michael, sitting back in his chair. He turned to the computer. "There are other things we haven't tried yet. Didn't Anteater say he was locked up?"

Parker nodded.

"So let's just try searching for him there."

"Where?"

"Well, *obviously*, I don't know that. But we can start by searching for—what's the right word for *asylum*?"

"'Psychiatric hospital'? Something like that."

Michael turned to his keyboard and typed something in.

"Okay, there are seventeen listed in New York State. Four in this part of the state."

"He could be anywhere, though," said Parker miserably. The constant dead ends they had been hitting were beginning to take their toll.

"Maybe. But he lived and worked near here. It makes sense he wouldn't be too far, right?"

Parker shrugged. He wasn't convinced, but it was as good a place as any.

"Now," said Michael, typing in something else, "we just need to find the patient lists."

"How are you going to do that?" signed Emma. *"They won't give them out."*

For the first time in a long time, Parker smiled. *"Just watch,"* he signed.

It took Michael only twenty minutes to hack into the servers of all four hospitals. A few minutes after that, the printer was churning out page after page of patient records.

"Schools and hospitals are always the easiest," said Michael. Nevertheless, he looked very pleased with himself.

"How many pages?"

Michael checked. "Four hundred eighty-nine. Some of them are outpatients, but I thought I'd print them all out, just in case."

Parker nodded. "If we each take some, it won't take too long to go through them."

"What are we looking for?" signed Emma.

"His name, I guess," said Parker. He picked up the stack that had already built up and shared it out between them.

"I guess it was too good to be true," said Michael glumly. They were sitting on the floor, surrounded by stacks of papers.

"We could have missed it," said Parker. "Maybe we should check again."

Emma shook her head and unmuted Effie. **Solomon Gladstone isn't an easy name to miss. Maybe we should look at other hospitals.**

Parker looked up at Emma, and his eyes widened.

"That's it!" he shouted. He leapt up and ran over to the computer. "They would have changed his name!" He looked up at the screen and found Solomon Gladstone's birthday.

"Twenty-seventh May, 1948," he muttered. He scribbled the date down on a piece of paper and ran back over to Michael and Emma, who were both looking at him with bewildered faces.

"Look again, but this time ignore the names. See if you find anyone with this date of birth. They might not have changed that."

"Ohhh," said Michael, clearly impressed. "Good plan."

Parker sat down and picked up the first pile of papers, and the three of them began their search again.

Emma found a match after only a couple of minutes. She held the paper up with a wide grin on her face.

"It's a woman," said Parker flatly.

Emma turned the page and read the notes. Her smile disappeared.

Parker gave her an encouraging smile. "We'll find it," he said. He picked up another batch of papers.

This time Parker was the one to find the match. Before Parker said anything, he checked—it was a man. Michael and Emma had picked up on his excitement, and they both rushed around to have a look.

"Simon Grimm," said Parker, reading the name out loud.

"Simon, Solomon," said Michael. "They sound kind of similar."

"And same initials," said Parker.

There were no other details about Simon Grimm on the page that Michael had printed off, and Parker was eager for Michael to try to find out more from the hospital computers. Michael, however, insisted they should look through the rest of the records first, in case there were any other matches. Parker reluctantly agreed.

There were none. As soon as he was finished with the last of the papers in his stack, Parker grabbed the one with Simon Grimm's name on it and jumped up.

"You'll be able to get more information about him?" he asked Michael.

Michael raised his eyebrows. "Do you really need to ask?"

"All right, all right," said Parker. He followed Michael over to his computer and watched, jittery with nerves, as Michael checked the notes he had scribbled down earlier, detailing how he had hacked into the server of Plotter Kill Psychiatric Center.

"What a horrible name," signed Emma. *"Why would they do that?"*

Parker translated for Michael as he answered her via Effie. **I know,** he said, shaking his head. **They probably feel bad enough without hearing that all the time.**

"It's the name of the river there. Plotter Kill River," said Michael as he typed.

Parker laughed as he told Emma. Emma, however, didn't seem to find it the slightest bit amusing.

They didn't *have* to name it after that, said Emma. Parker shrugged and nodded in agreement.

They could have just made up something, she continued. **Something happier. Like the Sunshine Center. Or Hope Hospital . . . Or . . ."**

Emma stopped as Michael turned. He was smiling. "Found it."

"Print it off."

"Already done," said Michael. He walked over to the printer, picked up the single piece of paper, and then placed it on the desk. The three of them crowded around to read it.

"Simon Grimm," muttered Parker. "Same date of birth. Admission date . . ."

They all looked up at the same time. *"Three years ago!"* signed Emma.

It was him, thought Parker, feeling as if he might burst with excitement. It was definitely him.

"Previous address," continued Parker. "Unknown." He read on. "Delusional Disorder? What does that mean?"

Michael reached over to his keyboard and searched for the term. He turned the screen for Parker and Emma to read.

"'Delusional Disorder—a serious mental illness in which a person is unable to distinguish what is real or otherwise. People with delusional disorder often have the false belief that they are being persecuted in some way. They often attempt to make contact with legal authorities. In extreme cases, people with delusional disorder can find themselves alienated from friends and family—either because they don't believe their concerns are being treated seriously or because they believe the people around them are somehow involved in the conspiracy against them.'"

"Wow," said Michael.

Parker felt himself go pale. "Read the notes section."

Michael glanced up at Parker and then began to read the rest out loud. "'Patient is highly dangerous. Extremely high risk of violence, particularly to unfamiliar persons. Only named staff may enter his room. Escape risk: high. Security level: maximum.'"

Parker read the notes and then reread them, not quite able to believe what he was seeing.

Finally he turned to Emma and Michael. "Well, this makes things a little more difficult."

"You *think*?" said Michael.

Emma tapped Parker on the shoulder. *"Maybe he wouldn't be like that to kids. I mean, if we're nice."*

Parker rolled his eyes. *"You think they haven't tried being nice to him?"* he signed back.

"What did she say?" asked Michael.

"She thinks if we're nice to him, he won't hurt us."

Michael started laughing, then saw Emma's face and stopped abruptly. "That's a nice idea," he said to her, "but I don't think it'll work."

"You have a better idea?" asked Emma.

Michael nodded. "Yep. We try something else."

Parker and Emma shook their heads—on this point, they were both in complete agreement.

"We *have* to go, Michael," explained Parker. "My dad said I could trust him."

"Your dad obviously didn't know this guy was some kind of an ax murderer."

"It doesn't say he's an ax murderer anywhere," countered Parker.

Michael scrunched up his face. "It kind of does, actually."

"No. It doesn't. And even if he were—which he's not—what choice do we have? It's our dad, Michael. You'd do the same."

"Not sure I would," said Michael. "Think about how worried I was about Aaron punching me. I'm not a fighter, Parker."

"You don't need to fight."

"You don't know that."

"Well, no," said Parker. "I guess I don't."

He felt his wrist vibrate.

"We have to try to meet him, Parker," said Emma.

Parker looked at Emma and then Michael as he weighed his options. In the end Parker came to the conclusion that there was only one possible course of action. Michael was right, but Parker and Emma were desperate. Desperation was always going to win out.

"We have to go," said Parker. "We don't need you to come. But could you help us get information on how to get past security?"

Michael nodded, and without another word he turned to his computer.

"They might have timetables or something," said Michael, opening up one window and then another. Then he froze.

"What's up?" asked Parker.

Michael pointed up to the corner of the screen.

Message from Anteater.

Michael clicked on it.

I am okay. They let me go. Where are you?
Have more to tell you. Think I know how you can
get to your dad.

The three of them looked at each other in surprise.

"What shall I write?" asked Michael.

He clicked reply and waited for Parker to say something.

But Parker didn't speak.

"Parker?" asked Michael, turning to face him.

"It might not be her."

"But it's from her e-mail address," signed Emma.

"They had her phone. They could have checked her e-mails."

Michael and Emma both mouthed *Oh* at the same time.

"May I?" asked Parker. Michael nodded and stood up to let Parker take his seat. Parker began to type.

Must check it's you. What is my father's name?

Parker clicked send. He turned to Michael and Emma, who both looked equally confused.

Before Parker had a chance to explain, the computer binged to notify them of a new e-mail.

It was from Anteater, and it contained only two words: *Geoffrey Banks.*

Parker stared at his father's name.

"But they already know that," said Michael.

"Yes," said Parker. "But Anteater didn't."

He opened up the page of Cassandra's Army and searched for Anteater. Her profile had been closed down. Every one of her posts had been deleted.

Anteater was gone.

CHAPTER NINETEEN

Parker had assumed that Michael was something of a wimp—happy to observe but quick to run if the situation turned on him. Given what Michael had himself told Parker, it was not an unfair assumption (and also quite understandable), but it turned out that there was something that could override this fear: the need not to feel left out.

At first Michael had agreed to do anything that he could to help them visit Solomon, as long as he didn't have to go anywhere near him. The following morning, however, while Parker and Emma were waiting for the cab that Michael had called for them (they figured that Brendan might draw the line at breaking into a psychiatric hospital in order to meet a violent madman), Michael told them that he had changed his mind.

"You really don't have to," insisted Parker. "I don't know what's going to happen."

Michael shrugged. "Yeah, but Emma's   you know . . . Well, what if something happens and she doesn't hear it? And she's only ten."

Emma lip-read this and thumped Michael in the chest. *"Tell him that ten for a girl is, like, fourteen for a boy,"* she signed to Parker.

Parker didn't have to translate—Michael was already apologizing profusely.

"You really don't have to come, Michael," said Parker. "You've done enough. I need Emma to get me in there, but we've got a reason to risk this. You don't."

"Yeah, well, it's fine. You'll probably need my help."

Parker shrugged. "Sure."

In truth he was delighted. Just because he had no choice about going on this crazy mission, it didn't mean that he wasn't a bit scared. Terrified, actually.

"Great!" said Michael, pulling out a large stuffed backpack from under the desk. "I packed some things in case."

Parker and Emma stared at the bag.

"Is that a . . . *machete*?" asked Parker.

"It's not real. It's rubber." Michael smiled. "But *he* won't know that."

"What else?" signed Emma.

"Walkie-talkies—seeing as I'm not part of the thought-reading gang. A laptop. Disguises."

"Disguises?" Parker narrowed his eyes. "You didn't bring the frog masks, did you?"

Michael looked insulted. "No. Hats. Scarves . . . um . . . shields."

"Shields? Really?" asked Parker.

"Did you read the notes on this guy?"

"Yeah. And I don't think shields are going to help."

Michael looked deflated. Emma gave Parker a stern look.

"But maybe I'm wrong," backtracked Parker. "Better to be safe than sorry, right?"

Michael nodded and pulled out a piece of paper from his pocket.

"There is one more thing." He smiled. "I found the codes for all the doors, including the one for a Mr. Simon Grimm."

Parker's mouth dropped open. "What?"

He snatched the paper and looked down the printed list of numbers. At the bottom of the page was a date. The codes had been updated three days earlier.

He looked up at Michael, then down again at the paper in disbelief. "Why didn't you say something?"

"That's what I'm doing."

"This is amazing, Michael!" Parker still couldn't quite believe it. Until now getting past the security doors had been the biggest hole in their plans.

"You're the best!" signed Emma.

It was probable that Michael hadn't understood every word that Emma had just signed, but he certainly got the sentiment. The corner of his mouth curled into an embarrassed smile. He shrugged.

"Thanks," he said. His phone beeped.

"Guess we're going to find out how much help they'll be soon," said Michael. "Cab's here."

* * * * * *

They spent the cab ride revising their plan in order to include Michael. Only the first part of the plan was definite: arrive at exactly midday. Michael had checked the staff roster and found that that was the time when the most members of staff were having lunch. Apart from that, and the floorplan of the hospital that Michael had found (on which Solomon/ Simon's small single room was marked with a large red X), they would have to improvise as they went along.

"We're here," said the cabdriver.

Parker looked up from the papers spread out on his lap and saw that the cabdriver was already pulling up outside the building. They had been so distracted that they had failed to stop him on the main road. Already, thought Parker with a sinking feeling in his stomach, things were not going according to plan.

"Here's fine!" said Parker. He was too late, though; "here" was already right outside the main doors.

Michael paid as Parker and Emma scrambled to collect all the papers. Parker jumped out and ran over to the left of the glass doors. He pressed his back against the redbrick wall, hoping he hadn't already been spotted, and waited for Emma to join him. Michael was last, somewhat slowed by the weight of the backpack on his back.

"Do you think they saw us?" asked Parker.

"If they did, they're probably wondering why we're standing in a line by the wall in broad daylight," said Michael. He pointed up to the security camera.

"Oh no!" said Parker as Emma turned to him with a look of utter panic on her face.

The problem was, there was nowhere for them to run to for cover. Green lawn stretched out from the building in all directions, with not even a tree trunk to hide behind.

"Let's try again tomorrow," signed Emma.

Parker shook his head and turned on Effie as he spoke to Michael. "We're here now. Let's just go in before anybody drives up. We have a better chance of hiding in there than we do out here."

But Michael was supposed to hide! said Emma.

"If they've seen the two of us, they've seen Michael, too. I say we just do what we planned and pretend that Michael is our friend."

"Pretend?" said Michael.

"I didn't mean that! I . . ."

"I know what you meant," said Michael. "I was joking. Come on, let's get this over and done with."

Of all the obstacles they had faced since his dad had gone, arriving at the secure room of the secure ward of a psychiatric hospital should certainly have been the most complicated. In reality, the opposite had turned out to be true. What actually happened was this:

* They walked in to find nobody at reception.
* They walked down the main corridor and past a

person—possibly a visitor—who smiled and bade them good afternoon as he passed.

* They reached the secure ward and watched through the glass doors as the nurse behind the counter stood up to answer the call that Michael had placed on his phone.

* Parker entered the code into the keypad, and the doors unlocked.

* They made their way to the far end of the ward, unnoticed, and through another set of doors that opened on Parker's first attempt. Though they heard people in the ward—someone singing, another person shouting—they saw nobody.

* They ran up the stairs and arrived at the only door on the small landing: Room 43.

Parker couldn't believe their luck.

"Not luck," corrected Michael as they approached the door. "I do not call staying up till three in the morning trying hundreds of passwords to get the codes *lucky*."

Parker gave Emma a put-my-foot-in-it-again look. "Sorry, Michael. Good work."

They all turned to face the door.

"What now?" signed Emma.

There was only one thing they could do—go in and find out if this was the man they were looking for. It seemed so simple, and yet not one of them made a move. Parker knew he should probably be the one taking the lead, but he couldn't quite bring himself to unlock the door—the fear of the unknown waiting for them on the other side had suddenly hit him.

"You're coming in with me, right?" he whispered.

Emma and Michael both shook their heads firmly.

"That was definitely not part of the plan," said Michael.

"*Please?*" said Parker. He was aware of how nervous he sounded. "Three against one."

"Against one what?" replied Michael. "Three against a normal human being, maybe. Three against a crazed giant, not so much."

There had been nothing in the records of Simon Grimm that had described him that way, but evidently Parker was not the only one who was imagining that he was at least eight feet tall. He pictured him drooling, too, for some reason—like a rabid dog. It was not a comforting image.

Parker raised his hand slowly to the keypad and then withdrew it quickly.

"Actually, maybe this isn't really such a good idea," he said.

We're here now! said Emma on Effie. **Think about Dad, Parker. Please.**

"We can wait by the door," offered Michael. "We'll leave it open. If anything happens, you can just run out. Or we can come and help you." He said the last part with little conviction.

Parker shook his head in resignation. "Fine," he whispered. "I'll do it. But *don't* close the door."

Michael nodded, and Parker reached out to punch in the

numbers, but once more he stopped abruptly. He turned to Michael.

"Maybe I'll take one of those shields."

Holding the disappointingly small plastic shield in front of his chest, and with the rubber machete tucked into the back of his jeans, Parker entered the six-digit number that Michael held up for him to read.

Click.

Parker turned to Michael and Emma, who were also both holding their useless shields in front of them, and nodded.

"Good luck," whispered Michael as he pulled down on the handle and swung the door open.

CHAPTER TWENTY

Upon entering Room 43, Parker found himself facing a small corridor that led out onto a room, of which all he could see was a desk piled high with books and a window on the back wall overlooking the green lawn. On his right was the open door of the bathroom. Parker, still standing in the doorway, leaned slightly forward and craned his neck to look inside. The bathroom was empty. Parker turned to face the window again and waited a moment but heard nothing. He took another step. Still nothing. Parker turned to look behind him, and Michael—his feet still very much on the other side of the door—motioned with his head for Parker to keep going.

Parker took a deep breath and started to walk forward, his fear deepening as each step took him farther away from the safety of the door.

The room began to open out in front of him, revealing a small table and a chest of drawers, but still no sign of *him*. Another step, and Parker reached the end of the tiny corridor.

He paused and listened, but the only sound he could hear was the loud thumping of his own heart. Half hoping that Simon/Solomon wasn't there after all, Parker took another deep breath and stepped into the room.

He was there.

For a moment—seconds possibly, though it felt longer—neither Parker nor the man said a word. They both stared at each other—Parker frozen midstep and the man, in a dark blue dressing gown, looking up from the armchair he was sitting in. Parker should have been the first to speak—after all, he was the one entering unannounced into the room—but he wasn't capable of saying anything; fear had rendered him speechless.

On a positive note, the man wasn't drooling. And he didn't appear unduly tall. However, both of those things would have been less unsettling than what Parker found instead. The man was, far and away, the strangest looking person who Parker had ever set eyes on.

His skin—even his lips—were gray. Not gray as in pale and sickly looking—gray as in the color of an elephant. Unlike an elephant, however, the man's skin did not appear to have a single wrinkle. It was as smooth as Parker's own, smoother even, and yet, perhaps because of his full head of shocking white hair, the man appeared to be old. He also had no eyebrows, and from where Parker was standing, it looked like he had no eyelashes, either. Most disconcerting of all, however, were his eyes; the left eye was twice the size of the right and a brilliant blue, pierced by a tiny black dot at its center. The right eye was completely black. It was entirely mesmerizing and terrifying at the same time, and Parker might well have stood there all day had the man not suddenly opened his mouth and let out the most terrifying yell.

"Aaarggghhhhh! We're under attack!"

In response, Parker let out an involuntary scream and half stumbled, half ran back into the corridor, where he tripped, jumped up, saw the same terrified looks on Emma's and Michael's faces, and then lunged forward in the direction of the door. And then he heard the man laughing.

Parker froze midrun.

"Kid! It was a joke! Come in."

Parker and Michael locked stares, both wide-eyed and both clearly unsure what they should do next. They were, Parker realized, completely and utterly out of their depth. He would have run out, no question, if it hadn't been for one thing—the man had an unmistakably English accent. It was coincidence enough to keep Parker listening.

"Are you still there?"

"Yes," squeaked Parker.

"Come back—I don't bite!"

All Parker heard was the word *bite*. He shook his head slowly at Michael and Emma and mouthed the words *no way*. Michael replied by holding up his hands as if to say, *What choice have you got?* and waved Parker forward. *Easy for him to say,* thought Parker as he turned stiffly around. With fear prickling every pore of his body, he stepped tentatively back into the room.

The man was still sitting in the armchair. He was now smiling.

"I thought the war had started," said the man. His voice was not threatening. It might have even sounded friendly had Parker not been expecting the man to lunge forward in a sudden attack.

Parker's eyes went down to where the man was looking and realized he was still holding the shield.

"Oh," said Parker, suddenly realizing what the man meant. "This . . . It isn't . . . ." He felt himself turning red as he quickly hid the shield behind his back.

The man laughed again loudly, and his mouth opened to reveal a set of brilliant white teeth and a tongue the same gray hue as the rest of him.

"Good thinking," said the man. "You don't want to be walking into the room of a madman unprepared."

Parker could tell the man was teasing him, but he was still too scared to find it amusing.

"So . . . I'm guessing you must be my new doctor."

"Me? No! I'm only twelve," said Parker, before realizing that the man was smiling again. *"Oh."*

"Tough audience," muttered the man with a mock frown. "Are you going to tell me why you're here, or do I have to guess?"

"I . . . um . . . well . . . I don't . . . Areyousolomongladstone?" blurted out Parker.

"Was that a word?"

Parker shook himself and tried again. "Are you Solomon Gladstone?"

At the mention of the name, the man pursed his lips and leaned forward in his armchair. His eyes, or rather his eye—the blue one—narrowed.

Parker's grip tightened around the handle of his shield.

"How do you know my name?"

The answer was in the man's question and, as Parker realized this, his face dropped.

"It's you," whispered Parker.

"It was the last time I checked."

The man waited for Parker to look at him before continuing.

"I have to admit, I'm curious. It's been a while since a child carrying a shield came in asking for me by a name nobody in this hospital even knows. Are you going to tell me what . . . what . . . what . . . what . . . Alberta!" shouted Solomon as his hand flew up in the air and slapped the back of his own head.

Parker leapt away terrified, and Solomon finished his question as if nothing in the slightest bit unusual had just happened.

"Is going on?"

"What?" whispered Parker. He'd lost track of what he was

being asked sometime around the time Solomon had shouted out "Alberta" and smacked his own head for no good reason.

"It's the way I unstick myself," explained Solomon.

"What?" repeated Parker. He was aware of how inarticulate he sounded; he just couldn't seem to do a thing about it.

"I get stuck on words sometimes—a side effect of my condition. Sounds like you might know what I mean. For some reason, a quick slap round the head and the word *Alberta* seem to get me back on track."

"Is that where you're from?" asked Parker in a quiet voice.

"Never even been there. But *Madagascar* is a bit of a mouthful, and *London* just makes me think of rain."

"Okay . . ." said Parker slowly. Clearly, the man was a complete basket case.

"Back to my question . . . Why are you here?"

"My dad told me to find you."

For a moment Solomon said nothing.

"Your dad?" he asked finally.

Parker had a feeling by the way Solomon was looking at him that he might already have a suspicion as to who his dad might be.

"Yes, sir. Geoffrey Banks."

Solomon's smile had completely disappeared. He closed his blue eye and dropped his head. "What's happened to him?"

"He's been taken. To a place called SIX. He said you'd know."

Solomon raised his hand slowly and rubbed his forehead. He didn't look up.

"Do you know where that is?" asked Parker.

Solomon, still hunched over with his hand on his head, nodded slowly.

"Can you tell me how to get there?"

Solomon didn't respond.

"Please help me. My sister and I need to find him."

"How could this happen?" muttered Solomon. He seemed to be talking to himself.

"Mr. Gladstone, please. I just need to know where to go. You're the only person who can help me."

Parker waited until, at last, Solomon looked up.

"What do you know about SIX?"

Parker shook his head. "Nothing." Anteater's conspiracy ramblings were hardly worth mentioning.

"Then you'd better sit down," said Solomon. He motioned to the sofa opposite him. "Your friends can join us too if they'd like."

Parker's head snapped around, and he caught a glimpse of Michael and Emma just before they ducked back into the corridor.

"Michael!" called Parker. "Come back."

It was a few seconds before Michael and Emma reemerged, both looking sheepish.

"It's okay," mouthed Parker.

* * * * * *

"Let's start with your names," said Solomon. "I'm guessing that you're Parker, and you must be the lovely Emma."

Emma smiled and nodded.

"How do you know . . ." Parker stopped as he realized his father must have told him.

"You can lip-read?" asked Solomon.

Emma nodded.

"Do I need to speak slower?"

Emma shook her head. She didn't seem as nervous from the sight of Solomon as Parker would have expected.

"And you are?" asked Solomon.

"Michael," whispered Michael. "I'm just a friend."

Solomon glanced up at the clock on the wall. "We have an hour before they come to take my lunch away. Can you stay an hour? Is there anyone waiting for you?"

"No," replied Parker. "We're here on our own. We can stay."

"Good, because there's a lot I have to tell you."

"How do you know my dad, Mr. Gladstone?" asked Parker.

"Okay. That's a good enough place to start. And call me Solomon, please. I taught your father and mother when they were at university."

"Our mum?"

"Yes. Brilliant scientist. Your dad, too . . . but your mother was something else. Quite a team."

"Do you know that she . . ."

Solomon tensed his jaw. "Yes. I know."

Solomon turned to look out the window. He didn't

speak for a while, and Parker, Emma, and Michael—not knowing what else to do—sat in silence and waited. When Solomon finally turned back, Parker saw that his eyes were moist.

"I'm so sorry," said Solomon. "It must have been so hard for you both."

"It's okay now. . . . Thank you," said Parker, feeling slightly awkward. "When was the last time you saw them?"

"I saw your mother three years ago"—he took a deep breath before continuing—"just before her accident."

"And Dad?"

Solomon's lips pursed into a tight sad smile. "Last week."

"Last week? But," said Parker, *"how?"*

"You're not the first to find out that it's not that hard to get in here. I gave him the codes and he'd come visit me between checks."

"But if you know the codes, why don't you just leave?" asked Michael.

Solomon pointed to himself. "I can't exactly go about unnoticed these days. I have everything I want . . . want . . . want . . . want . . . Alberta!"

Solomon slapped his head, and Michael leapt up off the sofa. He was stopped from running only by Parker reaching up and grabbing his T-shirt to pull him back.

"It's okay," whispered Parker. "It's a stutter thing."

Michael looked no less horrified, but he allowed Parker to pull him back down to the sofa.

"Sorry, did I scare you?"

Michael shook his head, still too terrified to speak.

"It takes a bit of getting used to," said Solomon. He laughed. "I even scare myself sometimes. Now, where was I?"

"You were telling us why you don't just leave."

"Ah yes. I have everything I need here."

"But are you actually—"

"Mad?"

Parker nodded.

"Depends on your definition of *mad*, I suppose. But, technically, no."

"So why are you here?"

"Not by choice—at least, not originally. I said a few things some people didn't like, and I was given two options. This was the better of the two."

Parker could guess what the other was.

Emma tapped Parker's shoulder. *"Has he always looked like that?"* she signed.

Parker grimaced but realized he had no choice but to translate. Also, he did actually want to know, himself. "She wants to know why you . . . um . . . look like you do? Were you born like that?"

Solomon chuckled. "No. I had an . . . Well, actually—it's a long story. It will make sense after I explain everything. I'll start with SIX. But first, I need to say something. I'm afraid what I'm going to tell you is going to upset you."

Parker drew a sharp breath. "Is he dead?"

"No! No, sorry—I didn't mean that. He's not dead. I don't know that for a fact, of course, but I'm almost certain he isn't."

Parker and Emma both sighed in relief.

"The thing is, I'm going to help you as much as I can. I promise. But I don't know if I'm going to be able to help you get to your father."

"It's okay," said Parker. "You don't have to come with us. Wherever he is, we'll get there. We just need to know where to go."

"I'm afraid it's not that easy. But if there's any way at all that I can get him back to you, I'll do everything I can to make it happen."

Parker nodded. "Thank you."

"And now—SIX." Solomon paused, as if searching for the right words. "I suppose there's no easy way to say this. SIX— the place your father told you about—is the name of a planet."

Michael gave a loud sigh. "Here we go again."

Parker, though equally disappointed, turned and glowered at Michael. "Let him speak."

"Again?" asked Solomon. "You've heard this before?"

"Yes," said Parker. "We read it on a Web site."

"*Really?* What did you read?"

Michael butted in. "That SIX is a planet. That all the money is going there instead of here, and that's why there's no money for anything. That it's a place where the rich are going to escape to when Earth is finished."

Solomon sat up straight and shook his head in surprise. "You already know it all?"

"Well, it's obviously not true," said Michael.

"Actually—hard as it might be to believe—it is all very true."

Michael groaned. "Oh, come on! A planet? In what galaxy, exactly?"

"Michael!" exclaimed Parker.

"This galaxy—the Milky Way. In the constellation Libra, about twenty-two light years away from Earth."

"Hmm. And you get to it *how*?" Michael no longer looked terrified, just irritated.

"Ah. If you liked that, Michael," said Solomon smiling, "you're going to *love* this. You get there by teleportation."

"Of course," said Michael. "And how does that work? Oh wait—I think I know this already! You stand in a blue light and say, 'Beam me up,' and then you're eating moon cheese with apes."

Solomon looked thoroughly amused. Parker, however, was not finding it so funny.

"Michael, stop!"

Solomon laughed. "It's okay. Really. It is quite a lot to take in. And the answer, Michael, is not a blue light. The method of teleportation devised by Avecto"—he looked at Parker and Emma—"the company your dad works for—is called avection. It works by analyzing matter as it breaks it down—"

"Not possible," interrupted Michael.

"And then rebuilding it exactly on the other end."

"Can't happen."

"The process is almost instantaneous."

"Impossible."

"Improbable," corrected Solomon, "but most certainly not impossible."

"And how do you know this?" asked Michael.

"Because I've been teleported myself."

Michael rubbed his chin and nodded. "Interesting," he said. "And—just out of curiosity—if you can do this, then why exactly haven't you teleported yourself out of here?"

"Well, it's not that simple."

Michael rolled his eyes. "It *is* that simple. You haven't done it, because it's not true."

"Michael!"

Parker grabbed Michael's arm and dragged him up and over to the corridor.

"What are you doing?"

"The guy is a nut case, Parker! Out of his mind. A complete lunatic! Did you hear what he was saying?"

"I don't care, Michael! I need to hear this out. Even if it's not true . . ."

"Which it's not."

"I still need to hear it! Don't you understand that?"

Michael shook his head. "What's the point?"

"The point is—I haven't got a choice. If you don't want to hear it, just leave! Okay?"

Michael thought about this for a moment. He grimaced, then sighed. "Fine, but don't expect me to believe it."

"You don't have to. Just let me listen."

The two boys made their way back to the sofa.

"Sorry," said Michael as he sat down.

Solomon smiled. "It's fine. A questioning mind is nothing to apologize for. Would it help if I explained how it works?"

Michael hesitated, and Parker nudged him with his elbow.

"Yeah. Okay. Why not?"

"I'll do that then. But first—if you'll humor me for just a moment—let's assume what I'm telling you is true so I can finish explaining to Parker and Emma what I know about what's happened to their father. After that, I'll go through the technicalities and you can ask as many questions as you like."

All three of them nodded.

"Good. Where were we? Ahh, yes. So avection is a type of teleportation. It was invented about thirty years ago by a man called Warren Bowveld—"

"That's the name of my dad's boss!" interrupted Parker.

"Without the number. Your dad's boss is Warren Bowveld III, son of Warren Bowveld Junior and grandson of Warren Bowveld Senior. But that's where the similarity between the three men ends. Senior was a brilliant man of science; Junior, a man of numbers; and Warren Bowveld III . . . Well, I'm not sure anybody's worked out where that man's talents lie yet."

"Which one discovered SIX?" asked Parker.

"That would be Senior," replied Solomon. "Having

discovered how to teleport, he began to send cameras out into space. A couple of years later, they found SIX."

"Why SIX?" signed Emma.

"SIX is the first perfect number in mathematics. Do you know what a perfect number is?"

"I do," said Parker. "It's a number that is the sum of its divisors. One plus two plus three equals six."

Solomon looked taken aback. "How old did you say you were?"

"Twelve."

Solomon smiled. "I suppose I shouldn't be surprised—you are your mother's son, after all."

Parker felt himself turn red.

"SIX," continued Solomon, "is the only planet that has been found—to date—that can support human life. Apart from Earth, of course. For this to happen, a huge number of things have to be true—air, water, a solar system like ours, for example. The list is very long, and the chances of finding a planet that ticks all the boxes are miniscule. That's why, when this planet was discovered, they named it after the first perfect number—because all the numbers aligned perfectly."

"Do people live there now?" asked Emma. Parker translated.

"Some—not many though. It's still very much under construction. For a long time after SIX was discovered, it was used just for research. Senior, you see, had no interest in making any money from his work, but his son, Junior, did not feel the same way. When his father died, Junior decided to make SIX into a luxury destination. Paradise for those who could afford it. He gathered together a group of very wealthy investors and set to work. Five years ago Junior died, and his son—your father's boss—took over."

Solomon stopped.

"I need a cup of coffee," he said. "Anyone?"

They all shook their heads.

"Good," said Solomon. He stood up slowly. "I've only got one mug."

He tightened the belt of his dressing gown and shuffled over to the small kitchen area in the corner of the room. Parker noticed that his gray ankles were visible between the gap of his red pajamas and open-backed brown slippers. He had been so distracted by everything that Solomon was telling them, this was the first time since sitting down that he had been reminded of Solomon's strange appearance. It also reminded him of where they were. He looked up at the clock and realized that time was passing quickly.

"How is my dad involved in all of this?" asked Parker.

"Your father," said Solomon as he dipped his spoon into the coffee jar, "was employed by Avecto to solve a very big problem for the company."

The kettle *bing*ed, and Solomon was silent again as he finished making his coffee. He walked back over with the steaming white mug and took his seat again.

"Avection works perfectly the first time around. If someone

is teleported, it will rebuild them on the other side *exactly* as they left, down to the holes in the socks they're wearing. That's why there are people up there working on building SIX . . . SIX . . . SIX . . ."

Parker steeled himself for what was coming.

"SIX . . . SIX . . . Alberta!"

Solomon sighed. "I apologize; it really is exhausting. The people there now, however, can't ever come back—at least not for the moment. Because avection—on humans—is an extremely complicated procedure. A body can be rebuilt once, but try it again and imperfections start to show up."

"What do you mean?" asked Parker.

"It's a bit like a digital image. Every time you distort a picture on the computer—say by rotating it, or making it small then big again, the file loses some of its detail. The more you repeat the process, the less detail the image retains."

"Interpolation," said Michael.

"*Exactly*. Very good, Michael," said Solomon, clearly impressed. "Avection has the same problem. It's fine for inanimate objects or small living things—you could teleport a car back and forth many times over before you'd ever see a difference—but humans are rather more complicated. There is so much information, as you can imagine, that while it's perfect the first time, the second time is generally disastrous. In fact, with one exception, nobody has ever survived a second teleportation."

"*Who's the exception?*" asked Emma.

Parker and Michael, however, had already worked it out.

"So *that's* why you look like that?" asked Parker.

"Ohhh," signed Emma.

Solomon nodded. "Yes. For reasons that I don't have time to get into now—I was teleported to SIX and back again. I made it—but as you can see, not unscathed."

Michael groaned, and they all turned to look at him in surprise.

"What's the matter?" asked Parker.

He looked pained. "This is *so* annoying. I really don't want to, but I'm actually starting to believe him."

Solomon laughed. "It's all true. You can check I haven't painted myself gray if you'd like." He held out his gray arm.

Michael shrunk back. "It's okay. Just keep talking."

"There's not really too much more to tell you. Your father, Parker and Emma, was employed to work out a way of making multiple teleportations possible. And he wasn't given a lot of time to do it. For years the investors have been asking to visit SIX so they can check on the progress themselves, but nobody is willing to take a one-way trip in case they get there and don't like what they find. Bowveld's been desperately trying to fix the problem, but he hasn't been able to solve it—or rather, the people working for him haven't been able to solve it. A couple of months ago the investors confronted Bowveld and told him that they were stopping all funding if he didn't start getting them up to SIX—and back again—within a few months."

Parker thought back to Saturday and his father telling him that his presentation hadn't gone well.

"Dad didn't do it, did he?"

Solomon shook his head. "No. The investors came to see him perform a second teleportation, and it didn't work. He called me on Sunday to tell me."

"How?" asked Michael with narrowed eyes. "There's no phone here."

"Ahhh," said Solomon. He reached behind him, dipped his hand into the back of his armchair, and pulled out a cell phone. He smiled.

"Technology—it's a wonderful thing," he said. He put the phone back before continuing. "Bowveld was furious—but not quite as furious as the investors. He blames your father—even though he's managed to do some wonderful work in the space of three weeks. The investors have given Bowveld a month to sort out the problem—or Avecto Enterprises is finished. This time—to make sure that he takes it seriously—they have told him that they want to see *him* being avected to SIX and back again, or they'll have him arrested for fraud. Bowveld had to agree—he had no choice—and now he can't risk your father not meeting the deadline."

"So what's happened to him?"

"Now that I don't know—apart from what you've told me. If he's gone to SIX—which it sounds like he has—I would guess that it's because Bowveld wants to make sure your father fixes the problem."

"How would that help?"

"Bowveld is a nasty piece of work. I'd guess he knows that if there's one thing guaranteed to get your father to fix the problem, it's knowing that he has to get back to you two."

Parker was too stunned to say anything. His mind was spinning, and he could see by how white Emma's face had gone that it had had the same effect on her. It was left to Michael to speak.

"If this is all true—and I'm not saying it is—but if it is, then what are they supposed to do?"

Solomon shrugged. "You'll have to wait. I know it's not what you want to hear, but if your dad can fix it—he will."

Parker dropped his head. He felt sick. "And if he can't?"

Solomon leaned forward and put his hand on Parker's hunched shoulders. "He will. I hate to say it, but Bowveld is right. There is no way your father won't find a solution if he knows that you're here. And he has help up there—he won't be on his own to work it out. He has a month before the final presentation. Wait until then."

Parker looked up. "A month? What are we supposed—"

Solomon put up his hand to quiet him. "I've just thought of something. . . ."

He stood up and walked over to the window.

"Solomon?" asked Parker.

"One moment," said Solomon, with his back to them. "I need to think."

Parker felt his wrist vibrate. He pressed down on Emma's light.

What's he doing? asked Emma.

No idea, replied Parker.

They watched Solomon muttering to himself, then shaking his head, then muttering some more. Finally he turned around.

"I don't know why I didn't think of this before."

"What?"

"Your father—he must have told you to come to me for a reason. Did he say anything else?"

Parker shook his head. "He got . . . The call got cut off. Why?"

"I think I know why he sent you to me; he knows that I'm the only person he can trust to pick up messages from him," said Solomon.

"You can talk to him?" asked Parker, shocked.

"No. Not exactly. But it's possible to send a message back in one of the shipments. There are weekly teleports to and from SIX. Avecto sends people from Earth to work there once a month, but there is a weekly shipment of cargo and data from Earth to SIX and back again once a week. If it's hidden well enough, it's possible to slip a message in there." Solomon rubbed his forehead. "That's definitely it—it has to be. You need to find Lina."

"Lina?" asked Parker. He knew exactly who Solomon meant—his father's assistant—but it was a surprise to hear Solomon say her name. "How do you know her?"

"I know her well. Or, should I say, I know her father well. We worked together at Avecto for many years. He left just before Junior came in and turned everything sour. He found out what happened to me when Lina started to work there and managed to find me a few months ago. In fast, he's the reason I have the cell phone."

"But if you knew, why didn't you tell my father what this place was like?" Parker could feel himself starting to get angry. "Why did you let him go and work there?"

Solomon bowed his head. "It's worse than that, Parker. I'm the one who told him about the problems they were having. That's why he came to Avecto and offered to help solve the avection issue."

Parker couldn't believe what he was hearing. "*Why?* Why would he do that?"

Solomon didn't answer immediately.

"I think," he said finally, "that's something your father needs to explain to you himself. Right now, we just get ahold of Lina."

"How?" asked Parker.

"I'll call Lina's father—I can trust him. I'll call you tonight and let you know more."

Solomon pulled out the cell phone from behind the armchair. "What number can I call you on?"

Michael started to read out the numbers, and Solomon punched them in one at a time. It was only then that Parker noticed that Solomon didn't have any fingernails.

"Done," said Solomon. He put the cell phone back and looked up at the clock. "You have to get out of here. We don't need any more complications."

They all stood, and Solomon shook hands with Michael and smiled. "I'll have to save the science bit for another time, I'm afraid."

"How convenient," said Michael with a small shrug. The sarcasm from earlier, however, was gone. Parker suspected that Michael, like himself, might have started to believe Solomon.

CHAPTER TWENTY-ONE

True to his word, Solomon called that evening during dinner. As upsetting as it was to accept, they had all agreed—despite how farfetched it sounded—that Solomon really did seem to be telling the truth. It was a lot to digest for Parker and Michael. Emma, however, had believed Solomon from the outset. *"You can tell from his eyes that he's telling the truth,"* she had explained. "Which one?" Michael had replied.

"No phones at the table, Michael!" snapped Hilda.

"Sorry, Hilda!" said Michael as they all jumped up. "Can we be excused?"

Hilda looked over at the almost untouched plates of food on the table. "But you haven't finished . . . "

They didn't hear the end of her sentence—they were already running out of the room. Parker took the ringing phone from Michael and answered. At the same time, he pressed down on his wrist so that Emma would be able to hear.

"Yes?"

"Parker?"

"Yes."

"It's Solomon."

"I know. Hi. Did you speak to Lina's dad?"

"Straight to the point—just like your mother. Yes, we spoke earlier, and he just called me back. He's spoken to Lina."

Parker nodded at Michael. *"He spoke to her,"* he mouthed.

"She's very upset. She must be doing a good job of hiding it though—Bowveld doesn't seem to suspect that her loyalties lie with your father."

"Did she find a message from Dad?"

"No, no. The shipments of data from Avecto arrive on Thursdays—tomorrow. She's going to have a look and see what she finds."

"How will she know what to look for?"

"If he's sent a message—she'll find it. It'll be marked with a symbol."

"What kind of symbol?" asked Parker, intrigued.

"A diamond with a smiley face on it."

"Sorry?" asked Parker. He had expected Solomon to say a string of numbers or something a little, well, less silly.

"It was the logo of the science team when your parents were my students. The Glad Stones—get it?"

Parker and Emma smiled. Michael was watching them with a sulky face—clearly annoyed at being left out of the conversation.

"And the message will be coded?" asked Parker. "Will Lina know how to work it out?"

"I'm sure she could if I told her how to do it. But I think—for her own protection—it's best that she doesn't know any more than she needs to. I've told her to bring whatever she finds to you—if there is anything. I'll talk you through it over the phone. Can you meet her tomorrow afternoon? She suggested the Paradise Mall—very apt, I think. Do you know it?"

"Yes," said Parker. "I know it. What time?"

"That I don't know—after she finishes work, I imagine. I'll let you know as soon as I hear from her. In the meantime I think you should both stay out of sight. You're not going to school, are you?"

"No," said Parker. Much to Michael's annoyance, he had exhausted his excuses with Hilda and would have to go in. Emma and Parker planned to hide in the tree house for the day.

"Good. Keep the phone on you, and I'll call as soon as I know anything more."

"Okay."

"And, Parker?"

"Yes?"

"Are you both doing okay? I know this must be a very hard time for you two."

"We're fine," said Parker. He decided not to mention that Emma had gotten upset earlier, or his own dark thoughts that had been plaguing him. "Thank you for helping us."

There was a pause, and Solomon's voice, when he spoke again, was tight and serious. "It's the very least I can do, Parker. The very least. I just wish I could do more."

There was another pause. "Now," said Solomon, "go and relax. Try to take your mind off things for tonight. We'll talk tomorrow."

Parker thanked him again and hung up the phone.

The following day dragged on and on. Parker and Emma sneaked into the tree house, unnoticed by Hilda, and spent the day watching the television, the clock, and the phone. Though it was a fine day and they would have loved to visit Polly and ride around on their bikes under the clear blue skies, they didn't dare risk being caught by Hilda. By the time Michael came back from school—annoyed and tired from the effort of avoiding Aaron all day—Parker and Emma were going out of their minds with boredom.

"He didn't call, then?" asked Michael.

Parker and Emma shook their heads. "Still too early, I suppose," said Parker.

Michael groaned, echoing both his and Emma's frustration at having to wait. He seemed as disappointed as the two of them, and Parker was once again reminded how lucky he'd been to find such a good friend just when he needed one most.

Michael flopped down on the sofa beside them and joined them in the same cycle of watching the television, the clock, and then the phone again.

In the end, realizing that they didn't need to hide from Hilda anymore now that school was finished, the three of them left the tree house with the plan to go distract them-selves and ride their bikes. Of course, the moment they stopped looking at the phone, it rang.

Parker answered and, following the strict instructions that Michael had given him earlier, put the phone on loud-speaker. He also turned on Effie.

"She's got it," said Solomon.

"What?" said Parker.

"She found the symbol I told her to look for—on a memory stick in the shipment. She managed to sneak it out, but she doesn't know what's on it. I'm sure it'll be there though—it has to be. Can you meet her in an hour? Is that too short notice?"

"No," said Parker. It was Brendan's day off, but he hoped they'd be able to get ahold of him. If not, they'd get a cab. One way or another, they'd be there.

"She'll meet you by the carousel at the mall—do you know what she means?"

Parker knew exactly where that was—at the front of the mall. It was always surrounded by people.

"I don't think you should be the one to go though, Parker."

"I have to go! What do you mean?"

"I have no idea if she's being watched. Can Michael meet her instead?"

Parker, though he hated the idea of not being involved, understood why Solomon was asking this. He looked over at Michael, who shrugged. "Sure."

Michael, thought Parker, seemed to be growing braver by the hour since this whole thing had started.

"Good," said Solomon. "She'll be having a coffee at one of the tables by the carousel. Parker and Emma can tell you what she looks like. She'll be there at six o'clock. She'll wait if you're late."

"We won't be," said Parker.

"Call me when you've got it."

"We will," said Parker. "Thank you."

"Of course," said Solomon.

Though it made sense that Michael would meet Lina, there was no way that Parker was going to be kept in the dark about what was going on at every step of the way. In that sense, it seemed he and Michael were much the same.

"Make sure it's working," said Parker as he handed Michael the spare cell phone that Michael had found in his house. They were sitting in the mall parking lot—having easily convinced Brendan to skip out on sitting at home in favor of escorting them on the next part of the adventure.

Michael took out the set of in-ear headphones from his pocket and connected them to the handset. He fitted the side with the microphone attached into his ear and called the phone Parker was holding in his hand. Parker answered on speakerphone.

"Testing, testing, one, two, three," said Michael into the microphone. His voice boomed out of the other cell phone, making Parker jump.

"Definitely working," he said, turning down the volume. "Make sure you don't hang up."

"I won't," said Michael. He opened the passenger door and climbed out. "Back in a moment," he said. His voice came out as an echo from Parker's hand.

Parker smiled. "Good luck. And, Michael?"

Michael stopped halfway through closing the door. "Yes?"

"Thank you."

Michael shrugged. "You're welcome," he said, and slammed the door closed.

Brendan turned to Parker from the front seat. "I'm going to follow him. Just in case," he said.

Michael heard Brendan through his headphones. "I don't need you to check on me."

"You won't even know I'm there," called out Brendan. He opened his door and turned back to Parker. "Don't go anywhere. I'll lock the doors."

Parker nodded. As soon as the door closed, he unmuted Effie and turned to look at the cell phone as Michael began a running commentary.

"I'm walking. . . . I'm walking up to the entrance . . . Still walking. I'm at the doors. I'm walking through the doors. . . ."

"You don't have to tell me everything," whispered Parker, then realized he didn't have to whisper. "Just make sure I can hear when you meet Lina."

"Oh . . . okay," whispered Michael. He went silent, and the

sound of his voice was replaced by the sounds of the busy mall. Parker and Emma waited. Then waited some more. Parker was regretting asking Michael to stop his commentary but decided not to say anything—he would hear when Michael met Lina; he just had to be patient.

And then the phone went silent. Michael had hung up.

Parker's eyes widened as he stared at the phone.

"What happened?" signed Emma.

Panicked, Parker looked down at the phone and wondered whether ringing Michael might bring attention to the hidden cell phone at the wrong time. He decided to count to sixty and then try him. He got to twenty-five seconds before he lost patience.

"I'm calling him back," said Parker.

He pressed redial and waited as the phone began to ring. Michael didn't answer. Parker tried again and waited.

Still no answer.

He was about to press redial once more when the phone began to ring.

"What happened?" asked Parker.

"I was going to the bathroom," whispered Michael. "I was desperate."

"Why didn't you tell me?"

"You said you didn't want me to tell you everything."

Parker sighed. "Fine. Tell me everything."

"I'm walking back out into the mall. . . . The carousel is in front of me. . . . There are about . . . hmmm . . . eight children on the carousel. There are approximately . . . fifty tables. I can't see her yet. . . . I'm almost there. . . . I'm looking. . . ."

Michael went silent.

"I see her."

Parker looked at Emma and gave her a thumbs-up, then realized she was already listening to his thoughts. He didn't normally forget Emma was on Effie, but she had been unusually quiet. She must be listening to him with it muted, he thought.

"*I am,*" signed Emma.

"Are you Lina?" asked Michael in a hushed voice. Parker snapped his attention back to the phone.

"Hi," said Lina's voice. "Michael?"

"*Yes.*"

"It looks more suspicious if you stand with your back to me and whisper," said Lina. "Come and sit down."

Parker listened as the sound of a chair being scraped across the floor filled the car.

"How are Parker and Emma?" asked Lina.

"They're okay," said Michael.

"I've been so worried about them. . . ." Parker heard her gulp and realized that she was crying. "I didn't know what to do."

"Are you okay?" asked Michael. Parker could hear the awkwardness in his voice.

Lina sniffed. "Yes . . . I'm sorry. It's just been such a relief to hear that they're okay. I couldn't find out anything."

"They're fine," said Michael. "They're staying at my house."

Lina sniffed again. "I'm so glad. . . . I thought they were on their own."

Parker had no idea she cared about them that much.

"How much did Solomon tell you?" asked Lina. She was whispering now, and Parker leaned in to hear.

"Everything," replied Michael.

"Everything?" asked Lina.

"Yes. The teleporting thing and that his dad is on another planet. Is it true?"

"Yes," said Lina. "Did he say anything else—about SIX? About who's on SIX?"

Michael paused.

"The people who are working there," said Parker. "Is that what she means?"

Michael repeated the question to Lina.

Lina paused.

"Yes . . . yes, that's what I mean. He's not on his own. Tell them that."

"They know already," said Michael.

"Good. Here . . . the carrier bag is by your feet now. Solomon asked me to add some info on SIX for you too. I got the only thing I could find that wouldn't go noticed if it went missing."

"Thanks," said Michael.

"Tell Parker and Emma that it's all going to be okay,"

Even at a distance Parker could hear the uncertainty in her voice.

"You should go now," said Lina. She sounded as if she were crying again.

"Okay," said Michael. "Bye."

Michael had already looked in the bag before he got in. He climbed inside, followed soon after by Brendan, and pulled out a plastic box.

"What's this?" Michael asked.

"You're joking, Michael, right?" said Brendan, peering through the divide between the front and back of the car. "Please tell me you're joking."

Michael shrugged.

"It's a video," said Parker. Brendan sighed in relief. "They used them in the olden times . . . instead of DVDs."

"Olden times!" said Brendan. "Watch your language!"

"Sorry," said Parker. "They used them a long time ago."

"That's better," muttered Brendan.

"How are we supposed to watch it?"

Emma smiled as Michael turned to Brendan.

"Brendan? Can you play this?"

Brendan shook his head. "Haven't seen a VCR in years . . ." He looked at Parker with narrowed eyes. "Not since I was a young man . . . back in the *olden* times."

Emma nudged Parker.

"It's fine," said Parker. "I've got one at home."

"You do?" asked Michael.

"Yeah, I collect old machines and stuff."

"You're not going back there," said Brendan. "I'll go."

"Really?"

"Who else? It sounds like I'm the only other person apart from you who knows what a VCR is."

Parker gave small smile in apology. "Sorry."

"Ah, it's all right, son. I was only joking. I'll drop you off back at the house and you can give me your key."

"Thanks," said Parker. He turned to Michael. "What else is in there?"

Michael reached into the bag and pulled out a memory stick. It looked much like the one Anteater had given them—except this one had a picture of a diamond with a smiley face drawn in its center in Wite-Out.

Michael shook the bag. "That's all there is," he said.

"I'll call Solomon," said Parker as Brendan started the engine.

While Brendan drove to Parker's house to get the VCR, Parker, Michael, and Emma took the memory stick up to Michael's room. Parker called Solomon again. He answered on the first ring. Parker turned on the speakerphone and laid it on the desk.

"Are you at a computer now?" said Solomon.

"Yes," said Parker. "Michael's just putting the memory stick in."

"Done," said Michael. He sat down in his chair and clicked on the icon that appeared—a nondescript white square.

Parker watched the window open, and a long list of numbered files appeared.

"There are hundreds of files," said Parker.

"There will be," replied Solomon. "Each one is the data for every person and object avected since the last report. Each of the files should be labeled with a very long number—is that right?"

"Yes," said Parker.

"Good. Look for a file that ends in the number 1983."

Michael scrolled down the list. He and Parker spotted it at the same time.

"Found it!" said Parker. His heart, he realized, was racing.

"Found it?" asked Solomon. He sounded almost as surprised as Parker. "Open it up!"

Michael was already a step ahead of him.

"More numbers," said Parker. "Pages of them," he added as Michael kept scrolling down, looking for the end.

"The numbers are broken up into sections—like paragraphs. Yes?" asked Solomon.

"Yes," said Parker.

"Find the paragraph that starts with a comma. There should be commas separating all the numbers, but there should be only one paragraph that begins with a comma. It'll be there somewhere."

"How do you know this?" said Parker as they all leaned in and checked each paragraph.

"Encryption course I used to teach. Thought it might

be useful for the kind of work many of my students went into—turns out I was right. This is one I devised—Gladstone Code—I used it to set the assignments to give my students practice. Any one of my students would know how to—"

"Got it! It starts comma, fourteen, twelve—"

"Stop—it can't be done over the phone. Print it off," said Solomon. "Each number corresponds to a letter. Write this down . . ."

Parker grabbed a pen and a piece of paper that Michael handed him.

"Write down the alphabet at the top of the page."

Parker did as he was told.

"The letters in Gladstone are the first letters of the alphabet—so put the number one under the letter *G*, two under *L*, three under *A*, and so on. Are you writing this down?"

"Yes," said Parker.

"Then go back to the beginning of the alphabet and continue from there. Put the numbers in sequence under each letter, from ten up to twenty-six. Skip the letters of my name, obviously. So *B* equals ten, *C* equals eleven, skip *D* and *E*, *F* equals twelve, and *Z* will be twenty-six."

Parker scribbled the numbers onto the page. "I've done it."

There was a pause. "Now you just have to work it out. If you see a zero on its own, ignore it. Double zero stands for a full stop. That's it."

"I'll call you back when I've worked it out," said Parker.

"Actually," said Solomon, "if you don't mind, I'll wait.

There's not much going on here and I want to hear what he says."

"Okay," said Parker.

"Take your time," said Solomon. "There's no rush."

Michael walked over to the printer and brought back the sheet filled with numbers. Parker took it from Michael and placed it next to the code. He set to work.

A	B	C	D	E	F	G	H	I	J	K	L	M
3	10	11	4	9	12	1	13	14	15	16	2	17
N	O	P	Q	R	S	T	U	V	W	X	Y	Z
8	7	18	19	20	5	6	21	22	23	24	25	26

```
, 14, 12, 0, 25, 7, 21, 3, 20, 9, 0, 20, 0, 9, 3, 4, 14, 8, 1, 6,
13, 0, 14, 5, 6, 13, 9, 8, 18, 0, 3, 8, 4, 9, 13, 3, 22, 0, 9,
12, 7, 21, 0, 8, 4, 25, 7, 21, 00, 14, 0, 8, 9, 9, 4, 0, 0, 6, 7,
16, 8, 7, 23, 6, 13, 9, 25, 3, 20, 9, 5, 3, 12, 9, 00, 18, 0, 2,
9, 3, 5, 9, 17, 3, 16, 9, 5, 21, 20, 9, 6, 13, 9, 0, 25, 13, 3,
22, 9, 5, 7, 17, 9, 23, 13, 9, 20, 0, 9, 6, 7, 5, 6, 0, 3, 25, 7,
21, 6, 7, 12, 0, 20, 9, 3, 11, 13, 7, 12, 10, 7, 23, 0, 22, 9, 2,
4, 00, 23, 7, 20, 16, 14, 0, 8, 1, 7, 8, 12, 14, 0, 24, 14, 8, 1,
6, 13, 14, 5, 10, 21, 6, 8, 7, 18, 20, 7, 1, 20, 0, 9, 5, 5, 17,
3, 4, 9, 5, 7, 12, 3, 20, 00, 23, 0, 7, 20, 20, 14, 9, 4, 12, 7,
20, 0, 18, 3, 8, 4, 9, 14, 12, 14, 11, 3, 8, 6, 5, 7, 2, 22, 9,
14, 6, 00, 8, 9, 9, 4, 25, 7, 21, 0, 6, 7, 5, 9, 8, 4, 6, 13, 9,
17, 0, 6, 7, 17, 9, 00, 20, 9, 18, 9, 3, 6, 00, 12, 14, 8, 4, 0,
23, 3, 25, 6, 7, 5, 9, 8, 4, 18, 3, 8, 4, 9, 6, 7, 17, 9, 13, 9,
20, 9, 00, 2, 14, 8, 3, 11, 3, 8, 0, 13, 9, 2, 18, 00, 14, 12,
14, 12, 14, 24, 0, 6, 13, 14, 5, 23, 9, 11, 3, 8, 3, 2, 2, 11, 7,
17, 9, 10, 3, 11, 16, 00, 14, 12, 0, 8, 7, 6, 0, 3, 6, 2, 9, 3,
5, 6, 23, 9, 23, 14, 2, 2, 0, 10, 9, 6, 7, 0, 1, 9, 6, 13, 9, 20,
00, 6, 9, 2, 0, 2, 18, 3, 8, 4, 9, 14, 2, 7, 22, 9, 6, 13, 9, 17,
00, 14, 17, 14, 5, 5, 6, 13, 9, 17, 00, 5, 7, 5, 7, 20, 20, 25,
12, 7, 20, 23, 0, 13, 3, 0, 6, 14, 3, 17, 18, 21, 6, 6, 14, 8, 1,
6, 13, 0, 9, 17, 6, 13, 20, 7, 21, 1, 13, 00, 18, 2, 0, 9, 3, 5,
9, 5, 9, 8, 4, 6, 13, 9, 17, 3, 5, 0, 3, 18, 00, 14, 16, 8, 0, 7,
23, 14, 12, 3, 0, 0, 8, 25, 10, 7, 4, 25, 11, 0, 3, 8, 4, 7, 14,
6, 25, 7, 0, 21, 0, 11, 3, 8, 00, 1, 9, 7, 12, 12, 20, 9, 25, 00
```

Parker had been so intent on deciphering the message that he didn't stop to read the whole thing until he was finished. As his arm had been resting on the page as he wrote, neither Michael nor Emma had managed to look at it either. They all leaned in and, in silence, read the whole thing to themselves.

"What does it say?" asked Solomon.

Nobody replied.

"Hello? Are you still there?"

Emma and Parker were too shocked to speak, and it was left to Michael to answer.

"Yes," replied Michael. "We're still here."

"What does it say?"

Michael paused, as if waiting for Parker to jump in, but Parker said nothing. His eyes were just reading the same part of the message over and over again:

```
NEED YOU TO SEND THEM TO ME. REPEAT.
FIND WAY TO SEND P AND E TO ME HERE.
```

"He wants you to send Parker and Emma to SIX," said Michael finally.

It was Solomon's turn to go quiet.

CHAPTER TWENTY-TWO

Parker walked away from Michael and Emma, who looked as shell-shocked as he felt. He took a seat on the gray leather sofa in Michael's room.

Questions were pouring into his head so quickly that there was no time to formulate any answers—was he really going to be teleported? Would it hurt? What would SIX be like? Was it really another planet?

Did he even want to go?

Michael seemed to understand that Emma and Parker needed time to think. He didn't say a word, and Parker barely registered the moment he left the room.

His wrist buzzed.

Do you think it's true? asked Emma as soon as Parker answered.

I don't know.

Do you really think Dad's on a different planet?

I don't know, Emma. I really don't know.

But teleporting—you really think that can happen?

Emma's questions echoed his own. It was too much.

I can't think, Emma. I *need* to think.

He hung up the call.

Parker had no idea how long Michael was gone from the room. However long it was, it wasn't long enough. When Michael returned, Parker was no closer to answering any of his questions than he had been when Michael had left. If anything, he was even more confused.

"Do you want to watch the video?" asked Michael quietly.

Parker looked up and saw that Michael was holding a VCR—the one he had built himself. It was strange seeing something so familiar so out of context, and it only added to Parker's sense of disquiet.

Parker nodded. There was, however, no urgency as he stood and followed Michael and Emma up the stairs to the gallery. He sat down on one of the beanbag chairs—his mind so full and yet so empty—and waited as Michael hooked up the VCR and turned the television on. It was only when the screen came to life—white lines flickering against black—that his attention turned from his thoughts to the video playing.

What do you think it's going to be? asked Emma on Effie.

Parker shrugged. **I don't know,** he said. **Let's just watch.**

Don't forget to repeat everything—I don't want to miss anything.

Okay, said Parker as bold white letters appeared across the screen.

The words dissolved into the black, and the film cut to an opening sequence of a chaotic street scene in Manhattan—traffic at a standstill, horns honking, and swarms of people dodging cars and stepping over litter on the sidewalks.

"Imagine," said a woman's soothing voice, "a world without traffic jams."

The scene cut to a factory with black smoke pouring out of a tall chimney stack.

"Imagine no pollution, no recessions, no wars, and no protests. Imagine no shortage of natural resources."

Parker watched the images of war victims, angry rioters, foreclosure signs, and closed-down gas stations flashing on the screen. He'd already heard enough about SIX to know where this was going.

An image of a blue planet appeared.

"Imagine you could create your own perfect world. Imagine the possibilities."

Three gold letters appeared on the screen: SIX.

"Discovered in 1981," continued the woman's voice, "the planet SIX lies in the Milky Way galaxy in the constellation of Libra."

The planet on the screen grew smaller until the entire galaxy was visible, and a straight red line appeared that connected the two labeled planets: Earth and SIX.

"This extraordinary planet—the first and only truly habitable planet ever discovered—is over nine billion years old, twice the size of Earth, and orbits a sun only slightly smaller than ours."

Parker watched as the camera zoomed back in on SIX, breaking the cloud cover to reveal a brilliant turquoise sea dotted with large islands. It looked, thought Parker, like somewhere in the Caribbean, with one notable exception: all the trees and plants were shades of purple.

"With its shallow waters, temperate climate, an abundance of natural resources, and vibrant vegetation, SIX is the planet that nobody ever thought would be found—a place even more hospitable to humans than Earth."

The scene cut to a brilliant white waterfall cascading into a blue lagoon.

"You'll find no treacherous dark rocky landscapes here. No aliens. No toxic air. You can forget everything that the movies have told you, because SIX is science fact, not science fiction."

Michael nodded his approval. "Good line," he said.

The film cut to a landfill.

"This is Earth today. It is accepted now that the damage done to our environment is irreversible. Soon—within our lifetimes—our planet will become uninhabitable. *Now* is the time to think about you and your family's future."

A clean white laboratory appeared, sunlight sweeping in through the tall glass windows in the background. Sitting around a table, a group of smiling but serious-looking people in white coats were conducting a meeting.

"Over the last decade, Avecto Enterprises has been laying the foundations that will move our vision of paradise into reality. We are now ready to enter the next phase of our ambitious plan—the building of a new world of a magnitude and magnificence never seen before."

The video went back to sweeping panoramic shots of blue waters, purple forests, and pure white beaches.

"Avecto Enterprises is now inviting investment in this magical paradise—a once-in-a-lifetime opportunity to purchase land on which to build your own perfect nation."

A quaint street scene of redbrick buildings and strolling couples appeared.

"Perhaps you'll choose to model your territory on the care-free days of the 1950s."

The image was replaced with a futuristic landscape of glass buildings and wide plazas.

"Or you might prefer a futuristic state-of-the-art way of living. Whatever your vision of paradise is, Avecto Enterprises can make it a reality."

The scene cut to a computer-generated view of a city center with wide empty avenues and buildings made of wood and glass, separated by squares of water and purple-leaved trees dotted with bright colorful flowers. A large glass archway formed a glistening rainbow over the scene. It was only when the camera zoomed in that Parker was able to see the archway was, in fact, a building made of glass. Running along the outside of it, a clear tube filled with glass capsule elevators delivered workers to their office buildings.

"This is Great Bowveld, the heart of SIX. Here, all nations will be able to work together to ensure that the practical needs of our generation and of generations to come are met. Taking the best of what we have here, then discarding the worst, we will be able to provide the finest standards of living. Together we can make this new world the very best that it can be. Together we can make sure that the mistakes made on Earth are never repeated. Together we can create paradise."

The film cut to a man sitting reclined on a sleek leather armchair, looking out of his floor-to-ceiling window at the blue skies and equally blue waters in the distance.

"Imagine a world of luxury. Imagine a world created to your vision of perfection."

The blue planet appeared on the screen.

"Imagine SIX."

The screen went black and the gold letters of SIX appeared above the words PRACTICE MADE PERFECT.

"*Wow*," whispered Michael and Parker at the same time.

"It actually looks kind of cool," said Michael.

Parker didn't respond, but he was thinking the same thing. He had been so focused on the process of getting to SIX, and on the thought of not being able to return, that he had not stopped to consider exactly what living there might be like. By the looks of it, it would be just like Earth, but better. And surprisingly familiar.

"Do you think it's true?" asked Parker finally.

"Are you okay?" asked Michael.

Parker turned, confused, and saw that Michael was looking at Emma. Emma, in response, wiped the tear running down her cheek and sniffed.

"I don't want to go, Parker," said Emma, her lip trembling as she signed.

Parker put his arm around his sister. "It's going to be okay," said Parker. "I promise."

CHAPTER TWENTY-THREE

Parker awoke the next morning with a sense of clarity and calmness that took him completely by surprise. The same could not be said for Emma, who clambered down from the bunk bed with bleary eyes. She looked like she hadn't slept all night.

Parker, having already showered and dressed (in the treetop tower), put down his toast.

"You okay?" he signed.

Emma shook her head and walked over to the sofa where Parker was sitting. She glanced down at the plate of toast and croissants that Michael had brought up for them before leaving for school, then turned away.

"What are we going to do?" signed Emma.

"We're going to go. We have to."

"Really?"

Parker shrugged and switched on Effie. **What choice do we have?** he asked. **We can't hide here forever. We haven't got anyone else to go to. We have no money,** and, even if we did, at some point somebody's going to notice two kids living on their own.

But shouldn't we wait?

For what? asked Parker calmly. **Dad's message said he wasn't going to be able to fix it in time. How long are we supposed to wait?**

Emma stared at Parker as if he'd gone mad. Parker sighed.

What Dad said makes sense—if he fixes it, we can all come back together. If not, at least we're with him.

Emma shook her head. **So you think it's true?**

Don't you? asked Parker.

I don't know. I thought so, but it's all so crazy. Do you really believe it?

Not really. Well, I'm not sure. But that doesn't matter. What difference does it make if we go along with it? If it's not true, nothing's changed. If it is, then we go spend some time in paradise, right?

That's not paradise!

I don't know, said Parker with a shrug, **I think it looks nice.**

It doesn't look like nice to me, Parker. Just a few rich people running away from everything they've messed up here—how is that paradise?

Dad's there. That's all that matters right now.

Emma looked ready to argue back and then, as Parker's logic began to sink in, the fight seemed to leave her. She dropped her head and slumped down next to Parker.

What if we end up like Solomon? Her thought was weak.

If what Solomon says is true—then that won't happen.

And if it isn't?

Parker shrugged again. **It's a risk I think we have to take.**

Emma thought about this as Parker picked up his toast and took a bite. Finally she leaned over and grabbed a piece herself. **Okay,** she said. **Let's do it.**

It's not so bad, Emma, he said. He smiled. **What's the worst that can happen . . . happen . . . happen . . . ALBERTA!**

Emma stared at Parker and then, in spite of their nerves—or perhaps because of them—they both began to laugh.

From the moment Parker made his decision that morning, his mood had lifted. All the tension and fear—despite what they might be about to be putting themselves through—had inexplicably disappeared. Perhaps it was that they finally had a plan. It was a crazy plan, sure, and it might not even be possible, but it was still a plan. Over the course of the morning, his calmness began to rub off on Emma, and by the time Michael returned from school, the two of them were happily teaching Polly new tricks in the field next to the tree house.

"I'm coming with you," called out Michael. The expression on his face was thunderous. "I *hate* that school."

Parker patted Polly on the head and stood up. He waited until Michael reached them.

"Really?" asked Parker. His face broke out into a wide grin. "That's great!"

Michael sighed. "No. I wish I could though. Aaron is such an idiot."

"What happened?" signed Emma.

"He tried to take my money again."

Parker raised his eyebrows. "Tried?" he asked.

"I didn't let him."

Parker's mouth dropped open and then curled into a wide smile. He thumped Michael on the back. "No way! What did you do?"

Michael gave a heavy sigh. "I punched him."

Parker took a step back and stared at Michael. "You *punched* him?"

Michael nodded. "And now I have three days detention."

Parker laughed—more out of shock than anything.

"It's not funny," muttered Michael. "My parents are back tomorrow. They're going to kill me."

Parker gave Emma a sideways grimace. "Sorry, Michael," he said. "I don't think it's funny—I just didn't think you'd do something like that."

Michael looked up at Parker with wide eyes. *"Me neither!* I don't know what happened—one moment he had his hand on my throat in the corridor, and then next he was lying on the floor."

"You knocked him out?"

Michael nodded slowly, and before Parker could stop himself, he let out a laugh that he immediately covered up with his hand.

"Sorry," said Parker. "What did Aaron do?"

"He cried a bit. I feel really bad."

Parker saw Emma turning her back to them to hide her giggles. Michael looked over at her and then back at Parker with narrowed eyes.

"Why are you two in such a good mood, anyway?"

"We've decided we're going to SIX."

It was Michael's turn to look shocked. "You spoke to Solomon?"

Parker pursed his lips. "No. But if he says he can get us there—then we're going."

"But it's probably not even true!"

"Probably—but not definitely. I can't think of any other good reason that Solomon looks like he does."

Michael sighed. "Me neither. I've looked up all his symptoms, and I can't find any condition that's even close to it." He paused. "So what now?"

Parker shrugged. "I guess we wait for Solomon to call."

"It's all arranged."

Those were Solomon's first words when he called that afternoon, and they took Parker completely by surprise. He had expected to discuss his decision with him, perhaps, or to hear Solomon's ideas for getting them there—he had not expected to hear that it had all already been arranged.

"*What?*"

"I spoke to Lina. If it's going to happen, it has to happen straightaway."

"But . . . why?"

"There is one trip for new personnel scheduled every month. That's tonight."

"Tonight?"

"It's that, or we wait another month."

Parker didn't say anything. He looked at Emma, and she seemed just as surprised—and unsure—as he was.

"Parker? Do you want to go?"

Parker hesitated. "Yes . . . I think so . . . but I didn't think it would happen . . ."

"So soon?"

Parker nodded and then remembered that he was on the phone. "Yes," he said.

"You don't have to go. You really don't. We can work something out here. Your father will understand."

At the mention of his father, Parker's resolve returned. "No. No—we want to go. What's going to happen?"

"Okay. Good. Listen carefully—there's a lot to do before we go."

"We?"

There was a pause. "You'll need an adult to accompany you. Children would never be sent to SIX on their own."

"So why couldn't Dad have taken us?" asked Parker. As he asked the question, he realized he already knew the answer.

"Your dad did not go willingly. And if you were there, what incentive would he have to sort the problem out?"

"I get it," said Parker. "You're coming with us?"

"Well, I *could* do with a holiday," he answered.

Nobody laughed.

"Parker. I have nobody here to stay for. I want to do this." He paused. "I need to do this."

"Won't another teleportation hurt you?"

There was a slight pause. "I'll be fine. I have a resistance to it, remember? And it's not like I could end up looking much stranger than I already do."

"But . . . why would you take the risk?" asked Parker. He wasn't sure why he would try to sow seeds of doubt in Solomon's mind if this was the only way they were going to see their father again. Solomon, however, had clearly already made his mind up.

"I'm not taking any risks—I know what I'm doing—and it's not up for discussion. If you're going, I'm going."

Michael leaned into the phone. "How are you going to get out, though?"

Parker hadn't even thought about this.

"Well, that's the easy part. I go out every night."

"Really?"

"The night attendant is saving up for a new car and I need

some fresh air—it's a mutually beneficial arrangement. There are some things to work out, though."

"Like what?"

"You both need to look different. Lina doesn't think Bowveld will be there—he doesn't bother with the run-of-the-mill stuff—but in case he, or anybody else who might recognize you is."

"What do we have to do?"

"There's not much we can do with you both. Change your hair. Dress you different. Lina has arranged for her sister to meet you. If it's a problem to meet at Michael's, we can meet at a hotel—"

"No," interrupted Michael. "Here's fine. My parents aren't back till tomorrow."

"What about Hilda?" whispered Parker.

"I'll speak to Brendan—he'll make sure she isn't around."

"If you're sure, Michael."

"I am."

"Okay, I'll need your address."

Michael told Solomon, who then repeated it back to make sure he'd written it down correctly.

"Lina's sister's name is Mai. She'll come to yours by cab at eight. She'll fix you two up. When you're ready, she'll call a cab—I've sorted out all the money for that with Lina—you don't need to worry about anything."

"And then?"

"Then you'll all come to collect me. I'll be waiting by the

road—Mai already knows to call me when you're near. She'll fix me up, and the cab will take her to her house. Mai doesn't know anything about what's actually happening, and Lina doesn't want her any more involved than she needs to be."

"Why does she think she's doing this?" asked Parker.

"Filming for a promotional video. It's the best we could come up with. You don't need to say anything—pretend you know nothing about it."

"Okay," said Parker. He couldn't imagine Mai would buy that explanation, but if that's what they had agreed on, then he wasn't going to argue.

"We'll take another cab from the hospital to the train station and board the bus to the Avecto Terminal. There'll be other people there who'll be on the same trip—so you both need to keep up our story the whole way."

"What's the story?" asked Parker.

"I'll explain when I see you. We'll have plenty of time. That's all. I'll see you at nine."

"Wait," said Michael.

"Yes?"

"Can Brendan take us from here? He can take us all to collect you."

"Who's Brendan?" asked Solomon.

"Michael's driver," replied Parker before Michael could respond.

Parker saw a brief grimace cross Michael's face as he glanced over at Emma.

"He's not just a driver," said Michael. "He's . . . well . . . he's more like family, really."

Parker could see that Michael was embarrassed.

"Can Brendan be trusted?" asked Solomon.

"Yes," they all replied in unison.

"Definitely," added Parker. "He knows everything."

There was another pause.

"Okay," said Solomon. "I don't see a problem with that."

"I'll call Brendan," said Michael.

"If there's any problem—just let me know, and we can go back to the original plan."

"There won't be," said Michael.

"Well then, I guess that's that. I'll see you at nine."

"Wait!" called Parker. "What do we need to bring?"

"Nothing. Just yourselves. Lina's taken care of everything on her end, and I've made a few phone calls to some old friends. Everything is taken care of."

"So that's it?" asked Parker.

"I think that's—" Solomon stopped talking. "Someone's coming, sorry. I have to go . . . go . . . ALBER—"

The line went dead.

CHAPTER TWENTY-FOUR

Mai arrived at ten minutes past eight. Brendan stood with them at the doorway to greet her. He had convinced Hilda to go home and take the night off while he took over her duties.

Parker watched as Mai paid the cab driver and, with Brendan's help, started to pull out bag after bag from the backseat.

"This is going to be an interesting makeover," whispered Michael to Parker.

Parker was thinking the same thing. Mai looked nothing like her sister, and it wasn't just that she was shorter and stockier than Lina. Where Lina was elegant and understated, Mai was an explosion of fabric and colors. She had streaks of fluorescent pink running through her black hair, matching pink lipstick, and some kind of multicolored tutu over blue-and-green patterned leggings. Her top half was wrapped up in a bright yellow-and-green striped shawl. Emma looked delighted.

"Hi!" said Mai as she hauled a collection of bags up the

stairs. Behind her, Brendan was struggling with at least five suitcases.

Parker hurried over and took some of the bags from Mai.

"Thanks! Are you Parker?"

Parker nodded. "What have you got in here?"

"Lina wasn't sure your exact sizes. She told me to get some options. Now, where can we go do your hair?"

"My parents' bathroom is the biggest," said Michael.

"Whoa!" said Mai as they walked into Michael's parents' bathroom. "This is bigger than my apartment."

Parker wondered if Michael ever got tired of hearing this. If he did, he didn't say anything.

"This is going to be so much fun!" said Mai. She dropped the bags by the door and dragged over an armchair from the corner of the room.

"Right. Let's do you first," said Mai.

Before Parker had a chance to object, he found himself sitting on the armchair while Michael ran around placing towels at his feet and Mai pulled out box after box of alarmingly bright hair colors.

"Is that all of them?" asked Parker.

"Uh-huh. You don't like them?"

"Don't you have a blond or something?"

Mai shook her head. "Even if I did, that's not going to work on your hair in one go."

Parker sighed. "Fine," he said. "That one then."

From the corner of his eye, he could see Emma smiling as

he pointed to a vibrant red box. He had no choice; apart from the jet black dye—which was too close in color to his own brown hair—it was the only one that might pass as natural.

"I'll have to do your eyebrows, too," said Mai as Parker replaced Emma in the armchair. "Or it'll look strange."

Michael smiled. "Yeah, Parker—it'll look *really* strange if you don't do your eyebrows."

Parker shot Michael a deathly glare. "Just do it," he said to Mai.

"It's not that bad," said Michael. Parker knew it had to be that bad if Michael was trying to make him feel better about it.

"It's awful," he said as he stared at himself in the mirror. In fairness, the color and side parting were so different that he could barely recognize himself, so, in that sense, it was a job well done.

"I love mine," signed Emma. She was standing next to him, smoothing the new black fringe that hung just above her eyes. *"I just wish I could have kept my glasses the same color."* Mai had painted the rims of Emma's glasses with black polish. It was surprisingly effective.

"Clothes," called Mai from the adjoining bedroom.

"Can't wait for this," muttered Parker. He took one last look at himself, sighed, and followed Emma out of the room.

"Lina said she wanted you both to have a completely new look, so I—"

"No way," said Parker. "I'm sorry."

He could hear Michael's muffled laughter as Mai took a deep breath and quietly returned the pink vest and lime green shorts to the bag.

"Don't you have anything, um . . . normal?"

Mai frowned and rummaged through a bag on the floor. "This?" she asked, holding up a pair of red trousers.

Parker shook his head.

"What about this?"

Parker knew she was doing them a favor, but he couldn't help the irritation building up inside him. "The whole point is we're supposed to blend in and not draw attention to ourselves. I just need something regular but different from what I normally wear."

"You can have something of mine," suggested Michael.

"*Yes!*" said Parker. "Great. Pick something I'd never normally wear."

Michael left just as Emma emerged from the bathroom, having already changed into her clothes.

Parker's shoulders dropped at the sight of Emma wearing a black turtleneck and black trousers. "Why couldn't you have picked something like that for me?"

"Lina said you wear dark clothes and she wears bright—I picked the opposite." She turned to Emma. "Do you like it?"

Emma grinned.

"Then," said Mai, "you're all done."

Emma shook her head. *"Tell her there's one more thing,"* she signed to Parker, then ran out of the room.

"Will it rub off?" signed Emma. Parker translated.

Mai squeezed out the last bit of pink face paint from the now flat tube onto her brush.

"No," answered Mai as she began to dab the back of Polly's hind leg—the only remaining white patch visible on Polly's skin. "Once it's dried," continued Mai, "it should be okay. Just don't rub it too hard."

Parker pressed down on his wrist. **Is this really a good idea, Emma?** he asked. He wanted Polly to come with them just as much as Emma did, but it didn't seem like the best idea, given that they were doing everything they could to not draw attention to themselves.

I'm not leaving her, Emma replied firmly.

"All done," said Mai. She stood up to survey the now rosy pink pig and shook her head. "This is now officially the strangest night of my life."

Brendan was waiting by the car when they finally emerged from the house. Emma and Parker carefully lifted Polly onto the floor of the passenger seat and put her down on the towel that Michael had provided—"just in case." Once she was settled, Emma and Michael climbed into the car, and Parker, wearing a navy blazer, dark trousers, and a white shirt, rolled his new suitcase over to the back and lifted it into the trunk. Both his and Emma's suitcases were stuffed full of the clothes Mai had brought—none of which Parker had any intention of ever wearing. Mai seemed to think that they needed different outfits for the shoot. Parker guessed the real reason was that turning up without luggage would arouse suspicion.

Brendan slammed the trunk shut. "I can't believe we're doing this," he said.

"Me neither," said Parker. He walked around to the passenger door and climbed in to find Emma crying.

"What happened?" asked Parker, alarmed.

Emma looked up at Parker and signed.

"Oh," replied Parker awkwardly. "I'll . . . um . . . miss you too, Michael."

Michael grimaced and gulped loudly, and Parker realized he was trying to stop himself from crying too.

"You okay?" asked Parker.

Michael coughed quietly and shook himself. "Fine. Sorry." He forced a smile. "It's not like I'm not going to see you again anyway, right? I'll see you when you come back."

"If we come back," added Parker quietly.

"When you come back," corrected Michael.

"Come back from where?" asked Mai from the front passenger seat. "How long are you filming for?"

Parker had completely forgotten Mai was there. "Oh . . . it's going to be all night."

"Oh. Right," said Mai. She turned to Brendan. "Kids are weird," she muttered.

Brendan smiled. "They sure are," he said. He looked up at the rearview mirror. "Got everything?"

Parker nodded.

"Then let's do this," said Brendan.

As they had agreed with Solomon on their way there, Brendan turned onto a dirt track a short drive past the hospital's entrance and switched the headlights off. Almost immediately Solomon stepped out from behind a tree and hurried over, a small leather suitcase in hand. Even under the darkening sky Solomon's appearance was alarming, but at least Parker knew what to expect. Brendan and Mai, despite both having been forewarned about Solomon's "condition," were both clearly shocked. Parker heard Brendan draw a sharp breath, but he said nothing. Mai's reaction was not quite so restrained.

"What *is* that? Is it contagious? I'm not touching him."

"He's not contagious," said Michael.

"He's fine," insisted Parker.

Mai shook her head in disbelief. "My sister owes me. Big time," she said as the door next to Parker opened.

"Perfect timing," said Solomon, smiling. "Wow," he said, looking at Parker and then at Emma. "You really do look different."

He leaned forward and introduced himself to Brendan, who shook his hand—apparently over the shock—and Mai, who managed to squeak out a small hi.

"You've got quite a job on your hands," said Solomon. Mai nodded, and at the same time Polly—who until now had been resting quietly by Emma's feet—grunted.

Solomon flinched in surprise and then looked down. For a moment he said nothing.

"Either I'm sicker than I thought, or there's a pig in the car," he said finally.

Emma nodded, and Polly, with perfect timing, gave another loud grunt.

"She's our pet. We want to take her with us," explained Parker.

Solomon sighed. "You can't take her. No animals allowed—not even pets."

"But . . ." signed Emma, *"we can't leave her."*

"I don't know what to say, Emma," said Solomon. "It can't happen. I'm sorry."

Emma's eyes filled with tears. *"But what's going to happen to her?"* she signed. Parker translated.

"She can stay with me," interrupted Michael. "I'll take good care of her, I promise."

A tear rolled down Emma's cheek, but she didn't respond. Parker guessed that she, like him, had known it would be unlikely that Solomon would say yes.

"Are you okay?" asked Solomon. He placed his hand on her arm. "I'm so sorry."

Emma wiped her cheek with the back of her hand and nodded. Solomon, perhaps realizing that there wasn't much more he could do to comfort her, leaned forward to Brendan.

"Okay if we find somewhere away from here to stop the car?" asked Solomon.

"No problem," said Brendan. He put the headlights back on and turned the car around.

"I'm not going to miss that place one bit," said Solomon as they drove past the gates of the hospital.

Mai looked past Brendan and did a double take upon seeing the sign.

"That's a psychiatric hospital," she said.

"Just visiting a friend," said Solomon calmly.

"At night?" whispered Mai.

"He's a bit of a night owl," replied Solomon.

Mai didn't respond, but Parker could see her face in the mirror. She looked terrified.

"Okay here?" asked Brendan. "Or do you want me to go a bit farther?"

"No, this is fine. If you could just switch on the lights so Mai can work her magic. Mai?"

Mai hesitated for a moment and then opened the car door. Up until then, Parker hadn't given any thought to how Solomon could possibly disguise the way he looked. Mai was really going to have her work cut out, thought Parker. Judging by Mai's face as she climbed into the back, Parker figured she knew it too.

"I don't expect miracles," said Solomon. "Just a bit of color to my skin and lips. Did you bring the glasses and wig?"

Mai nodded and reached into one of the bags by Parker's feet. She handed Solomon a dark black wig speckled with gray, and a pair of sunglasses.

"And I found the stick, too," said Mai. She pulled out a small folded white stick and handed it to Solomon.

"I don't know how you managed all that in one afternoon. Excellent work, Mai. Thank you."

Mai gave a small smile. It was clear that Solomon's charm was starting to work on her.

"You're going to pretend you're blind?" asked Parker. "Won't they take the glasses off before they, er, start filming?"

"No, it doesn't matter what you're wearing," said Solomon. He stopped talking as Mai reached out and gingerly dotted Solomon's gray face with blobs of beige. Parker had many more questions, but he couldn't find a way of wording any of them without giving the game away, so he kept silent until Mai was finished.

Solomon slipped on his glasses and brushed his hand over his new hairdo. Mai held up a mirror to him, and Solomon inspected his new look.

"You are very talented, Miss Chan. Very talented indeed."

Parker couldn't believe the transformation. Solomon looked—almost—normal.

Mai blushed.

"Mai's cab should be there now," said Solomon to Brendan. "First gas station you come to on the Thruway, heading north."

"I know it," said Brendan. "Let's go."

Solomon spent the rest of the short journey making idle chat with Mai about her family. As soon as he'd waved her off with a reminder to send his best to her father and closed the door, he turned serious.

"Right, lots to do. Brendan, we have to be at Syracuse train station by half past ten—we can't be late."

"Plenty of time," said Brendan, pulling out of the gas station. "No traffic at this time of night."

"Good, good," said Solomon. "Thank you."

He turned to Parker and Emma. "We have a lot to discuss. First, you're sure you want to do this?"

Parker and Emma nodded. Though nerves were starting to set in, the whole plan still seemed somewhat surreal. It was hard to believe, even though they'd said yes, that this was not some kind of a game. Believing it was made it easier to go along with it all.

"Very well," said Solomon. "You'll need passports and papers."

He pulled three passports from the inside of his suit jacket. "They're just for show. It's important that you follow me in line and don't give your papers to anybody but the person I give them to. Understood?"

"Yes," said Parker.

"You're my children. I'm widowed. My name is James Marsh. You are Jennifer Marsh and Aaron Marsh."

Parker groaned as Michael let out a small laugh.

"Aaron?" asked Parker. "Do I have to be?"

"Not my choice—that's what the passports say. Jenny and Aaron. Okay?"

Parker and Emma nodded.

"Parker, if you need to speak, you'll have to put on an American accent—can you do that?"

"Not really," said Parker. "I'm no good at accents."

"Do your best—they're not going to be testing you. Maybe try not to speak too much."

"I won't speak at all," said Parker.

"Okay, that's fine—I'll do all the talking. Emma—you are not deaf," he said. "That'll draw attention to you. Just stay close to me and let me do all the talking. That goes for both of you."

"What if they realize it's us?" asked Parker.

"They won't," said Solomon. "Nobody's going to be expecting you to board the flight—they call it a flight, by the way. They won't be looking for you, or even know about you, probably. This is just the standard weekly departure for people going to work there. As long as we all keep our heads down and do our best to blend in, we'll be fine."

A bright-red-haired boy, a mute girl, and a blind father. Parker couldn't see how they could possibly blend in.

"Will it hurt?" signed Emma. Parker repeated the question.

"No, I promise you—you won't feel a thing."

"Will Effie still work when we get there?" asked Parker.

"Effie?"

Parker pointed to his wrist.

"Oh. Yes, absolutely. You arrive exactly as you left."

"We're here," called Brendan.

"Then all we have to do now is say our good-byes," said Solomon as Brendan pulled up at the drop-off point outside the busy station.

"Michael," said Solomon. "I was sorry I didn't get a chance to answer all your questions from the other day. I had—"

"That's okay," interrupted Michael. "Sorry I was rude."

Solomon smiled. "Not rude—inquisitive and skeptical—both excellent qualities." Solomon reached into his pocket and pulled out a small gold key with a small brown tag hanging from it. He held it out and placed it into Michael's hand.

"What's this?" asked Michael.

"This," said Solomon, "is a key to my laboratory. The address is on the tag. I haven't told anyone about it until now."

"Laboratory?" asked Parker.

Solomon nodded. "When things began to take an unsettling turn at Avecto, I began to do some work of my own."

"What work?"

"I started work on an Avectron."

"You built a teleporter?" asked Michael incredulously. He was still staring at the gold key resting on his outstretched hand.

"No. I started work on it, but I was never able to finish it."

"But . . . why are you giving it to me?"

"Two reasons," said Solomon. "One: I'm a man of my word. I promised you an explanation, and this will explain everything. And two: I wanted to know this information would be left in capable hands."

"I don't understand," said Michael. "What do you want me to do?"

"Finish my work," replied Solomon.

"But I don't know anything about this stuff," said Michael. His eyes were wide with confusion.

Solomon smiled. "You'll work it out."

Then, before Michael had a chance to reply, he turned to Brendan. "Thank you for taking care of them. And for driving us tonight."

"Not a problem," said Brendan. "My pleasure."

Solomon opened the car door and stepped out as Michael silently put the key in his pocket. "Take care, Michael," said Solomon. "Parker, Emma, you should say your good-byes here."

Emma leaned over the front seat and gave Brendan a kiss, then turned to Michael and gave him a hug. Michael leaned forward but kept his arms at his sides, clearly feeling awkward. "Bye—" Michael held up his hand and slowly signed the letters *E-M-M-D*.

Emma smiled. *"Bye, Michael,"* she signed back. She got out of the car, leaving only Parker to say his good-byes.

"Thank you, Brendan. For everything."

"You're welcome, Parker. It's been quite an adventure. You ever need anything, you know where I am."

Parker turned to Michael. He didn't know where to begin.

"See you later, Aaron," said Michael.

Parker smiled. "Ha ha," he said. His face turned serious. "Are you going to do it?"

Michael knew what Parker meant. "I'm going to try."

"So I'll see you there then, right?" said Parker. "This isn't good-bye."

Michael shook his head. "I don't know. I hope so."

For a moment neither of them spoke.

"Michael," said Parker finally, "thank you. I'm really—"

"Yeah, yeah. I know. Me too. Just go. Send me a postcard or something."

"I'll have to work out how to write *Wish you were here* in Gladstone Code."

Michael didn't respond immediately, and Parker realized he had tears in his eyes.

"So," said Michael gruffly, "have a good trip." He held out his hand.

Parker gave a small laugh and shook it stiffly. "It's been a pleasure working with you," he said in a businesslike voice.

"Yeah, yeah," said Michael. "You too."

Parker slid along the seat and stepped out. He leaned in, waved good-bye one last time, and closed the door behind him.

CHAPTER TWENTY-FIVE

"You have your tickets?" asked the man standing by the shuttle bus marked AVECTO CONVENTION.

"Yes, sir, I do," said Solomon in a strange, thick accent. Parker guessed it might be an attempt at a Southern accent. A terrible attempt.

Solomon reached into his jacket and pulled out a stack of papers.

"Aaron," drawled Solomon, "find the tickets, son."

Parker took the papers and mumbled something along the lines of "Yes, Dad." He didn't trust himself to speak up— though he wasn't sure his attempt at an American accent could be any worse than Solomon's.

Parker rummaged through the papers and realized he had no idea what he was looking for.

"Want some help with that?" asked the driver.

Parker nodded and handed the papers to the man, who took them and swiftly pulled out three pieces of paper.

"You're all set. You can leave your bags there," he said,

pointing to a pile of suitcases by the door. He handed the papers back to Parker. "Your dad need any help getting up there?"

"No, siree,' said Solomon. "My boy can sure show me the way."

Parker tried not to look as horrified as he felt. Fortunately, the driver didn't seem to pick up on anything out of the ordinary and had already turned to take the tickets of the two men in jeans and sweatshirts who had just arrived behind them.

Parker and Emma took their three bags and dumped them on top of the pile of suitcases. He grabbed Solomon's elbow and hurried him up onto the bus. There were maybe ten people on it—two women and the rest men, all sitting on their own at window seats. Every one of them looked up as they walked along the aisle to the row of empty seats at the back, but nobody said anything.

Parker let Emma take the seat by the window and then sat down himself and turned to whisper to Solomon.

"I don't think you should speak too much."

"Really?" replied Solomon. "I thought I sounded quite convincing."

Parker shook his head. "Not really. Sorry."

Solomon nodded. "I'll try toning it down a bit," said Solomon. "Thanks for letting me know."

The two men who had just boarded took the pair of seats in front of them.

"I don't get why they can't tell us how long the flight is," said the man in front of them.

"Right. Or at least which continent this place is in—it's not like that's going to blow their cover."

Continent? thought Parker. *Oh.* He pressed down on his wrist.

The men in front of us don't know about SIX.

What? replied Emma.

They think they're going to another continent or something. Just listen.

The men were now talking in hushed tones, and Parker leaned forward to listen. He repeated the conversation back to Emma.

"I don't know what it is—something just doesn't feel right," said the man by the window.

"I agree, man. The money's good though."

"I know, but we don't even know where we're going. I thought they'd have told us more by now. It's freaking me out. Maybe we should just leave now."

"Seriously? Come on, Joe—that's crazy. With the money they're paying us, we can do a couple of months—build a few walls or whatever they want—and come back with enough in the bank to take the rest of the year off. Whatever it is—it can't be that bad."

"It could be."

"Or not. Let's just go check it out—we don't have to stay the whole year. Okay?"

"Fine. But if I don't like it—I'm on the next flight back. You with me on that?"

"Sure, man, whatever."

Parker sat back and looked at Emma with wide eyes. **They have no idea.**

You have to say something, said Emma.

No way! said Parker. **We can't say anything.**

But they can't come back! They think they can leave.

Parker tensed his jaw and glared at Emma. **No way. And anyway, what am I going to tell them—"By the way, you're actually going to a different planet?" You think they're going to believe me?**

Emma shrugged. **You have to try, Parker. What if they have family here?**

Parker shook his head. **Then they'll see them when Dad works out how to teleport back. We can't bring any attention to ourselves right now.**

Emma bit her lip as she thought about what Parker was saying.

Okay. You're right, she said finally.

Parker leaned back in his seat and muted his thoughts on Effie. That fact was, he didn't like it any more than she did, but right now they had to think of themselves. If there was one thing Parker was certain of, it was that they wouldn't get a second chance to do this if they messed it up.

Emma nudged him. He turned to look at her, and she nodded in the direction of the front of the bus. He turned and saw—to his surprise—another child: a girl about six years old.

Both her parents were dressed in dark colors, both with the same serious look on their faces.

The girl saw Emma, and her face broke out into a wide grin. She tugged on the sleeve of her father's coat.

"Look, Daddy, there's another girl here!"

"Keep your voice down, Lily," said her father. "You can talk to the girl later."

Lily dropped her head but didn't say a word as she took a seat next to her mother.

"That's everyone," said the driver as he climbed back onto the bus. He sat down in the driver's seat and closed the doors. "We'll be there in about an hour."

One the men in front of them sat up. "The airport is ten minutes away," he called out.

"Private airport," the driver called back as he started the engine.

In their rush to leave, Parker hadn't given much thought to where they would be leaving from. At a push, he would have guessed that it would be from the offices of Avecto. It quickly became clear, once they crossed a security checkpoint and turned onto what appeared to be a completely empty field, that he would have been wrong. It seemed that Parker was not the only one confused—everybody on the bus, with the exception of Solomon and Lily, had their faces pressed up to the windows, searching the black landscape for anything that might resemble a terminal.

Parker could hear the two men murmuring urgently between themselves as the bus began to slow down, and Parker wondered if they were getting ready to make their escape. For their sakes, he hoped they were. The only problem with that, Parker thought, was that there was nowhere to run to—only what appeared to be miles and miles of grass in every direction. There were no streetlights, no people, no buildings, and no other vehicles. In the distance Parker could make out the faint glow of light from the security booth. It was the only visible light, barring the white headlight beams from their bus.

"What kind of an airport is this?" called out someone at the front.

The driver didn't respond. Parker turned to Solomon, and he leaned down and whispered in Parker's ear.

"The terminal is undergound. We're almost there."

Oh, mouthed Parker. He turned and signed to Emma what Solomon had said, and she raised her eyebrows in surprise. They both returned to staring out the window, searching for what might be the entrance. They didn't have to wait long.

Even under the full beams of the bus—and now knowing what to expect—the entrance to the terminal was not immediately obvious. It appeared, at first, as a far-reaching narrow black rectangle laid down on the grass. As the bus continued its approach, it became clear—to the alarm of everybody in the bus—that it was a hole. It was only when the bus looked like it was about to drop that Parker—who was not the only one gripping his armrest—realized that it was, in fact, a sloped runway.

"What is this?" asked someone as the bus began a smooth descent down into a long tunnel.

"The terminal is coming up," called out the driver. "Everything will be explained there."

Parker glanced around at the rest of the passengers on the bus and saw the same concerned expressions on the faces of all of them. As unsettling as this was, thought Parker, at least he knew what was really happening. He couldn't begin to imagine the confusion of anybody who didn't.

The black hole became a black metal wall ahead of them. The bus slowed down as it approached, and then came to a standstill. From where Parker was sitting, he wasn't able to see exactly what the driver was doing—though it seemed, from the way he was leaning to the side and murmuring something, that he was addressing an intercom.

The black wall slid open slowly, and a strong white light poured out from behind it. Parker could see nothing more, except what appeared to be a smooth white floor ahead of them. The bus started moving once more, and the white floor opened out to reveal an equally white room. It was, thought Parker, not unlike Michael's basement, except even shinier and sparser—if that were possible.

The bus parked and the doors opened. The driver stepped out, and one by one the passengers realized he was unloading their bags from the cargo. Everybody, except for Solomon, took this as their cue to leave.

"No rush," said Solomon. Ahead of them, the aisle was already full, as everybody waited to get off the bus. Parker watched as the two men in front of them had moved far enough along not to hear them. He turned to Solomon.

"They don't know they're going to SIX," whispered Parker.

"Who?"

"Those two men. They think they're taking an airplane somewhere."

Solomon nodded. He didn't look the least bit surprised. "Some don't, some do. It depends on what their level of security clearance is."

He pulled out the papers from his jacket.

"This," said Solomon, pointing to a large letter *I* on the right side of the ticket, "stands for 'informed.' That means that we know where we're going and how we're going to get there. Some tickets have *UI*—'uninformed.' I'm guessing that's what will be on those men's tickets. There's one other level—but they don't need tickets—*R*. Stands for 'resistant.' They may or may not know all the details—but they definitely do not want to go."

"Like Dad?" asked Parker.

Solomon nodded. "Come on, let's go."

The two men the last passengers apart from themselves— were now climbing down the stairs of the bus.

Solomon stood up and started to lead the way.

"You're supposed to be blind," said Parker.

Solomon shook his head and smiled. "Well remembered, Aaron."

"Thanks, Dad," said Parker. He sidled past Solomon and pretended to guide him forward and down the steps.

The driver was pulling out the last suitcase. Parker went over to their three bags, which were now lined up next to one another by the front wheel of the bus. His wrist buzzed.

What happens now? asked Emma.

Parker shrugged just as her question was answered. A wide smooth white door that Parker hadn't noticed slid open and a woman with blond hair—tied up into a neat bun— wearing a dark green suit and bright red lipstick stepped out. Everybody turned to face her.

"Ladies and gentlemen," she said with a warm smile on her face. "Welcome to the Avecto Terminal. My name is Grace, and I'll be your hostess today."

"Where are we going?" demanded a bearded man in an ill-fitting brown suit.

Grace walked up to him and placed her hand gently on his arm. "We'll explain everything inside."

She led the way toward the door, the man walking beside her.

"Did you have a pleasant journey?" Grace asked the man.

"It was fine—except nobody knows what's going on."

She wrinkled her nose and smiled apologetically. "I know—I'm so sorry. I wish we could make it less of a mystery, but it has to be that way for security. I hope it wasn't too unsettling."

The man shrugged and mumbled something along the lines of "It's okay."

Parker dropped back as he realized that Emma—who had taken on the task of guiding Solomon—was at the back of the group. Slowly, they followed the group through the doorway and into a warmly lit large space filled with tall plants, soft music, and rows of shiny black leather seats. On the far wall from where they came in, beside a set of steps leading up to another floor, a thin curtain of water fell gently in a small pond. Parker could see large orange fish gliding through the water.

This is nice, said Parker on Effie.

I know, said Emma. **It's not what I expected.**

Everybody seemed to be thinking the same thing, and the group visibly relaxed as they made their way over to the seats. Even the jumpy man who had been sitting ahead of them on the bus looked impressed.

Grace stood in front of them as everybody found their seats and settled, and three men, dressed in the same green uniforms, joined her at her side. One looked older than the rest—they were all smiling.

"Can I go look at the fish?" said Lily loudly, her back turned to the back of the room. *"Please?"*

"Sit down, Lily," muttered her mother.

Grace laughed. "It's fine. She can go and look. Just be careful."

Lily looked at her mother, who smiled and nodded. Lily beamed, jumped, and picked up her small red backpack carefully with both hands.

"You can leave it here," said her mother.

Grace hesitated for a moment and then nodded. She ran off.

Parker turned his attention back to Grace.

"Good evening, everybody, and welcome. We're delighted you're all here with us today, and we hope that your journey to SIX will be pleasant and smooth. Yes?"

Parker turned and saw that the jumpy man had his arm in the air.

"Where is SIX?"

A few people—*I*s, Parker guessed, shifted uncomfortably and looked away. Grace, however, seemed unfazed by the question.

"It will all be explained soon. I'm afraid at the moment I'm not at liberty to say anything for security reasons—just in case any of you should choose to leave before we board."

"Does that happen much?" asked the bearded man.

Grace shook her head. "Never, but we still have to be cautious."

Parker wondered if backing out at this point was really an option.

Grace turned to the three men at her side. "This is David," she said, introducing the older man, who smiled and gave a small wave. Grace leaned forward to look past him. "And

William and Nathan. If you need anything at all or have any questions, they'll be more than happy to help."

She turned back to face the passengers.

"Your luggage has already been delivered to the cargo hold, and we'll be ready to leave as soon as we've run through security."

Parker felt himself tense at the mention of security.

"We'll be calling passengers up to board by name. It shouldn't take too long. In the meantime, please do help yourselves to the complimentary drinks and snacks." She pointed to a full cart parked at the end of the first row of seats. "And one last thing. The bathrooms are over there, if you need to go, so please do make use of them before you board. Now, if there's anything . . ."

Something seemed to have caught Grace's eye, and everyone turned to see what it was.

"Why is the bag moving?" she asked. She was looking at the red backpack on the empty seat.

Parker couldn't see what Grace meant. Lily's mother looked down at the backpack with a confused look on her face and shrugged. "I don't see anything moving."

As soon as she spoke, the backpack shunted a fraction to the right and stopped again.

Lily's parents' eyes widened, and her father's head snapped around to the back.

"Lily!"

Lily, who was kneeling down by the pool of water, looked up.

"Come here!"

Lily stood up slowly and started to walk over. She look terrified.

"Now!"

Lily jumped and ran over.

"What's in there?" asked Lily's father.

Lily looked down at the backpack.

"Nothing," she whispered.

Her father reached over and picked up the bag. Lily's bottom lip began to wobble as her father zipped it open and, with a disapproving glance up at Lily, pulled out a small cardboard box with holes in the top of it.

"I didn't want to leave him," said Lily.

Grace walked over to the family and watched as the father opened up the top of the box.

"Oh!" said Grace. "Oh, dear."

Lily's mother turned to her daughter as her father began to apologize to Grace.

"What were you thinking, Lily? We told you he couldn't come."

Parker tried to get a look inside the open box.

Can you see? asked Emma on Effie.

Parker shook his head.

Grace sighed and knelt down next to Lily.

"Honey, I'm so sorry—but he can't come with us."

Lily looked up at her father. "Daddy? Please?"

She started to sob, and her mother took her hand and

pulled her onto her lap. She stroked her hair as her father turned to Grace.

"Is there no way? It's only a hamster," he said.

Grace shook her head. "I'm sorry. The instructions were very clear—no pets at all. You'll have to leave him."

She leaned forward and took the box from Lily's father's hands.

"No!" screamed Lily. She tried to reach forward, but her mother held her tightly.

Parker watched as Grace handed the box to William and whispered something in his ear. William nodded and walked away, leaving Lily screaming and sobbing behind her.

Parker heard muffled sobs. He turned to see Emma with her head down beside him, her body shaking with her sobs.

Emma? What's wrong?

Emma didn't answer. Instead she covered her head with her hands and kept crying.

Emma? Tell me what's wrong.

Finally, Emma lifted her head. She stared at Parker for a moment, her eyes red and her cheeks wet with her tears.

What's the matter?

I'm going to miss Polly, she said. And then she began to cry again.

Parker, not knowing what else to do, patted his sister awkwardly on the back.

She'll be okay, he said. **Michael will take care of her.**

Emma nodded but didn't say anything back as Grace

stood up and walked over to the long counter on the side of the room. She returned almost immediately, holding three purple drawstring bags.

Grace knelt down in front of Lily, who was still crying.

"Here you go, sweetie," said Grace.

Lily looked at the bag and then started crying loudly again.

Lily's mother took the bag. "Thank you," she said.

Grace placed her hand gently on Lily's mother's shoulder. "Why don't you take her over to the back until she calms down. We'll call you in a little while."

Lily's mother nodded, and she and her husband stood up.

"Poor kid," muttered a woman behind them.

Parker turned his head to watch as they made their way over to the pond at the back, when he saw, out of the corner of his eye, Grace walking over to where he was sitting.

"Here you go, honey," said Grace as she handed Emma one of the purple bags. "Are you okay?" she said upon seeing Emma's face.

"She's nervous," mumbled Parker.

Grace nodded. "You'll be fine," she said to Emma gently. She turned to Parker. "Would you like one too?"

Parker nodded, took the remaining bag, and then quietly thanked her. Grace smiled and walked back over to the counter where David, the older of the three male Avecto employees, was already waiting. Parker opened up the bag. Inside he found a coloring book, pens, candy, cards, and a handheld electronic game player.

He pulled it out and showed it to Emma, who gave a small smile and then turned back to her thoughts, leaving the purple bag unopened on her lap.

Parker didn't get to play his new game for long. They were the first to be called.

"Here we go," said Solomon. He had been surprisingly quiet since arriving at the terminal. Parker wondered if this had something to do with him commenting on his accent.

They walked over to the counter.

"I'll take this one," said David. "James is an old friend of the family."

Solomon nodded.

"Ah, how nice!" said Grace. She looked down at the list in her hand and called out another name as David ushered them over to a computer farther along the counter.

"You have all the papers with you?" asked David.

Parker nodded and placed the stack of passports and papers that Solomon had given him on the counter.

David checked the passports but made no comment on the fact that the pictures clearly didn't match any one of them. Parker stood in silence as David began to tap on his keyboard. He looked up and handed the passports and tickets back to Parker.

"You're all set. If you just go to William over there, he'll show you to your seats."

"Thank you," said Solomon in a quiet voice. "Thank you so much."

David looked down at his screen. "You're welcome," whispered David. "It's good to see you again, Dr. Gladstone."

"Thank you," said Solomon. He turned and let Emma lead him over to the open doors where William was waiting. They were halfway across the room when they crossed paths with Grace, leading one of the women passengers over to the counter.

Grace stopped and placed her hand on Solomon's arm. "Have a wonderful journey," she said with a bright smile.

Solomon smiled. "Thank you . . . you . . . you . . . you . . . you . . ."

Parker's eyes widened in horror as Grace watched Solomon with a look of growing concern on her face as he continued to repeat the word *you* over and over.

Solomon had no choice. He raised his hand, and Parker and Emma tensed as he slapped the back of his head and let out a loud shout.

"Alberta!"

Startled, Grace jumped back—just as Solomon broke into song.

"Albertaaaa! I'll miss you, Alberta! My beautiful land . . ."

Solomon nudged Emma to move on, and the three of them quickly walked off, leaving Grace behind them, looking perplexed.

Solomon stopped singing and breathed a quiet sigh but said nothing as they approached William. He took their tickets from Parker.

"Follow me," said William.

CHAPTER TWENTY-SIX

Parker's nerves returned as they walked through the door-way into a long black corridor, past four closed doors marked SAPPHIRE, DIAMOND, TOPAZ, and RUBY. They stopped at the door marked EMERALD. William pressed a gold button, and the doors opened to reveal another long corridor with silver metal doors running along both sides.

"We've put you all together in one of the family rooms," explained William. He led them down to the end of the corridor and pressed another button. The door opened to reveal four narrow black leather beds side by side in the center of the room.

"You don't need to do anything at all," said William. "Just lie down on the beds. You can leave your bags and anything else you don't want to carry on you anywhere on the floor—they'll be there when you arrive. There's no need to stay completely still, but we'd prefer it if you didn't move around too much."

William pointed up to a large white rectangle that took up most of the ceiling.

"The screen above you will turn on in a moment and show you a film—it will tell you when we're ready to go—" William stopped. "Oh. Sorry, sir. I wasn't thinking. The film has full audio too—you won't miss anything."

"Thank you," said Solomon.

"Is that all okay? Do you have any questions?"

Solomon shook his head. "No, we're fine."

"Do you need me to help you onto the bed?"

"No, no. My daughter can help me. Thank you."

"All right, then. Your flight will leave first—in about ten minutes," said William. "If you need anything at all, there's a button by your headrests to call for assistance. Enjoy the flight."

Solomon thanked him and William left the room. He waited until the doors had closed, and then he turned to Emma and Parker.

"We did it." He smiled.

Parker and Emma were too nervous to smile back.

"Ten minutes?" asked Parker.

"They don't want passengers getting restless. It will be fine," said Solomon. He walked over to the first bed and lay down.

Parker hesitated for a moment and then lay down on the bed next to Solomon. Emma took the one next to him. She turned to face him, and Parker felt his wrist buzz.

This is weird, said Emma.

I know. So weird.

I thought they'd put wires on us or something, said Emma.

Parker smiled. **Maybe it's a television show—one of those ones that pulls pranks on people, and in a moment Dad's going to walk in laughing with a camera crew.**

Emma's mouth dropped open. **I bet that's it! Oh no, Parker! We're going to look like idiots.**

Parker rolled his eyes. **Dad would never do that to us. That's, like, the meanest prank ever.**

Maybe Dad didn't know about it.

Emma. It was a joke. A television show would not kidnap Dad.

I don't know. Remember that show where a man pretended that he'd died and then he jumped up in his coffin when everybody was crying at the funeral?

Okay. That was pretty bad. But this isn't like that—I know it isn't.

Emma didn't look convinced. **Fine. But, if it is, we'll pretend like we knew it was a prank all along. Okay?**

Fine, said Parker.

There was a pause.

Parker?

Yes?

I'm scared.

Parker responded before he'd had a chance to mute his thought. **I'm scared too.**

Really?

A bit. But it will be fine. Let's just lie back and pretend we're at the cinema. I'm going to try to sleep.

Sleep?

Well, maybe not sleep—just rest. Thinking about things isn't going to help. Try it.

Okay, said Emma. She smiled at him as she pressed down on her wrist to end the call, then turned to face upward. Parker watched her close her eyes, then he turned to do the same.

After only a few minutes the silence in the room was broken by the sound of lapping waves. Parker opened his eyes and watched as the screen above him brightened. A gentle beach scene appeared—not unlike the one they had seen on the video Lina had given them.

"Welcome," said a soothing voice accompanied by subtitles at the bottom of the screen. "Your journey will commence shortly. In the meantime, please lie back and relax."

The gentle music grew louder, and the lights in the room dimmed to ultraviolet. Above him, on the screen, relaxing scenes of sand dunes, gently stirring water, and leaves blowing in the wind played. Parker could swear he could smell lavender.

Before long all his nerves had disappeared. Hypnotized by the combination of sights, sounds, and smells, Parker let himself fall into a half sleep.

He had no idea how long he'd been lying like that when the peaceful state he had fallen into was interrupted by the sound of Solomon's voice.

"Parker," whispered Solomon.

Parker turned his head to face Solomon. "Yes?"

"Your wrist thing—is it on? Can Emma hear anything at the moment?"

"No," said Parker, "it's not on."

"Good. Leave it off for a moment. I need to say something. You can tell Emma when you get there—I don't want to upset her now."

Parker stopped himself from sitting up. "What's wrong?" he asked.

"When we get to SIX, I need you to take Emma and get out of the terminal there quickly. Leave me. Do you understand?"

"*What?* Why? They don't know who you are."

"Just do what I say. Leave with Emma and find your father straightaway. Your wrist thing will work there—exactly as it did here."

"But . . . *why*? . . . What about you?"

Solomon didn't say anything for a moment.

"Solomon?"

"Parker, I wasn't being completely honest with you about the effects of a third teleportation on me."

"What do you mean?" asked Parker.

Solomon stared back at Parker but said nothing, as if he were waiting for Parker to work it out for himself.

Parker tried to remember what Solomon had told him, but his mind was still groggy from his near-sleep, and he couldn't recall the conversation at all. Eventually, though, he remembered and, when he did, the true meaning behind Solomon's words came to him all at once—clear and devastating, like an invisible punch to the stomach that knocked his whole body forward and pushed all the air of out him, leaving him unable to breathe.

A third teleportation was going to kill Solomon.

When Parker finally spoke, his voice was weak. *"Why?"* It was all he could manage to say.

Solomon seemed to know that Parker had worked it out. "Because I had to."

"Your flight will commence in two minutes. Please lie back, relax, and enjoy."

A surge of panic ran through Parker.

"You can't do this!" he said. He leaned over the side of his bed, his head spinning and his heart thumping loudly as he searched for the assistance button.

"Parker, stop!" said Solomon. "I'm going! If I don't go—you don't go."

"But why, Solomon . . . Why would you do that?" He couldn't help himself; he was starting to cry.

Solomon took a deep breath. "I had no idea that they were going to take your mother."

Parker wiped his cheek with the back of his hand. "I don't understand. . . . I don't understand what you're saying."

"I was the one who asked your mother to come and help with the work we were doing. If I'd known—if I'd had any idea at all that they were going to send her to SIX—I wouldn't have done it. I promise you."

"What?" whispered Parker.

"Your mother, Parker. She's on SIX. She's alive."

Parker stared at Solomon. His whole body was shaking. He couldn't breathe. He couldn't think.

"One minute to avection."

"When I realized, I went after her," continued Solomon, talking quickly. "I went to SIX, and they sent me back, think-ing it would kill me. When it didn't—they locked me up. I couldn't get ahold of anyone until Lina's father made contact with me. I called your father and explained everything. That's why your dad came here and offered to fix the problem of multiple teleportations. He made a deal with Bowveld—he'd fix it and she would be allowed to return."

Parker was crying too hard to speak.

"I'm so sorry, Parker."

"Please, Solomon," said Parker, struggling to get his words out. "Please don't do this. . . ."

"Avection commencing in ten seconds."

"It's okay. I'm not scared. I'm ready, Parker. I've had a good run."

"But . . ."

"Five . . . four . . ."

"Send my love to your parents."

Solomon smiled and turned to look up at the screen. Through his own tears, Parker saw a single tear run down the side of Solomon's face, drawing a line of gray as it ran down his beige cheek.

"Avection initiated."

"Solomon!"

Parker never had a chance to thank him.

Everything turned black.

CHAPTER TWENTY-SEVEN

When Parker regained consciousness, he didn't immediately remember what had just happened. His whole body was tingling—the sensation stronger in some parts than in others. It was distracting. Something in his mind, though, was reaching out to Parker. Something unsettling. He was too dazed to work out what it was.

When he was seven, he'd had his tonsils out. Coming around from the general anesthetic, he'd felt as if he'd woken up inside a dream—conscious, but not conscious. It was this same feeling that he was experiencing now. He moved his head slowly to the side and stared down at his left hand. It had no fingers. He watched with interest, but no alarm whatsoever, as his thumb slowly appeared, followed by the next finger, and then the next.

He became aware of the loud humming noise only when it stopped. At the same time, the vibrations in his body disappeared. Parker felt his head begin to clear.

Slowly he began to remember—fragments of sights, sounds,

and conversations coming together like tiny pieces of a huge jigsaw.

A little girl crying. A long dark tunnel. A woman in a green uniform. Grace, that was her name. The smell of lavender. Solomon singing.

Solomon.

Parker's head snapped around.

Just for a moment Parker thought he was mistaken. Solomon was there right next to him. At first glance he looked the same as he had the last time Parker had seen him. He was staring upward and wearing his suit, which appeared perfectly intact, and the skin that was visible was still the same beige color of the makeup that had been covering him. Then he saw that Solomon's hair was gone.

Parker sat up straight. It was only then—when he had full view of Solomon's body, that the full horror of what had happened became apparent. All the features of Solomon's face had disappeared. Just two black holes for his nostrils and one for his mouth. No eyes, no nose, no lips. No ears. He looked so blank—so unhuman—that Parker couldn't really think of it as Solomon—not until he heard a noise coming from the black void of Solomon's mouth—a single, long, drawn-out gasp for breath.

He was still alive.

Parker's first instinct was to jump up and run to Solomon's aid, but fear, and the knowledge that there was nothing he could possibly do to help, rendered him frozen. Staring helplessly, Parker watched as the gasp ended and Solomon's body began to shake.

Finally, with one last violent convulsion, Solomon's body came to rest. There was no more movement, no noise, no nothing.

Solomon was gone.

The finality of that thought barely had time to register when Parker realized that the doors would open soon. Solomon's words came back to him:

Take Emma and get out of the terminal.

He hadn't checked on her, but then she hadn't called him on Effie. *Please,* thought Parker as he turned around, *let her be awake and alert.*

She was, Parker found, already sitting up. Her head was bowed, one hand holding her other, palm up.

Parker jumped off the bed and stepped over to her.

She didn't move.

He reached out and grabbed her arm. She lifted her head slowly. Her eyes were wide but her expression was blank, as if she were in a daze. For a moment Parker thought that she must have seen Solomon, but then she lifted her hand in front of his face and turned it to show him her wrist.

Parker stared at it and then, silently, looked down and turned over his own hand. It was the same.

Three glowing dots of light.

He had been so focused on what was happening to Solomon that he hadn't had time to think about what Solomon had told him.

He saw Emma press down on the light for him. He answered it and put his own thoughts on mute.

It's broken; it's just noise when I try to press it, she said. **I saw it when I woke up. I thought Mum was here.**

She looked up at Parker.

Parker? Are you crying?

Parker hesitated. *Just repeat exactly what Solomon told you,* he thought. His hand was reaching out to unmute Effie when a sharp gasp from Emma interrupted him. Parker looked at her and saw that her eyes were fixed in the direction of where Solomon's body was lying.

She began to scream.

Parker didn't have a chance to explain anything. She was still screaming as the doors opened and a brilliant white light swept into the room.

Shocked into silence, they both froze as a silhouetted figure stepped forward and revealed himself.

It was a young man, maybe only a few years older than Parker. He was staring at Parker and Emma with a look of concern, or confusion, on his face. Perhaps both. Parker registered this before he looked down at the purple blazer the man was wearing. There, embroidered in gold on the breast pocket, were three bold letters: *SIX.*

Despite having seen the effects of the avection on Solomon and despite everything that had happened up until that point, it wasn't—for some reason—until he saw the number on the jacket that it all suddenly felt real to Parker. Any uncertainty he may have had about anything he had been told disappeared at that very moment.

He was here. On SIX. And beside him, a man was lying dead.

"Everything okay?" asked the man.

His voice snapped Parker into action. He grabbed Emma's arm as he pressed down on his wrist.

We have to go!

Emma didn't react.

Emma! We have to get out of here!

He pulled her arm and she stepped forward.

"Fine, thank you," said Parker.

His voice wasn't able to hide his panic. Before the man could say anything else, Parker took Emma by the arm and hurried her past the man and out into the corridor.

Parker checked behind him. The man had his back to them. He wasn't moving. Parker could guess why.

Parker looked around him. On the other side of the corridor, the side he had just come from, a line of doors ran both ways. At one end, a door blocked the way; at the other, an open turning. Parker had no way of knowing which one would lead to the exit. He chose to head in the direction of the turning. He grabbed Emma—who was still numb with shock—and began to run toward it just as a shout rang out from the room they had just left.

"Assistance needed!"

Though Emma was by his side, it was only because Parker was dragging her with him.

"Emma! Please! If they find we came with Solomon . . ."

She stopped just as they reached the turning in the corridor.

He's dead, she said flatly.

Yes. Emma, listen to me. We have to find Dad.

Dad?

The mention of their father seemed to have woken up something in Emma.

Yes, Dad. Please, Emma. I'll explain everything—but we need to get out of here.

Emma looked at Parker, and her eyes began to well up with tears. She nodded.

Okay.

She understood.

On the count of three, we run. Don't stop until I say. Ready?

Yes, said Emma.

Okay, one . . . two . . . three . . . go!

Parker and Emma ran forward, turned at the same time, and broke into a sprint toward an open archway.

They were almost there when two large men in black jackets appeared. They both glanced over at Emma and Parker as they ran straight past them in the direction of the shouts for help.

Parker knew it wouldn't be long before they came back for them. He sped up, and Emma, now looking completely focused, did the same.

They didn't stop. Not when they ran out into an empty lobby, nor when they saw the three large gold letters on the wall or the purple trees dotted around the space. They didn't even stop when their wrists began to vibrate.

Parker was the first to speak.

Dad! Where are you?

Parker? Is it really you?

Daddy?

Emma?

It was the moment they'd both been waiting for ever since their father had been taken, but Parker had no time to celebrate as a shout came from behind them.

Stop them!

Keep running, Emma!

Parker! Where are you?

We're at the terminal. They found Solomon.

Daddy, said Emma. **He's dead.**

There was a moment's silence.

Get out of there now.

We're running. We don't know where to go.

Are you in the lobby? Can you see the gold letters on the wall?

We just passed them.

Keep going. You'll see some elevators on your right and then a row of doors. Take the . . . second one—you'll find stairs. Go down one flight and you'll see the exit door ahead of you. It leads you outside. There

are restaurants and cafés all along the seafront. **Find somewhere to hide. We're on our way.**

Okay, said Parker. He went to speed up, then realized that Emma was starting to fall behind.

Emma! Hurry up!

Emma nodded, and Parker saw her will herself to go faster.

Parker pointed to the entrance **See it?**

Yes, said Emma. They both sped up.

Parker wasn't sure when he lost Emma. One moment she was next to him, the next he was running through the door of the stairwell on his own.

Parker spun around and saw—just before the door slammed shut—Emma kicking wildly as the two men they had passed earlier dragged her away. Both men were looking around them as they pushed Emma forward. Parker realized that they hadn't seen him.

He could have run down the stairs. He could have found somewhere to hide. Then, when his dad turned up, they could have gone back to get Emma together. That may have been the sensible thing to do but, for Parker, there was never even a moment of doubt in his mind. He opened the door and stepped back out into the lobby.

CHAPTER TWENTY-EIGHT

We're on our way; that was what his father had said. It was all Parker could think about as he sat with Emma in the avection chamber, on the bed farthest from where Solomon's lifeless body still lay untouched.

When they'd told their father they had been caught, he'd repeated it.

We're on our way.

We're.

Meanwhile Parker and Emma could do nothing but wait, their backs turned away from Solomon, the two guards watching their every movement closely. So far a stream of people had come and gone. Some had asked them questions, none of which either Parker or Emma had answered. Not one of them seemed to have any idea what it was that had happened to Solomon. They were all in agreement, however, that whatever it was, it was very serious indeed. Now they were waiting from someone in senior management to arrive.

Parker stared down at his wrist. The middle light was still

on. Of everything that had happened in the last hour, this was the most surreal of them all. He had dreamed about this happening for three years, and yet he couldn't bring himself to press down on his mother's light. Not that there would have been any point anyway; Effie's signal couldn't get past the thick walls of the chamber.

While they'd waited, Parker had told Emma everything that Solomon had said before the avection. She had reacted in much the same way as he had—with shock and then tears. After that they had sat next to each other in silence—both lost in a tornado of thoughts—until the doors opened and a group of people walked in, headed by an extravagant-look-ing large woman in a black tunic, oversize sunglasses, and swathes of gold jewelry hanging from her neck and wrists. Her dark brown perfectly styled hair bounced as she strode into the room.

"Where is he?" she asked. She didn't acknowledge Parker or Emma.

The man in a dark suit on her right—a tall pale man with a long face and closely set eyes—motioned to his right. Parker had met him earlier when he'd attempted to question Parker and Emma. He had introduced himself to them as Anderson. Parker guessed, by the fact that he was the only other person apart from the woman not wearing a purple blazer, that he was more senior than the rest of the people in the room. Apart from the woman, of course. Just by the way she conducted herself, it was clear that she was very much the one in charge.

The woman said nothing. Parker, along with everybody else in the room, turned to watch as she walked over to the body of Solomon. She removed her sunglasses and held them out to her side. A young woman with red hair ran forward and took them from her.

"What do we know about him?" asked the woman as she prodded Solomon's body.

"His papers say that his name is James Marsh—a fifty-eight-year-old NASA engineer from Florida. He's blind and widowed. It's about all we know," said Anderson.

"Are those his children?" asked the woman without looking away from Solomon.

"Yes," said Anderson. He walked up to the woman and, though he kept his voice down, Parker was still able to hear what he said. "They're not talking. We think they're in shock."

The woman turned around. "I'd like you all to leave."

Nobody argued. They all turned and walked straight out.

"You too," she said to the guards. "Out."

One of the guards appeared to hesitate. "Are you sure that's safe?"

"Don't be ridiculous," snapped the woman.

"Yes, President. Of course. We'll wait outside," said the guard as he withdrew quickly from the room.

Parker stood, pulling Emma up with him.

"Not you. Sit down."

Parker said nothing but sat back down slowly. The woman walked over to them and waited until the doors closed.

Parker steeled himself. She did not look like somebody who was going to accept their silence easily. It was, though, the only thing he could think of doing. He would call his father when they were out of the chamber, but for now they were on their own once again.

"I am Genevieve Bowveld—President of SIX. I want you to answer my questions—do you understand?"

Parker was surprised to hear the Bowveld name—but he didn't allow himself to show any reaction.

"How do you know Solomon?"

The question was so completely unexpected that Parker flinched in surprise. It was the first time he'd reacted in any way since they'd been brought back to the chamber. Annoyed with himself, Parker looked down at his lap.

"You might as well tell me now," said Genevieve. "One way or another, we'll get the information from you."

Her voice was slow and threatening.

"His name is James Marsh," said Parker quietly. "He's my dad." He didn't look up.

"No," said Genevieve. "His name is not James Marsh. His name—as you full well know—is Solomon Gladstone. And Solomon Gladstone did not have any children. It may not be obvious to the thickheaded people who work for me, but I know a multiple avection when I see one. We've only ever sent back one person who survived. That person, as I'm sure you know, was Solomon Gladstone. So, I'll repeat my question—how do you know Solomon?"

Parker shook his head.

"Very well. Then answer this for me—who are you?"

"Aaron Marsh," said Parker. "My sister is Jenny Marsh."

Emma kept her head down.

If she doubted this, Genevieve didn't mention it. "Why did Solomon bring you here?" she asked instead.

Out of the corner of his eye, he saw Emma's hand going to her wrist.

Don't tell her anything, she said.

I won't, replied Parker.

Genevieve was silent. Parker didn't dare to look up.

"You leave me no choice," said Genevieve as she walked away.

Parker's head snapped up, and he saw Genevieve pressing a button in the wall. The doors slid open. The group of people outside saw her and straightened to attention. She motioned for Anderson to come forward, then she turned and fixed Parker with a stare.

"Send them back," she said.

Parker's eyes widened.

Anderson looked equally shocked. "But that would be a second avection for them. It will—"

"I know what a second avection means, Anderson. Send them back."

Anderson shifted uncomfortably and glanced over at Parker and Emma. "But, Genevieve, they're just children."

"Are you arguing with me?"

Anderson shook his head. "No, President. Of course not. It's just that—"

"Do you know who that man is?" interrupted Genevieve, turning to face Solomon's body.

Anderson shook his head.

"I'll give you a hint, Anderson: it's a multiple avection."

Anderson thought about this for a moment until the answer came to him, and his mouth dropped open.

"*Solomon?*"

"Exactly."

"But why?" He lowered his voice. "And who are they?"

"They're not talking and, frankly, it's irrelevant—we're not running a day-care center. The whole matter makes me very uncomfortable."

"But—"

"We don't need this kind of complication on SIX, Anderson. My decision is final. I want those children gone."

Parker wondered if she was letting them hear this so that they would react. It almost worked—Parker was half ready to say something in protest—but he stopped himself; he didn't know what to say. He couldn't tell her the truth—he was sure that would be no more welcome than their silence. And talking would mean telling them that they had come after their father. He had no idea what trouble that might cause his parents. He decided to keep quiet until he could think of a better way out of it.

"When?" asked Anderson.

"Now."

Parker froze.

"Send them straight back," she continued. "Put them into one of the resistant chambers—they'll need to be strapped down."

Anderson leaned over and whispered something in Genevieve's ear. She nodded, and then they both stepped onto the other side of the doorway. Genevieve waved for everybody gathered outside to leave. They scurried off, and Anderson and Genevieve began a whispered discussion out of earshot of Emma and Parker.

Parker! said Emma on Effie.

Parker realized that he couldn't wait any longer. He looked at the open doorway.

Emma. We have to run.

They'll catch us.

We have no choice. We can't get ahold of Dad in here. Ready?

He looked over at Emma. She nodded.

At the same time, they both stood up and then, before Genevieve or Anderson had a chance to react, Parker and Emma ran out and down the corridor.

"Stop them!" shouted Anderson.

They sprinted back along the same corridor that they had run down only moments earlier. This time, however, they didn't even manage to reach the turning. The two guards must have been waiting right there, and they had called for backup—there were at least six guards behind them. The group of guards stepped out, and there was not a thing that Parker or Emma could do about it—they ran straight into them.

Genevieve walked over to them slowly as Parker and Emma kicked and struggled in an attempt to escape. She reached out to Parker's face and grabbed his chin, then lifted his face up to hers. Parker didn't stop struggling—his face contorted with the effort of trying to get away.

"Now that wasn't very clever, was it, darling?"

She looked up at the guards. "Sapphire. Now."

Emma began to scream as the guards dragged them over to the nearest door.

"Help!" shouted Parker as the door slid open and the guard dragged him inside. Parker twisted and kicked and tried to reach his wrist to call his dad as another guard stepped in to help. They each took one of Parker's arms.

"Somebody help us!" shouted Parker as the men dragged him into the chamber.

Emma screamed louder as the guard dragged her over to the nearest bed. She kicked and fought as hard as she could, but the man was too strong. Genevieve walked over and watched as the guard lifted Emma onto the bed. Another guard stepped in and pulled up a strap from the side of the bed. Emma was still screaming as he pinned her hand down and began to wrap the strap around her wrist. He was about to secure it when a voice stopped him.

"Let go of them."

Everybody froze.

Parker turned.

There, standing the doorway, was his father.

Parker could only stare, as if he couldn't quite believe it was really him. He heard Emma gasp, but neither she nor anybody else said a word as Parker's father stepped into the room and walked over to Genevieve.

"Let them go. Now."

Parker felt the grips loosen slightly on his arms, but the guards did not let him go.

Genevieve and their father locked eyes.

"Dr. Banks. This is all starting to make sense now."

"Give me my children."

Genevieve shook her head. "I'm afraid that won't be possible, Dr. Banks. Your children are unauthorized to be on SIX."

Parker watched, transfixed at the transformation of his father as he glared back at Genevieve. If his dad was scared, he had a good way of hiding it.

"My children are here because I am here," he said. "It seems you underestimated what I would do to bring my family together."

Genevieve narrowed her eyes at their father. Parker could hardly breathe. He had already seen what Genevieve was capable of.

"Get back to work, Dr. Banks. If you want your children, you will get the job done."

Parker's father looked down. For a moment Parker thought he was going to give up—that he was going to leave them here and do as Genevieve was telling him. But then his father lifted his head, and Parker saw the anger and steel in his father's eyes. His father would be doing no such thing.

"For three years," said Parker's father, his voice strong and low, "I have let you and your brother dictate the course of my life. I allowed it because I am a father and a husband. My children and my wife are all that matter to me. You see that as a weakness, but you are wrong. They are my strength, my reason for living, and I would have done anything to keep us together. Now they are here—we are here together—and you have no more power over me."

"How dare you?" asked Genevieve. "You listen to me—"

Their father put his hand up. "Stop."

Parker guessed that Genevieve was not used to being told to do anything. She closed her mouth.

"I think," said Parker's father, "that it's time for *you* to listen to *me*."

Parker's father paused. Genevieve did not respond.

"My children are leaving with me. Now. You will grant them full citizenship of SIX without restriction, by the end of the day. My wife, my children, and I will live here freely. There will be no more threats and there will not be any attempt to break my family up. In exchange, we will finish the work that you need us to do."

Genevieve opened her mouth to say something, then closed it again.

"If you do not keep to this arrangement," continued Parker's father, "then you will have to explain to your investors why a solution was never found."

He glared at Genevieve, his jaw locked tight. "I hope that I have made myself clear."

The whole room was completely silent as he looked away from Genevieve.

"Parker," he said. "Emma. We're leaving."

The guards appeared to hesitate. They all looked over at Genevieve, who didn't say anything.

Then, still staring at Parker's father, she gave a slow nod.

The guards stepped back, and Parker and Emma ran to their father.

Parker's father didn't say anything as he walked hand in hand with Emma and Parker down the corridor and through the lobby. They took the elevator in silence—their father stroking their newly dyed hair. He didn't say a word about it. He didn't say anything. When the elevator doors opened, he took them across the lobby and through the main doors. He didn't stop until they crossed the doors of the terminal and stepped out into the brilliant sunshine.

Parker found himself standing on a sidewalk made of sparkling white marble. Framed ahead of them by two towering palm trees with purple leaves was a pure white sandy beach that led out to the still waters of the bluest sea that Parker had ever seen. Parker turned to their father as he knelt down in front of them and took them both into his arms.

Parker and Emma wrapped their arms around his neck as their father gripped them tight.

"I'm so sorry," he said. "I'm so, so sorry."

In response Parker clung tighter, burying his head in his father's neck. They stayed like this until, finally, their father lifted his head. Parker saw his father's eyes were red, but he was smiling.

"I can't believe it," said his father. He gave a small laugh. "I can't believe you're here."

Parker looked at his father. He had to say something.

"Dad. Solomon told us that—"

"Your mother?"

Parker nodded.

Their father nodded back. "You do know that she had no choice?"

"I know," said Parker. "Where is she?"

Parker's father stood up. "She left as soon as I called her. She'll be here any . . ."

He stopped. Parker looked up and saw his father was looking down the sidewalk. He and Emma both turned their heads.

Even at a distance Parker knew it was her. She was running, black shoes in one hand, her head down.

And then she looked up and saw them.

For a moment they all stood frozen—staring at one another across the distance—as if none of them could believe this moment was real.

Parker let go of his father and ran toward her.

PART III

SIX

They had waded out at least a mile, and the water was still only up to Parker's knees.

As he waited for Emma to catch up with him, he looked down at his toes, tanned and clearly visible through the shallow water. He wriggled them into the smooth sand. There were no fragments of shells, no seaweed, and no fish. Not yet. There were talks about introducing fish to SIX, but that wouldn't be for a while yet. Parker had only been on SIX for two weeks, but already he knew it took a long time for anything to happen here.

He felt a splash of water hit him on his back, and he turned to see Emma grinning.

"We have to go back," she signed. *"Lunch is ready."*

Parker turned. His mother was standing on the deck outside their house—a white-stoned villa with wood-framed windows and purple ivy draped along the veranda that ran the length of the house.

She waved. Emma and Parker stomped quickly back

through the water and ran across the beach and up the wooden steps to where she was standing, two blue towels in her hand. In the two weeks since they had arrived, she had changed. She looked less gaunt, and she looked as if she had slept.

She wrapped one towel around Parker first and kissed the side of his head.

"I'll bring lunch out," she said as she wrapped the other towel around Emma. They had been offered a chef—most of the elite on SIX had them—but their parents had turned the offer down.

Parker and Emma sat down at the wooden table. There was no need to change out of their swimsuits—it was warm. It was always warm.

Their mother brought out a tray of bread, vegetables, fruit, meats, and two tall glasses of juice. She placed it in front of them and went back in, returning a few moments later with plates and cutlery.

"Geoffrey!" she called as she sat down.

Their father emerged from the house. He looked tanned and rested. He held up two thick books.

"Catalogs have arrived," he said.

He placed them on the table and sat down.

"What do we do with them?" asked Parker.

"Just go through them and mark whatever you need—clothes, toys. You can each get a computer too."

Parker and Emma both nodded, but neither said anything.

"And don't forget school starts next week," added their

mother. "So make sure you get everything you need for that—
I've left the list on the kitchen counter."

Parker's father looked down at his watch. "We need to eat
up, Sarah."

He reached out and grabbed a piece of bread, and the rest
of them followed suit.

"We'll be back around six," said their mother as she picked up
their empty plates.

"What are you going to do?" asked their father.

Parker shrugged. "Probably go to the club."

The Bowveld Country Club was where Parker and Emma
had spent most of their days since arriving. It had tennis
courts, six pools—one with slides and a wave machine—and,
sometimes, other children.

"Okay, good," said their father. "Have fun." He and their
mother both gave them each a kiss and left to go to work.

Parker reached over and grabbed the two thick catalogs.
He handed one to Emma, and then opened his and turned
on Effie.

Wow, said Parker. **There's so much stuff.**

He flicked through the pages and stopped at one filled
with colorful photographs—row upon row of every toy imaginable. All he had to do was place a tick under any picture
and, within days, whatever item he'd chosen would be his.
He should have felt excited, but instead he felt strangely
indifferent.

Look at this, said Emma. She raised her catalog up to show Parker a double page filled with pictures of bicycles. She had a sad smile on her face.

But no goats for Africa, said Parker.

Emma frowned. **Don't joke about it, Parker.**

I'm not.

His sister sat back in surprise and stared at Parker. **Really?**

Parker nodded, then quickly looked back down. Even though they were talking on Effie, it still unnerved him. The cameras and microphones were hidden, but they both knew they were there, listening to every spoken word—watching for any sign of rebellion.

Complete loyalty—that was a condition of living on SIX. They were the first wave of citizens. Soon—though the booklet didn't say when—the Exodus would be taking place, and those who had been given a ticket to SIX would leave Earth. The investors, and whoever they chose to bring with them, would arrive to live here forever. When that happened, it would be the responsibility of anybody already on SIX—of the Ambassadors, as they were called—to welcome the new arrivals and show them how good life on SIX was. In bold black letters, the booklet had clearly stated the penalty for not complying—expulsion from SIX.

Do you think we could ask for the money instead— and tell them to use it back on Earth? asked Emma, interrupting Parker's thoughts.

You know we can't, said Parker. **They'd throw us out of here before we even finished asking the question.**

So what are we supposed to do? Nothing?

Parker sighed. **I don't know. I just don't want to get us—or Mum and Dad—into trouble.**

Emma dropped her shoulders in defeat. Despondently, she reached out, grabbed a pen, and began to make marks in the catalog. Parker took the other pen and looked down for a moment, then gave up; he was too distracted. He closed the book and looked out at the white sand and sea.

Neither Parker nor Emma had said anything to their parents about how unhappy they felt about their new life. It seemed so—well—ungrateful. They had been reunited with both parents, after all, and in a world without crime or hunger, where everything they wanted was theirs at the mark of a pencil. And yet, or rather because of that, it felt so wrong.

The problem was that the more Parker learned about the Exodus, the more he felt disgusted at the injustice of it. Emma had been teasing him—during their talks on Effie— that he was sounding more like her every day, and Parker couldn't deny it. Everybody, it seemed, was in a state of frenzied excitement at the arrival of the new citizens—perhaps influenced by the propaganda on television and in the newspaper—and yet there had not been a single mention about the fate of the ones who would be left behind. Who, he wondered, would be picked? And who had the right to make those choices?

Of all the people Parker knew, he expected that Michael would be the most likely to end up here—purely by virtue of his parents' wealth. But what about his family and friends back in England? Brendan or Anteater? Or even Polly?

The more Parker thought about it, the more he thought of the Exodus as a lottery of the worst kind. And yet—*and yet*—he was already one of the winners. He was here, sitting in what was meant to be paradise—so why could he think about nothing but how to change things? Right now he knew he was powerless to do anything. Until that changed—and it was possible that wouldn't happen until he was older—he would just have to learn to stop thinking about his old life. In time, and with enough practice, he hoped he might eventually learn to be happy here.

Practice, after all, makes perfect.

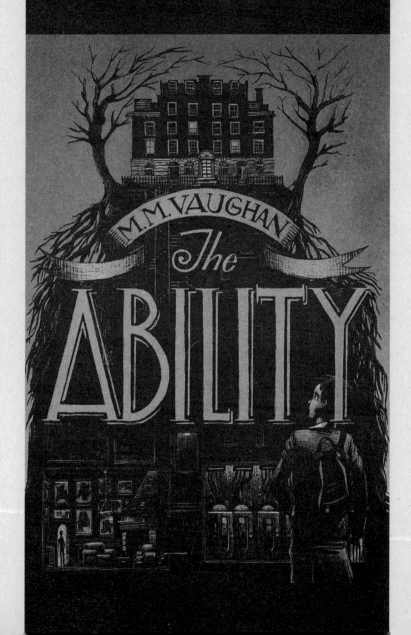

Thirty Years Ago

"I have a bad feeling about this," said Edward, tapping his foot nervously. The sound of his shoe hitting the metal floor of the van echoed all about the enclosed space, masking the sound of the waves that crashed furiously at the foot of the cliffs that stood not far from where they were parked. *Tap. Tap. Tap.*

Anna gave Edward a warning look as their teacher, Mr. Cecil Humphries, turned round from the driver's seat, his face red with anger.

"Stop that right now or I'll throw your shoes out of the window."

Edward didn't say anything, but the tapping stopped. Mr. Humphries turned to Miss Arabella Magenta, sitting next to him in the passenger seat, and sighed.

"Honestly, what have I done to deserve this? As soon as this year is over, I'm moving to the country—as far away from any brats as possible."

"We can hear you, sir."

"Good," said Mr. Humphries, without looking back.

Anna said nothing as the four other children whispered around her. She felt the anxiety of the group deeply and hoped the mission would end quickly so that they could return to their school, far away from this desolate, dark landscape.

At that moment, exactly as their carefully planned schedule dictated, Mr. Bentley Jones was carrying the briefcase full of money toward the cottage by the cliff. Their view of the cottage was hidden by the wall of trees behind which they had parked the van, but Anna could see exactly what was happening—it was her and Clarissa's job that night to use their Ability to keep an eye on their teacher.

"Mr. Jones is nearly at the cottage. There's a light on in the window."

"Good," said Miss Magenta. "As soon as he's inside, we'll get out and move closer."

"Why do we have to get out? Can't we just do it from here?" asked Danny nervously.

"For goodness' sake, we've gone over this a thousand times," said Miss Magenta, looking exasperated. "If we're going to wipe the minds of these people, then we need to be within twenty feet of them."

"Can't we just give them the money?" asked Danny.

Anna, Edward, Clarissa, and Richard all nodded in agreement.

"Don't be ridiculous," said Mr. Humphries. "It will only be a short time before they ask for more, and then when will it stop? If we don't want people to find out about the Ability—and believe me, we don't—then we have to use Inferno on them. It's the only way."

"But we've never even practiced it—what if it doesn't work?" asked Clarissa.

"It will," said Miss Magenta, irritated. "It's been tried out in Italy, where the rules are more relaxed, and it worked just fine. Where is he now?"

Anna and Clarissa remembered what they were supposed to be doing and closed their eyes.

"He's not there yet—probably another minute."

Anna kept her eyes closed and watched Bentley Jones striding forward, head bowed low as he fought his way through the invisible wall that the vicious wind and rain had created.

"Don't do that!"

Anna opened her eyes and saw Richard, who was almost twice the size of the other two boys, flicking screwed-up pieces of paper resting on his knee in the direction of Danny.

"What? I'm bored," said Richard, seeing the look of disapproval on Miss Magenta's face.

Anna sighed and closed her eyes. They had been class-mates for just over five months, and she was only slightly less irritated by Richard than she had been on day one, when he had spent the entire morning pulling her long braid of black hair and then laughing hysterically. Clarissa had told her it was a sure sign that Richard liked her—a thought that made Anna's stomach turn. The other two boys, however, Danny and Edward, had become her close friends. Edward was serious and calm, always trying to keep the peace between Richard and whoever he was irritating on any particular day; Danny, on the other hand, was sweet and clumsy, his head always stuck in a book.

"He's coming up to the door," said Clarissa. Everybody stopped and looked over at the two girls.

"Right, get ready to jump out. As soon as Mr. Jones gives the signal, you're all to leave the van and wait for our instructions. Understood?"

They nodded.

"Good. What's happening now?"

"He's knocking on the door. It's opening . . . It's . . . it's . . . an old lady in a dressing gown?"

"How strange. It's not exactly the image of a black-mailer that I had in mind," said Mr. Humphries to a similarly bemused-looking Miss Magenta.

"She's asking him if he's okay. Mr. Jones is holding up the briefcase," said Anna, trying to explain everything in as much detail as possible. "She's asked him if he'd like to come inside and warm himself up."

"And now?" asked Miss Magenta.

"He's gone inside, and there's a man there. An old man smoking a pipe. He's turning off the radio and walking over to Mr. Jones. They're shaking hands."

"What's the old lady doing?"

"She's putting the kettle on."

The group watched the girls intently as they took it in turns to describe the scene in detail. The old woman prepared the tea and carried the three steaming mugs over to the sofa on which Bentley Jones was now sitting.

"Mr. Jones says he's here to hand over the money. . . ."

"Yes?"

There was a pause.

"The lady said she doesn't know what he's talking about."

"Something's wrong. Something's very, very wrong," said Mr. Humphries, rubbing his hand across his greasy, thinning hair.

"I think we should get out and—"

Mr. Humphries was interrupted by the sound of the back doors swinging open. Two men in black hoods appeared before them. Anna, who up until that point had been watching the cottage in her mind, was taken completely by surprise. She screamed as the men reached inside and grabbed her, pulling her out onto the ground.

"It's a trap!"

Anna spun her head round in the direction of the voice and saw the figure of Bentley Jones rushing back toward the van.

The men grabbed her by the arms and legs and lifted her easily, then sped off in the direction of the cliffs, as she wrestled them in vain.

Danny looked about him at the others, all frozen in shock.

"Anna!"

He leaped out of the van before anybody could stop him and ran off in the direction of the men, the teachers and pupils following behind him.

Anna screamed as she watched Danny running to try to catch them, and then suddenly, without speaking, the men stopped. Anna watched as one of them moved his right arm around and lifted it up above her head. It took a moment for her to work out what she was looking at.

"He's got a gun! Danny, stop!"

Her voice was drowned out by the sound of a single shot fired. Anna watched as Danny fell to the ground. The men began to run again toward the cliffs, holding Anna tightly as she sobbed and tried to turn and twist her way free. Suddenly Anna remembered her Ability and closed her eyes, but it was too late. The men stopped and swung her backward, then forward, and released her. She flew up into the air, over the cliff's edge. The last thing that Anna saw, before she lost consciousness, was the black water of the sea looming closer.

"Quick, where's the knife?" said a deep voice that sent a chill down Anna's spine.

Anna opened her eyes and grimaced at the throbbing pain in her head. The ground she was on was moving and she realized that she was on a boat. It was pitch-black except for the light from a flashlight, resting next to her on the deck. She was lying down, her arms and legs tied, her clothes soaked and clinging to her skin. She shivered, then noticed that she was no longer wearing her jacket, which was now in the hands of a woman sitting at her feet. The woman passed the knife over Anna's head to a gloved hand.

Anna screamed as the man took her arm. She felt the blade cut slowly into her and then the sting as the pain began to register. Blood dripped down from her arm as Anna cried, tears running down from her emerald green eyes, and the woman leaned over to wipe her arm with the jacket.

"That's enough. Throw it into the sea. They'll find it in the morning."

"Why are you doing this?" asked Anna.

"Because, my dear, you and that Ability of yours are going to make us very rich indeed."

"They'll find me," said Anna, sobbing. "You won't get away with this."

"Oh, I don't think they'll look very hard. You'll be easily replaced."

"You don't know what you're talking about. They're my friends; they won't leave me."

"Look up."

Anna stopped crying and looked up. The cliffs loomed high ahead of them, and she could make out the light from the cottage window. Something near the building moved, and she squinted to try to make out what it was.

"That's right—that's the van you came in, with all your so-called friends inside, and it looks like they're leaving.

They've given up already," said the man, laughing.

Anna watched helplessly as the van drove off into the black night. It was at that moment that she realized the true hopelessness of her situation, and she began to scream, the sound of her anguish lost within the howling of the heavy storm winds.

Wednesday, October 17

Cecil Humphries, the government minister for education, despised most things, amongst them:

Cyclists.

The seaside.

Being called by his first name.

Weddings.

The color yellow.

Singing.

But at the top of this list was children. He *hated* them, which was rather unfortunate given that he was in charge of the well-being of every child in Britain. He knew, however, that the public was rather fond of them, for some reason he couldn't fathom, and so he had reluctantly accepted the position, sure that it would boost his flagging popularity and take him one step closer toward his ultimate goal: to take the job of his old school friend Prime Minister Edward Banks. Unfortunately for him, the public was far more perceptive than he gave them credit for, and kissing a couple of babies' heads (then wiping his mouth afterward) had resulted only in a series of frustrating headlines, including:

HUMPHRIES LOVES BABIES

(BUT HE COULDN'T EAT A WHOLE ONE)

The more he tried to improve his image, the more it backfired on him, which only intensified his hatred of anybody under the age of eighteen, if that were at all possible.

It was only fitting, therefore, that the person who would ruin his career and leave him a quivering wreck in a padded cell for the rest of his life would be a twelve-year-old boy.

If you are twelve, you have it:
the Ability to enter people's minds.

It's your choice whether you use it
for good . . . or for evil.

 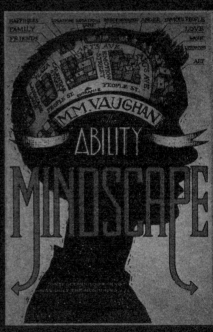